# WHEN I
# KILL HIM,
## JESUS CAN HAVE HIM

WHEN I KILL HIM, JESUS CAN HAVE HIM

E. Claudette Freeman, Editor
Contributing Authors: Shanier Adderley Souffrant, Stephanie Outten, LaShawn Hewlett-Wilson, Craig Stafford, L. Melissa Smith, Toni Seaton, Yolanda Davis-McCullough, Margarette Joyner

Copyright © 2018 Freeman Thomas Books, an imprint of Pecan Tree Publishing

ISBN: 978-1-7328311-5-5 (Paperback)
ISBN: 978-1-7328311-6-2 (Digital)
Library of Congress Control Number: 2019934438

All scriptures listed are King James Version or New International Version.

Cover and Interior Design by Dimitrinka Cvetkoski
Printed in the United States of America
First printing edition 2019
Freeman Thomas Books
Pecan Tree Publishing
Hollywood, FL 33020

# Contents

FREEMAN THOMAS BOOKS
A PECAN TREE PUBLISHING IMPRINT

FREEMAN THOMAS
B O O K S

WWW.PECANTREEBOOKS.COM
INFO@PECANTREEBOOKS.COM

# Introducing Your Storytellers

## *Lies We Live by Shanier Souffrant*

Trying to pen words that appropriately characterize Shanier Souffrant, can be quite a challenge. Shanier is very passionate about all things "Art". She stems from a multi-talented family of singers, actors, musicians and writers in which each piece of art has become a part of her. Most of her work evolves around teaching effective expression and communication through the arts. Shanier is also the author of the Secretly Broken series, which is a compilation of fiction novels about family and relational challenges. Her motto is; "There is truth in fiction. Truth will always lead to a win, but sometimes you have to ease people into it." This proves to be true each time someone reads her work and a character resonates.

Get to know Shanier at www.myshaniersouffrant.com

## *Sweet Like Candy by Yolanda Davis-McCullough*

Yolanda Davis-McCullough is the wife of Pastor Martai D. McCullough of the Greater New Bethel Missionary Baptist Church of Liberty City, Florida. She is an active member of her church and will often be seen surrounded by youth. She enjoys working with the youth and empowering them through the arts. Yolanda has a passion for the written word and can often be found somewhere enjoying a book.

## *The Podium by Stephanie Outten*

Stephanie Outten, Chief Visionary Officer of Cocoon to Wings Publishing & Coaching, serves as an author, publisher, coach and "Literary Doula." She guides existing and aspiring authors through birthing their literary masterpiece and leaving their story as their legacy. She is a Christian fiction author who birthed her first novel, "Is This the Way to Joy?" in 2016. She is a co-author in the Amazon Bestseller, "Soul Talk", and she is working on the sequel to her first novel, while also coaching new writers and publishing other authors' works. Her favorite quote, "When sleeping women wake, mountains move," has been the mantra that allows her to move mountains in her own life. Visit Stephanie at StephanieOutten.com for more information

## *Raven's Altar by L. Melissa Smith*

Although she has spent most of her writing career producing feature articles, press releases, editorials, letter writing and other nonfiction writing, writer and journalist L. Melissa Smith does periodically delve into fiction writing. Her novel "Love in Disguise" is a suspenseful Christian romance novel that deals with grittier, realistic issues of adultery, betrayal and deceit. In "Raven's Altar", Melissa deals with unlikely victims of domestic violence and shows that just because you grew up in the church, doesn't mean you are a Christian.

## *Hex and Hair Grease by Craig Stafford*

21st Century Thought Leader, Craig N. Stafford is an ex at-risk youth turned internationally recognized Author, Ordained Minister, Master Mason and Motivational Speaker. He has an affinity for folklore and has come to admit he's a closeted spoken word artist. Flash fiction is his niche with an emphasis on the supernatural and Black cultural references. Conversations with family and friends brings him optimal joy.

## *Don't Tell Me Nothing About My Pastor by Margarette Joyner*

Margarette Joyner, Founder/Executive Director of The Heritage Ensemble Theatre Company is blessed with many talents: Director, Singer, Playwright, Costume Designer, Set Designer, Collage Artist and Jewelry maker. As a Playwright she has written such plays as Message from a Slave and Sweet Chocolate and the Seven Christians. For two years, Margarette was also the face of Glory Foods and still has a cooking show on the Glory Foods website. She has worked on and off stages across the country for more than three decades and can be seen on numerous television commercials and documentaries. She graduated from VCU with a Master's Degree in Theatre and currently is a full time Certified Actor Interpreter at Colonial Williamsburg. When asked about her many talents Joyner responded, "I am humbled by the fact that God has chosen me to represent His work." Learn more about her theatre work at: theatreubuntu.wix.com/thetc.

## *I Know What You Did by LaShawn Hewlett-Wilson*

LaShawn Hewlett-Wilson is the author of Forbidden Fruit and Forbidden Fruit II: Betrayal can never be forgiven. Writing has been her passion since middle school; and is now her platform to share her stories with many. LaShawn loves writing romance novels because she can create stories surrounded by erotica, suspense and drama, which portray characters burning with lust, love and passion. When she's not writing, she's working hard as a realtor, and enjoys spending time with family and friends. LaShawn currently resides in Richmond, Virginia with her family and Yorkie. Learn more about LaShawn on her website: www.lashawnhewlettwilson.com.

## *Pearls and Shadows by Toni Seaton*

Toni Seaton, is a therapist/mental health consultant, presenter and Co-Founder of Tau Rho Omicron Christian Sorority Inc. She sits on the Board of Directors of Green Apple Accreditation of Children's Services. She is fascinated with studying different religions, cultures and the historical context where the two collide. She has served as a freelance journalist writing for FIU's Sociological Journal, Good News Goulds and the UrbanAmerica Newspaper. She's been published in the anthology "Multi Culti Mixterations: Playful and Profound Cultural Interpretations Through Haiku". She is founder of The Smart Cookie Collective. A group of women, "smart cookies" working together to deliver educational, coaching and consultant services.

www.smartcookiefl.wixsite.com/website

## *This Is Not Your House by E. Claudette Freeman*

E. Claudette Freeman is an award-winning journalist and an award-winning playwright. Her work has been featured on stages in Miami, Fl; Palm Beach, FL; Memphis, TN and Richmond, VA. She is the author of two works of fiction: PIECES AND ME: THE STUFF THAT WAKES ME UP AT NIGHT and PRECIOUS REDEMPTION: SHELTERED DELIVERANCE REVISITED. Freeman is also the author of two collections of journals and a non-fiction exploration of spiritual dreams, WHEN I DANCED WITH GOD. She is a sought-after literary coach and development editor. For more information, visit her website: www.eclaudetteliterary.com

# WHEN I
# KILL HIM,
## JESUS CAN HAVE HIM

# THE LIES WE LIVE
### Shanier Souffrant

### One Moment in Time
### Elena

A moment in time is what the singer's beautiful voice croons throughout the quiet eerie space in my husband's hospital room. Her voice is beautiful and so is the melodic music, but it still doesn't over power the beeps and the ticks coming from the many monitors that are attached to him. My Hank has always been one of her biggest fans and normally whenever we'd hear this song, he would stop in his tracks, grab me by my waist, pull me close and we'd sway like no one was watching. Today is different. The song takes me on another emotional roller coaster. I mean, like one of those rides that snatches you up in the air at a hundred miles per hour, then drops you just as quickly, taking away every inch of the breath that God himself breathed into you. She's asking for a moment in time and so am I.

I don't just want one more moment in time with him; I need it. There are so many unanswered questions, so much left undone. I want to know how all of the hopes and dreams that we shared can just vanish with one swift strike to the heart. We've fought through greater things, I've even sacrificed my own dreams, and for what. I thought one day in the end, we'd gain it all, together. But here I sit, watching the love of my life lie helpless as a machine pulls and pushes breath through his lungs. Turns out, the answers are not all up to me because I would have never chosen to let him go. Not like this. I want to hold on to this man, give God a chance to do what He does best and resurrect him from this unwanted rest.

"Oh Hank, baby, we had so much more work to do. Why choose this? Why?"

The hospital room's door flew open with my husband's older brother and my only confidant, Obediah St. James along with my two children standing behind him. I guess my wailing wasn't as quiet as it should have been for the intensive care unit, because there they stood interrupting the private moment I'd asked for. I was hoping my plea would somehow bring him back to us. However, stubborn is what stubborn does, which is whatever the hell it wants.

"Elena. Is everything okay?

"I'm not okay, Obie. Who would have ever thought that the great Roland Henry St. James would be lying here in this state? Your brother has made the choice to give up and I just don't get it. Something just doesn't seem right about this. You knew him. Probably better than I did. Why would he choose this?" I cried.

There was a ghostly shift in Obediah's expression. My discernment never steered me wrong, but this wasn't the time to assess my brother-in-law's thoughts. I need to get through this moment in time. When Hank's heart finally stopped, I'm afraid that my own will follow suit.

"Hank was a man of great faith, and people with faith don't just decide they don't want to fight anymore. And cremation? Is this a St. James thing, because I have never known island folks to burn themselves into ashes? I'm sure your mommy is rolling over in her grave about this."

There was that tension again in Obediah's face, except this time, his eyes quickly shifted away from me. I decided to put a tack in that for sure and address it with him later, when I have the strength to deal.

"Mommy, I need to go for a while, but I'll be back," My daughter Jacinta said as she carefully approached where I sat.

"I need to spend some time with the children." She knelt before me with a solemn countenance, "Rohan says they are asking for Papa."

Rohan Palmer was my daughter's husband and second in line to lead Agape Temple. He's a great speaker and the people really love him, but I'm not sure about how firm of a leader he would be. My daughter seems to wear the pants in that household.

"He's not sure what to tell them," she said. "I was thinking... maybe we should all go speak to them together. We can come back tonight for one last goodbye before they remove daddy's..." Jacinta gently patted my hand, then turned her gaze from me.

She couldn't finish her sentence, but I knew what she didn't want to say. I didn't want to come to terms with the fact that my husband chose to donate his organs to some stranger after death myself. Life Span, the organization that Hank signed his body over to, gave us seventy-two hours more after we agreed to release him. I'm in disbelief every time I think about it. I wonder if the person that gets a piece of my Hank even deserves it.

"And I have to head to the church so that I can prepare the statement for Sunday. Deacon Sanders is impatiently waiting for me to present something." My son and second heartbeat, Roland Jr. spoke as he gently caressed my shoulder. He's mine and Hank's first choice to run Agape Temple, but he'd rather work outside the four walls of the church. He and a few of his buddies started a street ministry called Rescued. I respect what he's doing, but I'm hoping he will put that aside to lead our family's legacy.

"I think Jacinta's right. Why don't you let us take you home to get some proper rest, mommy? You've been here for almost two weeks, and I know you haven't slept since daddy got here," Jr. said.

"I've slept as much as I needed to."

"Yeah, but I'm sure it wasn't well." Obediah interjected.

"How am I supposed to sleep well, when my husband is lying here with all of these machines connected to his body?"

I didn't want it to happen, but the break down coming on was inevitable. I'd held it together long enough, and at this moment, there was no controlling the flood of tears that were brought on by the gut-wrenching pain of losing my Hank.

"He doesn't want us to fight for him. Please! In God's name, tell me how am I supposed to sleep. Sleep? No." I screamed. "I need many more moments with him. I want to hear his voice or see those pale green eyes one more time." I looked over at Obediah, willing him to at least look at me, but he didn't. His eyes were fixed on the sight of nothing outside the window. I knew nothing was there for him to see but a blank canvas of a wall to the adjacent building and a small part of the parking lot. I've looked out the same window a time or two these past ten days.

"Do you understand that this man is all I've ever known? From eighteen years old, he's been my everything." Obediah finally turned to look at me, his eyes spoke something I didn't recognize or comprehend. I couldn't differentiate whether or not he was confirming my rant or just letting me know he understood. His gaze didn't last at all. He turned to the window once more. Something else seemed to hold his attention from the outside.

"Mom, I understand what you're feeling," Jacinta said. "He was our father and everything we've ever known too. But we have to get it together and somehow find a way to live on. God has allowed this to happen to daddy and we..." she grabbed her brother's hand pulling him to kneel alongside her, "have to learn how to hold each other up now."

How strange of Jacinta to say we have to hold each other up, as she just pulled her brother down to her level. That girl is too strong for her own good. I don't know whose gene pool she pulled from the most, Hank or mine. As far as looks, she's everything Hank. She is the spitting image of my husband in female form. Her tall slender build and light green eyes that sometimes turned a smoky grey whenever she became angry all came from her father. It's going to be even harder to look at her now.

The tears began to fall again. I've cried more in the last ten minutes than I have since Hank collapsed in his office at the church ten days ago. Through the tears I found his hand and held it tightly.

"I guess you've run your race. You've maxed out your destiny on this side of heaven my Hanky Boy. You've finished your course. Maybe you've even seen the glory of what eternity on that side looks like. It breaks my heart to know that you don't want to come back to us, I'll never understand or agree with your choices, but I accept it. You'll forever live in our hearts."

I gently kissed his hand and held it close to my face. I had one final hope that a miracle would happen. Maybe if he felt the warmth of my tears or my pulse, he'd be revived. Unfortunately, after several minutes of hoping and wishing, my miracle never happened. I still didn't want to let go of his warm, calloused hands. The machines were his lifeline, but Hank's touch was what kept the blood pumping in my veins.

"Sleep well my love. Sleep well."

## Harvesting
## Obediah

Elena, Roland Jr, and my niece Jacinta and her family all sat at the long dining room table having breakfast and morning devotion. I had the honor of sitting in my brother's chair at the head of the table.

My brother Ro's actions when he was alive always got past me and now after his death, he's doing the same just as well. Our mommy nicknamed him L.B. short for Lagniappe Boll'face. For years he thought she'd coined the name from a prominent military soldier that served with our father, but in reality, she was calling him quite the opposite. She confessed to me years later, along with an apology for creating a very demanding man child who pushed and manipulated people to get what he wanted. Although he and I were only a few years apart in age, he was considered mommy's bonus baby. She'd found out she was pregnant with him four months after our father died. My baby brother demanded a lot of my mother's attention, so growing up, I found myself bowing out a little more than I should have out of pity. That's how he actually got Elena, and eventually, I even became okay with that too.

I remember the day he came to me about starting a church. Mom didn't think he was the pastoring type and neither did I. I knew he enjoyed going to our friend Lucky's church when we were kids. Ro and I both loved going because it was a step away from the tight necked order of service at my mom's Catholic church.

When we came to the states, she made me promise to look after him and I did. I supported him and Elena when they started Agape Temple just one year after they arrived. They rented the church building owned by a Seventh Day Adventist congregation on Sundays. Things were slow for the first two years, but midway through their third year, they began to grow out of the building.

Agape had a combination of Ro's creativity and my practical eye woven all through the design. I did what I could to keep most of our family's traditional ways, but Ro never stayed in the box. That's how it's always been with us. I thought eventually he would get the value in us balancing one another out, but he seems to keep it coming with one uncanny idea after another.

Roland Jr. found a note to the family that was conveniently stashed in the top drawer of his office desk addressed to his family. He requested that his family sits Shiva, which is a Jewish custom that suggests we remain together under one roof for seven days to honor him. The more I think about it, the more I wonder about the irony of it all. Although we were all caught by surprise by his untimely death, he seemed planned and ready.

My nephew, Jr. stood with his father's bible in hand, as Jacinta lit a candle. We were on day six of this show, so they had an ease about the way things should go by now.

Elena spoke before they started. "I'm sure being in the comfort of your own homes would have been easier, so thank you all again for being here. Your father has always been a meticulous planner and it appears he's still at it, even after he's dead and gone. I never got why he did some of the things he did, but somehow it worked in all of our favors in the end." She graced the table with her pleasant smile, and I noticed as each day passed, there was more light pushing its way through the dimness in her eyes.

Jr. began to read the passage that his father had instructed for the day, except unlike the days prior, he was brief. Instead of expounding on the passage, he looked over at Jacinta's husband, Rohan and asked him to finish.

"I'm not sure if that's a good idea." Rohan said with hesitancy.

"Why not honey? You're just as much a part of this family as any of us. Daddy would have loved to hear you." Jacinta prodded.

"The thing is... he's not here and I was nowhere on his list of instructions. Let's just honor his wishes to the letter."

"I really think you should, Rohan. Jr. has passed this to you. Take the Bible and speak. Please." Jacinta spoke with a plastered smile, but the incite behind her words told Rohan and everyone else at the table that this was not up for further discussion.

Rohan took the bible that his brother in law handed him and reluctantly began to read Deuteronomy 24:19.

"May I please have the room for just one more brief moment." Elena stood from her chair, elegantly holding up a perfectly manicured finger to stop Rohan. She looked at him with a seriousness that I could definitely identify with. The words that have always followed that look have always cut to the core of any situation. "Is this something that you want to do?" Elena emphasized the word, you as her finger pointed at Rohan.

"If you guys wish to hear me speak, then I will speak."

Jacinta sat back in her chair and folded her arms. Jr. followed her lead with a smile and I just sat back and watched the show along with the children.

"My question was, is this what you want to do?" Elena asked again.

"Yes, Lady St. James," Rohan said as he attempted to straighten his posture. "I'd be more than happy to speak." He cleared his throat and began to read the passage once more before adding his thoughts.

By the time Rohan finished sharing, the entire table had wet glossy faces. I even dropped a tear or two. His illustration of the scripture was so profound, I think it even changed Elena's opinion of him.

"In closing," Roland Jr. stood to speak his peace. "Thanks bro. That was good stuff. I know my father didn't mention having you speak during this time of sitting Shiva... maybe his wishes were written before you were a part of our family, or maybe he was testing my leadership. I'm not sure, but I am sure that a true leader always does what's best for everyone and if I must say, by the looks on all of your faces, we needed exactly what Rohan had to share. I truly believe this was the best call."

Roland looked at his mother then continued.

"As the passage states, let us move forward with the harvest we've reaped. The Lord instructed the people to leave the bundles of the harvest if they so happened to forget them. Not to go back for them, but to leave them for the fatherless and the others that may be coming along the same path. We don't need to know why they were instructed to do such a thing, but it's necessary that I point out another scripture that comes to mind. One person plants, another gives water, but God is always there to provide the increase."

Jr. held his mother's gaze a little longer this time. He reminds me so much of myself. He's always respected his parents but has never backed down from his own principles.

"I didn't plan this. God and Daddy did. I won't be the one to pick up the mantle. Rohan is the right person to take Agape Temple to the next level. It's obvious, he's equipped, and he has the heart for Daddy's vision. It's not my calling, so don't ask me to do this."

"Jr. honey, God has called you to reap the harvest too," Elena pleaded.

"The harvest is plentiful mommy, but the laborers have to be positioned right. Not just put in a position."

I watched Jacinta smile as she looked on at her brother. Elena appeared to be intently listening to Jr.'s plea as I too nodded in complete agreement.

Elena called me out. "I assume you are questioning my view too, Obie?"

"Rohan is an amazing communicator and he has one of the strongest women standing alongside him," I motioned toward my niece, Jacinta. Pausing before I finished my statement, I had to make sure she understood me clearly.

"Just as Roland Henry St James had with you."

## *Enemies or Allies*
### *Elena*

Later that day after lunch, the family sat outside on the lanai to enjoy the beautiful weather. It was seventy degrees out and for once, South Florida was given a small glimpse of what the fall season felt like in every other east coast state. The disfavor I once had for the idea of Rohan becoming lead pastor at Agape Temple had diminished. My intentions were never to demean him any more than my daughter had, but the day can't come soon enough for him to stand up to her.

"Thank you, Rohan. Or, should I say Pastor Palmer? Your message really spoke to my heart this morning."

Rohan nodded his head and smiled. I'm not sure if he decided to forgo further acknowledgement because he was still digesting my approval, or he was just playing it safe. Either way, his actions showed me that he was indeed a smart man after all.

As I changed the subject, I could literally see his face rest with relief.

"Has anyone heard from any one from our staff?" I asked.

"I had a few missed calls from Brother Tarrin, but I let them go to voicemail," Jacinta said."

"Same here," Jr. said. "I did answer Deacon Sanders's call. I thought maybe he would know where I could find Daddy's laptop."

"Did you ever find it?" Obediah asked.

"I did, but it was wiped clean. I thought maybe I could pull some of his sermons up, but there was nothing on it."

"He's always protected that thing with his life," I laughed. "but I find that strange that all of his sermons were gone."

"Where did you find it?" Obediah asked.

"It was in the top drawer of his office desk along with those lists of instructions he gave."

"Obediah's face grew grim. It was the same solemn look he had when we were in Hank's hospital room the other day. Just as I was about to ask him about his change of mood, our doorbell rang. Rohan got up to answer.

"I wonder who that could be," Jr furrowed his brows as we all did.

"Might be one of those lackey board members who's finally decided to properly show their respect. Sending us a measly bunch of flowers is not the way you honor the man that lead you for years." The more I thought about the way our church had all but left our family alone angered me to the core. Hank was good to those people and for almost two weeks, not one phone call..."

Rohan stood at the threshold of the door and cleared his throat as if he wanted to warn us of our guest standing beside him.

I looked up to see my nemesis, Pastor Carla Moss standing there with the stern dry face that she always held. Carla wasn't like the other disrespectful, thirsty, ungodly women that desperately vied for my husband's attention. For that matter, I wasn't' concerned. She was a power-hungry young force that constantly tried to dumb me down. Over ten years ago, Hank hired her as Executive Director of Operations. In my opinion, he'd given her too much power, way too soon. In the beginning, I tried to cozy up to her. She was just a few years out of college, single and had moved to South Florida from the Midwest. I saw and understood her strength, so I thought it would be nice if I offered to mentor her. I remember her words and how they had cut like it was yesterday. "Thanks for the consideration ma'am, but I'll pass. My circle is closed. If I only associate myself with like-minded people, there's not much room for growth, don't you think? And besides, I'm sure there are enough women at Agape Temple who could use a hand or two in finding the right color shoes to wear with their fancy dresses."

Before I knew it, I'd kicked off one of my fancy shoes and threw it at her. That wiped the snobbish grin right off her face. Hank didn't like it and I didn't care. He knew and Carla learned that day of my quick temper. I remained cool, calm and collected, but whenever I felt disrespected or betrayed, somebody's going to feel my wrath. Carla didn't want to experience that anymore, so she stayed her distance and Agape Temple remained a safe place for us both.

Her approach was different today. She actually came with humility.

"Once again, I'd like to offer my condolences, Lady Elena. Pastor St. James was a great man." Carla said. Then she did something that almost pulled me out of the shock of having her in my home. She knelt before me and cupped my hands into her tiny palms. This was a posture that my children had always taken with me when they wanted to comfort me. It made me want to meet her parents just to tell them that they hadn't done such a bad job raising this young woman after all.

"I've done my best to keep everyone from bombarding you and the family. I thought it was best they give you all time to mourn privately." She paused a beat and batted her eyes.

So, she was the one that kept the flunkies away. "Thank you, I said on a forced exhale. Despite her effort a single tear fell. I didn't think the devil cried.

"Please know that everyone is praying with and for you through this challenging time."

She looked up at Roland Jr. as she finished her words of comfort.

"I have a schedule here," she said as she released one of my hands to fish an envelope from the pocket in her blazer. "This is a list of all of the ministry teams who will be ready to come by starting next week. They will assist you and the family in any way."

We both watched Jr. as he read the piece of paper.

"If I need to change anything, please let me know," she said.

Jr. looked up from the paper. "Thank you, Pastor Carla. We will take a better look at it later. I will get back to you if changes are needed."

Carla turned back to me and took both of my hands once more. The sincerity in her voice gave me the feeling that she had more to say and from what I sensed, it wasn't good news.

"I really don't mean to intrude any longer or more than I have to, Lady Elena, however I there's one more thing I need to bring to your attention." She paused and cleared her throat.

"Sister Sasha has gone missing. The authorities have been discreet thus far, but this morning, they came to search the church and now they've asked to search your home."

"Why here? She's been gone from Agape Temple for over three years." Obediah asked.

"For clues on her whereabouts, I presume."

"Sasha is an adult. Maybe she's decided to move on with her baby's ... her child."

"Obie!" I scoffed. People make mistakes, we can't condemn Sasha for having a child out of wedlock forever. That's not fair."

"I'm not condemning Sasha. I just think it's strange that she kept the father of her child a secret. I mean, what if its someone from the church? Don't you think they should get the same treatment as she did. I just don't want her taking the brunt of the shame but letting whoever this enigma may be get away."

It's not like Obediah to be so callous. Sasha wasn't blood but she was a valued member of the St. James's clan. When she'd gotten pregnant by some mystery sperm donor, the board decided she could no longer be a part of our leadership team. It took a long time for me to get over Hank allowing them to do that.

"Obie, maybe something has happened. I can't see her just up and leaving without at least saying goodbye to us," I said. Sasha hadn't been around much, but she still remained in touch with Hank once she realized how bad he felt about the way those self-righteous board members had cast her away.

Carla interrupted our exchange, "According to the detective, a friend had gone to her apartment and apparently there was some potential evidence of foul play that raised a red flag."

"Oh my God, Lord have mercy. Please Jesus, fix it." I cried. "I can't bear to lose another person so soon."

Obediah rushed over to comfort me. "Sasha is fine, Elena. I'm sure she'll show up. She lived in a secure building. It's not like some random person could gain access to her apartment. I'm sure for her, Ro's death was detrimental. She's got to find her way just like the rest of us."

Obediah was now sounding more like himself. He's a straight shooter, but he was still empathetic, unlike Hank who always felt he had to please everybody.

"I know, but if the police are saying there was suspicion of foul play, that can't be good."

"Try not to get worked up about this mom," Jr. said then turned to Carla.

"They can come, but not until we're done sitting Shiva."

Carla scanned the room, then fixed her eyes back at me. "Officially, they don't have to ask for your permission, but I'll try to hold them off for as long as I can. I don't think they have a warrant."

"At least until tomorrow at sundown," Jr. said. "Please give them my number and I will make the arrangements."

## *Food for the Soul*
## *Elena*

I decided to get out of the house to do a little grocery shopping. Tomorrow would be one year since my Hank left us, so I've invited the kids over for a memorial dinner. I haven't seen them as often as I'd like this past year. I see Jacinta and Rohan every Sunday at church, but Roland Jr has had his hands full with his own ministry. I only get to see him maybe once or twice a month. Obediah has been my constant for comfort since day one of our separation that last day of sitting Shiva. We've always been close, but our bond of friendship has grown these past twelve months to somewhat of a codependency. He doesn't know that I knew about his and Hank's bet from the first day the three of us met. I thought both of them were handsome, but it was Hank that grabbed my heart. He was the most charming brother that seemed to know exactly what he wanted, when Obie on the other hand, always played the role of perfect gentleman. At eighteen, that was the last thing I wanted, but now at fifty-six, it's everything I need.

It's been difficult for me as I try my best to keep our thing platonic. Using the words Our Thing even seems strange. However, it's not as difficult for everyone else around to label what we have . Those nosey church folks always find a way to meddle.  I've even caught some of those nosey board members hanging at the corner of my home on some weird surveillances.

There was something about Obie and me that just worked and I could feel he knew it too, but he never made a move. The only move he'd make was his calls to check in throughout the day just as he did now.

"Hello... Obie, hey. I'm just leaving the grocery store. Okay, sure. I'll be home in a few."

Obediah said that he needed to talk to me about something important. I tried a little prying because his tone concerned me, but he insisted we speak in person.

## *Return to Sender*
### *Elena*

Obie and I pulled into my driveway at the same time. He got out of the car with a large white envelope in hand. He tucked it under his arm to help me get the groceries out of the trunk.

"I didn't realize you were coming straight over," I said. The look on his face caused greater concern than the tone of his voice over the phone. Once we got the groceries inside, he motioned for me to have a seat at the breakfast bar.

"Obie, is everything okay?"

"I don't know Elena." He placed the envelope on the table but kept his hand on top. The small green writing in the top left-hand corner read Life Span. Seeing their envelope took me back to the day we said our final good byes to my Hank one year ago. It was the organization that Hank donated his organs to. I assume the puzzled look on my face is what made Obediah shift from his own hesitant posture.

He opened the envelope and handed me the one-page letter. I read it quickly, then looked up at him. He blew out a deep sigh and shrugged his shoulders. I slammed the paper on the table, then quickly picked it up to read it once more.

"What is this, Obie?"

"I'm just as baffled as you are." He replied.

"Harvey Steinberg?" I questioned. Wasn't that the gentleman who was in the hospital room with Hank, just before they moved him to a private suite?"

"That's him. He and his wife were a very nice couple."

"But why would he be sending money to Hank? And what records need updating?"

Obediah gave me his shut up and listen look. It was obvious he was just as confused about all of this as I was, but he appeared to have more answers than I had. He turned his phone toward me. There was a web page pulled up with the name Attorney Allan Starks. Under his name was the same address listed on the letter I'd just read. It wasn't until I saw the name that I was prompted to look again at the envelope. There was a big red stamp across the middle that said Return to Sender. Life Span wasn't sending the letter to Obediah or me, it was addressed to this Attorney Starks.

"How did you get this?" I asked

I don't know how it ended up in my office mail, however I have met this guy once. He was..." Obediah's voice faltered. "I remember meeting him one day at his office with Ro a few weeks before he died. He'd asked me to lunch that day. I was supposed to meet him at one that afternoon, but since my morning meeting was cut short, I came early and figured I would just wait for him in the lobby."

"Why was he using this guy? Larry has been our attorney for years."

"He'd told me this guy specialized in property law and preferred to keep his outside business separate from the church's."

"I'm still a little lost here. What outside business are we talking about Obie?"

"He was working on developing the land for low income housing on the property adjacent to Agape Temple. He never mentioned that to you?"

"Vaguely. But it was just an idea of his and Jr.'s. I didn't realize they moved forward with any planning."

"As a matter of fact, they had. I still have the plans in my office."

"Ok, so what happened that day?" I asked.

I didn't want to be short with Obediah but the conflicting expression across his face told me there was more to the story than he was willing to share causing that unwelcomed sick churning in my stomach to return.

"When I arrived, he was still in his meeting with the attorney. I had to take a call, so I asked his secretary for a room that I could get a little privacy. She led me back to a small conference room that was next to the office where Ro and the attorney were."

"I could hear them talking through the paper-thin walls and the conversation between my brother and this Starks was questionable. I couldn't make out the meaning of everything they were saying, but I clearly remember hearing the attorney say to him..."

Obediah abruptly stopped talking once more. The apologetic looks in his eyes told me this is where the story stops, and it did.

"I'm not sure, Elena. All I know is that this letter is very strange. The timing of it, how it got in my mail and the crazy indication that Ro and this Harvey guy somehow had a connection that none of us knew about prior to his death.

"What do you think the connection was?" I asked. I'm a pretty clever woman, but this was a little over my head. Not because I wasn't probably thinking the same thoughts as Obie, but I didn't want to believe that my husband would keep some god-awful secret that I may never find out the truth about.


### *Questions and More*
### *Obediah*


I unerringly remembered my brother and the attorney's words. Every single one of them.

"Thirty-eight years with someone is a long time my friend." The attorney stated. I watched him slide over a stack of documents, gesturing for Roland's signature. I kept still and quiet in an effort for neither of them would notice my presence. I wanted to get more but Ro's response muddled the conversation even more.

"First off, you're not my friend so keep your personal advice. You were hired to do a job that I hear you're the best at. Let's not mistake this for anything else."

"Suit yourself."

After a few more minutes of getting absolutely nothing concrete from their back and forth, I decided to let them know they had company. The attorney addressed me with a nod;  but Ro's expression resembled a staggered shock. It was obvious to me at that point that Ro had something to hide because he abruptly asked the attorney to only read the last page of the document he had in hand.

Before we were out of the office, he reneged on our lunch. My brother was as cunning as I was, he knew that our bite to eat would turn into a nice little questioning session that he didn't want to give answers to. He came up with the excuse about having to get back to the church for another meeting.

I was angry with him that day. I couldn't put my finger on it, but I knew he was up to no good and it got way under my skin. Hearing Ro talk of Elena in a negative connotation haunted me with the memory of the day he and I first met her. I was just shy of twenty-one and Ro was eighteen. Both of us had fallen head over heels at the first sight of Elena. Ro only saw it as a big win to be able to get the prettiest girl in the neighborhood, who was still untouched. But I saw so much more. She was what my mother called a Sweet too bad Red. She was a beautiful girl. Her skin was a caramel color and was as smooth as cocoa butter and she carried herself with a confidence unlike the other young ladies in the neighborhood. When Ro noticed my eye took to her just as strong as his, he challenged me to play our favorite card game,

All Fours. The winning team would get the first go at stepping to the girl. Lucky was with us that day, but he refused to be on either of our teams. His belief in the nickname we gave him stood true, so he and our other buddy Ian both bowed out.

Ro and I never got around to speak about that office encounter, but unlike our unspoken agreement to never let Elena know of our little competition at winning her heart, I had every intention on confronting him. I never got the chance. The next time I'd laid eyes on my brother was the day I got the call that he was admitted into the hospital.

## *Goat Cheese*
## *Obediah*

I followed the guard down the hallway, listening as the jingling of his keys echoed off the walls. We were in a minimum-security facility, but it still gave an unnerving feeling non-the less. Maybe my jitters came from the fact that once I finally tracked down Attorney Starks, I'd found him to be locked up in a federal prison. His secretary, the one I met that day in his office still worked in the same building but for a different attorney. Turns out, she was the one who slipped the incriminating letter concerning my brother into my office mail.

Starks only agreed to see me under the pretense of me telling him there was monetary gain. When Starks realized he wasn't getting what I had promised, he quickly clammed, claiming the only business he had with my brother was the low-income housing project and some other property he called Eden's Gate. I knew all about the first property he'd mentioned, but I had no recollection of anything pertaining to an Eden's gate. When he noticed my flustered expression he quickly called for the guard. I asked a second time about Eden's gate, but he gave me nothing. He just pushed himself away from the table.

"Eden's gate, what is it man?" I yelled once more before Starks rounded the corner to leave.

"Sorry I can't help you. I can't break attorney client privilege."

"You're in a federal prison for doing God knows what. I'm sure your practicing law on the up and up is not what landed you in here. Why chose now to do the right thing ?" I said sarcastically.

He chuckled, "Get home safe."

***

After driving around aimlessly for hours I'd finally grabbed the nerve to go to Elena's. I couldn't keep avoiding her and had to tell her something. The last thing I wanted was for Elena to think I was as shady as my brother was revealing himself to be, even in his death. Something Starks said instantly came to mind and I realized a key fact. Attorney client privilege doesn't hold when the client is dead. His taunting gave me the answer I needed? Whatever he and my brother had going on, I was determined to get to the bottom of it. I had to tell Elena what I suspected, even if it was farfetched.

## *Keys to the Truth*
### *Elena*

Obediah seemed remorseful as he left my home the day he brought that letter by. I couldn't pin down if it was because of what he didn't want to tell me or if he really had no clue and was disappointed in himself. He didn't even show up for  dinner later that evening. This is the first time in a week I've even talked to him and he tells me that he believes Hank is not dead. I'm afraid to admit to him the I got the exact feeling after reading the letter and the thought of it is not improbable. Someone has been receiving money in Hank's name or on his behalf. Based on the figures on those returned checks, they were receiving a healthy amount.

"I trust your intuition, Obie, but how do we even begin to prove this theory?" I asked.

"The detective working Sasha's case returned a box of his things. Where is it?"

"I put it back in Hank's office. Why?"

Obediah swiftly walked passed me and barreled through Hank's office door.

He was already rummaging through the box by the time I reached the door.

"Talk to me, Obie. What are you looking for?"

"The stuff in this box may not have been of any use to the police, but there may be valuable evidence for us in here."

Obediah held up a plastic bag with a gold key in it. He pulled it out and a small, oval shaped, engraved copper piece of metal hung from the ring that read, Cloak-and-Dagger.

My first instinct was to try the lock on Hank's old brief case. I held my hand out for him to give me the key but when I tried it, it didn't work.

I slipped the key in the pocket of my cardigan and pulled Obie up the stairs to my closet. There were a few pieces of luggage that Hank used a lot when he traveled that had locks on them, however the key didn't fit in either of those. While Obediah was putting away the last piece of luggage, he banged his elbow against the wall. The grimace on his face told me that it hurt really bad.

"That's some tough dry wall," he said. He rubbed his hand across the space and noticed a slight give to it. He pushed in on the area and a twenty-four-square inch piece of the wall popped out.

To our surprise there was a safe behind it. I took the key from the pocket, then tried the lock. That didn't work either.

"Wait, the logo on that safe has the same engraving on that key ring." Obediah said. He pulled out his phone, typed in the pass code, then handed it to me. I Googled the name and there it was, first on the search list, Cloak and Dagger Home Safety. I hit the call button and the phone just rang. When the answering service picked up, I hung up the phone and called again. This time someone picked up on the first ring.

I placed the phone on speaker, then handed it over to Obediah. I suddenly had no clue what my next step should have been.

"Thank you for calling Cloak and Dagger, where your privacy and security comes first." The gentleman nicely stated his greeting the first time, but by the third, he sounded agitated because neither of us spoke up.

Obie finally decided to respond.

"Ah, hello, I would like to have a tech out to my home. I seem to have lost the key to my safe."

The gentleman's voice returned back to its cheerful state, "I can have a tech come out to assist you. What's a good day and time for you, sir?"

"As soon as possible," Obediah replied. "Is two hours okay, sir?"

"Yes, that would be fine. Thank you." Obie gave the gentleman our address, confirmed the appointment time, then hung up.

The tech showed up earlier than we expected, but his customer service skills were the complete opposite of the representative that we'd spoken to on the phone.

I was already a ball of nerves, so when he said that he couldn't help me unless I gave some stupid password, I nearly lost it.

"I'm sorry sir, but my husband owned this safe and he's dead. I don't know what the password or pass phrase could be. Will you please help me?" I thought my desperate plea would move him, but to no avail, he just shook his head.

"It's strict policy that we get the password or phrase before assisting anyone in opening a lock, ma'am."

"There has to be something you can do," Obediah said. "Is there some type of hint for the customer, just in case they forget?"

"Obie was pulling for straws, but his clever question worked."

The tech tapped a few numbers on his tablet and for the first time he had a semi-pleasant expression on his face.

"I believe I can give you that information, but only because Mr. St James is deceased. Let's see," he rubbed his chin and began to hum a weird tune while waiting for the information to appear on his tablet.

"Mother's nickname." He let out a quiet laugh, along with a questioning gesture.

"What kind of hint is that?" I spat out but before I could say another word, Obediah cut me off and said quickly, "Lagniappe Boll'face."

I swung my head at Obie, questioning what the hell he'd just said.

He answered, "It's something my mother used to call him when we were young. I'll tell you about it later. Is that it?" he asked the tech.

"That's it," the tech answered. He looked down at his tablet and began typing again. A few seconds later, the safe's door opened and there was another small key hole. The key that you have is for that lock ma'am. Do you need help with it.?"

"No." I answered. I wasn't sure if I wanted a stranger around once I uncovered what was in that safe."

"Thank you, sir, I'll show you out." Obediah said.

## *Necessary Evils*
### *Obediah*

When I returned back to the closet, I found Elena sitting on the floor in a daze. She held her hand out to me and I attempted to help her up. She shook her head, but still held out her hand where the gold key sat in the center of her palm.

"Open it please. I couldn't bring myself to do it." She softly spoke.

There was one single line on each side, staining her face from the tears. Seeing her cry because of the loss of my brother was one thing; but watching her pain-filled eyes tear up because of his betrayal was another. I wanted to comfort her, but I knew that's not what she wanted. She needed me to be strong in this moment. Strong enough to pull back layers that I'm sure neither of us were ready for.

She watched as I took the key and slowly placed it in the hole. As the door popped open, I could have sworn I felt a chilling flow of air move through the room. I allowed my eyes to follow the resonating breeze before turning back towards the safe. I reached inside and brought out a stack of what appeared to be letters. I pushed my hand into the hollow space once more to pull out another stack the pushed the small door closed.

Elena, still sitting on the floor looked up at me and patted next to where she sat. I followed suit with the two stacks in hand.

We sat there going through detailed documents and bank statements that revealed Sasha, my brother's assistant, was his mistress. There was one envelope that held a deed to a parcel of land which was the missing piece to our complicated puzzle. The bright red and white folder had the two-word lettering spread across the front - Eden's Gate. Our theory of him being alive was not farfetched to say the least.

I couldn't make out exactly where this land was, but I knew someone who could help me find it.

Elena placed her hand on my knee and softly spoke again. My heart skipped a beat, but I couldn't show it.

"We need to go. And I mean like right now." Her tone was insistent; however, I knew full well that we couldn't just hop a plane to blindly search for him.

"Let me look into this place first, Elena. We have no idea what we could be walking into."

"I een scared Obie, and I know you not either," she said. Whenever she got angry, her Trini accent would come on strong. "That money that Hank hasn't been receiving these past couple of months may put him in dire straits. You know how eager he gets when his back is up against a wall. He's liable to do something stupid."

"I don't think he could top faking his death, Elena."

"Well I need to find him." Elena peered over at me, shaking her head as if she suddenly felt the pang of defeat. "We're too old for this Obie.

We're supposed to be in the prime of our lives, relaxing and living our dream. That was our plan."

Her eyes turned sad all of a sudden.

"Elena, that was probably your plan, but it's obvious my brother had something totally different in mind. We know he's always played by his own rules, but this is taking it too far."

She pushed herself up from the floor and stood over me smoothing out her clothes.

He may have started this, but I'm going to finish it. Apparently, he one monkey who een know which tree to climb. I gon show he ass doe."

The patois got stronger, which meant if my brother Roland was alive, he was in a world of trouble when they faced off.

"I'm going to make a few calls first? Then we can book our flights." I had to at least try to delay her wrath. Although, I was just as eager to find him to beat him down, my pain didn't mount up to the same rage as Elena's.

"You have twenty-four hours," she warned. "Ready or not, I'm on that plane by this time tomorrow. And Obie," she said with her finger nearly tipped at my nose.

"Uh huh, "I replied.

"Do not tell anyone about this. Especially my children. If that man is still alive, he won't be for long after I done wit' he and I don't want them to have to mourn their father twice."

Elena's usual calm manner was null and void. Her eyes now showed no mercy. I realize sometimes there are necessary evils, but I couldn't think of one single reason why he would do this. If my brother is still alive, he was about to face his real death by the hands of Elena St. James.

## Lady and the Dream
## Obediah

It had only taken one phone call to find the place where I suspected my brother was hiding, but I didn't let Elena know right away. I needed to see him first before unleashing his ferocious wife on him.

Her petite frame seemed to expand to that of a linebacker. The way she carried herself once she exited the airport in Trinidad, was intimidating. She briskly walked in front of me with her chest out, mouth tight and fist balled to each side. I told her that we would check in at the hotel first, then move about the island to ask around. However, that wasn't my plan. Once I got her settled in her suite, I managed to hop a cab and head toward the beach. My old friend Ian was there waiting for me. He'd called in a favor from his nephew who owned a small tourist boat to take me to a small island just off the coast that we called Centipede. When I spoke with him, I didn't tell him anything about my suspicions. I couldn't chance the possibility of Ro getting a heads up before I got to him.

Things were moving fast, so my plan was only partly thought out. Aside from the one-word question of why, I still hadn't a clue what I would say to Ro when I finally saw him. The two-hour boat ride gave me a little time to put my thoughts in order. I thought I knew my brother inside out, but I guess not, because here he was living a whole new life with a woman, I apparently knew nothing about. What would I say to Sasha, who until her last year of working with Ro I'd grown fond of? It was she who pulled away from me all of a sudden.

I shook at the thought, refusing to believe my brother would play with the lives of his children and grandchildren. How could he leave them? I knew he loved them. However, what I don't know for sure is if he really loved Elena or just because he'd finally beat me at something, she was the grand prize.

Ian remained quiet the entire ride, leaving me to my thoughts. He resurfaced to the front of the boat as it pulled into the makeshift dock. I hopped off once Ian's nephew tied us up.

"Do you know where you're going?" Ian asked as I hurried down the dock.

"I think so. If I'm correct, the place I'm supposed to meet my colleague is about a half a mile up the trail over there," I lied.

He handed me a device that resembled a walkie talkie that we used to communicate with as youths. I took it and thanked him as I turned away to trek up the road. Ian yelled out with the walkie raised, "hail me if you need anything."

"You got it, man." I raised the one he'd given me as an okay gesture.

Along the beach sat a few families beneath the shade of large palms. Just past them was an old boat yard with a group of fishing vendors selling their fresh catch for the day. I loved my life, but I'd be lying if I said that I didn't miss this part. I envied the peaceful island life and the natural beauty of living off the land.

Before long, I was right in front of my destination. Just beyond a slight bend in the road was a cluster of trees that hid a small yellow sign that read, LB164-354. I leaned in, looking closer for some type of entrance and for a moment I missed it. The cluster of trees was visibly a decoy for anyone passing by. It was obvious that you had to know where you were or what you were looking for in order to notice the ten feet wooden gate, surrounded by a slab of concrete wall on each side.

I tried the lock and the gate opened. There was a small entrance that was about six or seven square feet before the metal door in front of me. I rang the bell twice before someone came to greet me. It was a little boy who appeared to be about four years in age.

"Hello sir, welcome to Eden's gate," he said with a courteous twang of Tobagian patois. He was barefoot with no more than a pair of shorts and what looked like a toy whistle strung around his neck.

"A young lady ran up behind him with a panic in her voice, Sebastian, no. you can't open the door for st…"

WHEN I KILL HIM, JESUS CAN HAVE HIM

She stopped dead in her tracks as her eyes met mine.

"Sasha?"

Sasha's eyes opened as wide as silver dollars. She didn't say a word to me, she just scooped up the little youth, then ran off. I could hear his little voice trail off as they disappeared. "I okay, mummy. But I have de whistle."

I tried following behind her, but she'd lost me just as fast as I'd found her. The bottom floor of what appeared to be a three-level home had several entrances throughout the open breezeway. Each door that I tried was locked. I decided to meander my way to one side of the property with my finger on the talk button of my walkie as if it were a trigger. The place was huge, surrounded by a forest of trees and these bright green plants that folded over every time I passed one. If I were the one trying to flee someone, it wouldn't have been hard for them to find me because when I looked behind me, they had formed a pathway. I decided to go back to the open courtyard that was just beyond the breezeway and ran right smack into my ghost of a brother. He didn't appear to be as shocked as I was. I assume it was because Sasha gave fair warning of my presence.

"O," he said. His eyes shot right up at me. He formed a crossed look on his face, then hung his head, like he somehow became embarrassed at being found out.

"Ro," I replied, then squared off. I had my brother by a good four inches and ten to fifteen pounds. Unless he had some kind of militia hiding somewhere in the quarters waiting for me to strike, there was no way he would get the best of me. "What the hell man?"

He looked at me and I watched as Roland's expression sadden. He looked just as he did as a kid when our mother used to catch him doing something he shouldn't have been doing."

"Answer me," I yelled. "Why man, why?"

"I assure you I have reason."

I noticed he didn't say good reason. At least he was trying to be semi honest about something.

"Come," he gestured for me to follow him down another walkway on the north side of his house that lead us to a huge backyard with an area just beyond it that looked like farmland.

When he turned to see that I hadn't moved from where I stood, he begged.

"Please, Obie. Come. I know I have a lot of explaining to do."

"You bet your ass you do. However, I'm not sure that there will ever be a good enough explanation to clear you on this one my bruddah," My eyes were cast on the mass piece of land in front of us.

"Look at me, Obie," Ro said.

"I don't know if I can stand the sight of you right now." I walked beside him, step by step. "Just tell me why and no lies. Please."

"Two years ago, I met a man named Harvey Steinberg. It was a random encounter one day when Sasha and I were at a diner talking. He overheard us trying to figure out how we were going to tell my family about our son and offered to help. After hearing him out, I realized he needed me just as much as I needed him."

"I asked you to start from the beginning bruddah."

"I am starting from the beginning. Harvey offered me two million dollars and an escape from all of this just for my kidney. He's introduced me to his attorney, and we made it happen."

"That's not what I mean. I want to know how long this thing with you and Sasha has been going on?" I barked in frustration.

"From the time she came to work for me. We met months before and I figured hiring her as my assistant would keep her close to me without any suspicions."

"What? Ro, how could you? Did you ever love Elena or was she just another conquered quest for you?"

"I cared for her. But let's be truthful Obie, Elena was more of a business partner, not a wife. She's too bull headed for her own good."

"Are you kidding me? That woman made you her world. And what about your kids and grandchildren? They didn't deserve this."

"They can handle life without me."

"You have no idea how you've hurt them. They were devastated."

"I never doubted that they would hurt when I was gone, but I knew they would eventually be just fine over time. That's why I made the request for all of you to spend the first seven days together. I hoped it would allow you all to see how easy it was to fall in line without me around."

"What if they didn't want to know that, or to feel that kind of pain. After finding that stuff in your safe, Elena had to come to terms with the fact that the love of her life was planning a whole other one with someone else."

"You must be losing your touch, bro. I thought by now you would have wifed her up." Ro's voice became indignant while spewing his thoughts of my feelings for Elena.

"This is not a joke, Roland. You're dallying with people's lives like it's a game. Is that why you left that stuff behind? As some sort of reckoning? I mean, you must have known Elena would possibly find them."

"Sasha was supposed to go into the safe the week before we left but when I actually did have a health scare, she got side tracked, and had to rush to pack her and the baby's things"

"So, it wasn't a heart attack?" I asked rhetorically.

"No, it was a major anxiety attack. Everything that I had pending caused me to spaz out. Sasha forgetting that stuff in the safe was a little sloppy, but when the doctors that Harvey had on his payroll played their role in making you all believe I was on life support I figured we'd be okay to go on with the plan.

"Elena and I met Harvey and his wife the day you were admitted, then they moved you." My words wandered off as I thought of that day, it was also the same day I could have sworn I saw Sasha down in the parking lot of the hospital."

"Harvey really needed that kidney, man. Once I tested as a match, he wasted no time wiring one hundred grand in the account that Starks set up."

"Let me get this straight. You met this Harvey Steinberg and sold your soul just so you and Sasha could be together?"

"I didn't sell my soul. I donated a kidney. There's a big difference."

"What sweet in de goat mouth is sour in he bam bam," I recited one of our mother's usual reprimands to us regarding consequences.

"Look at me. Do I look like I'm missing out on anything?"

From my peripheral, I watched his hand wave over his property. I nodded with a look of disgust on my face. Ro didn't seem phased at all.

"This is all I've ever wanted and when I got the chance to get it, I took it."

"If this is all you've ever wanted, then why did you waste thirty-eight years of Elena's life before going after it? Why bring a whole family and a church into the mix?"

"Because I didn't realize it until I actually got the chance at it. And besides, the church and the family were all Elena's ambitions, not mine."

"She didn't force your hand, Ro."

"True, but I made promises to her and at the time I thought it was only right to honor them."

"Exactly." I scoffed. "You made promises, but you still left them. If I would have known that your heart wasn't in it. There is no way I would have bowed out."

"There it is," Ro said. An evil smile spread across his face. "I knew you still wanted her. Well, you can still have the lady and the dream. Nobody else has to know." Ro's sarcasm came out more like a plea for me to keep his secret.

"Elena's back on the main island and she had the same notion that I did. She's not leaving here without answers and I'm not going to be the one to give them to her. You are."

"Don't bring her here," Ro spat.

"I won't bring her here, I'm taking you to her."

"Just let it go, Obie. Leave it be."

"I'm sure you wish I would bruddah, but that's not happening. You selfish bastard!"

I'd heard enough of him trying to justify his actions. There was nothing he could say that would make me fall in line with what he was doing.

"Call me what you want. I've made peace with my life."

I hope he has, because when Elena sees him, he may meet Jesus or Satan for real this time.

"Go tell your new family whatever you want, but I'm not leaving Centipede Island without you."

## *Not a Word*
### *Elena*

When Obie sent the message to me saying that he was on his way back to our hotel with his brother in tow, I nearly passed out from the emotions that fisted my heart. I guess a part of me hoped this was all a farce. The thought of him making a mockery of our lives and everything we've built over the years took me somewhere I thought I'd never go.

I paced the floor for a few hours, trying to sort out the aftershock of finding out that the man that I thought had left me by death, only left me for someone else.

When I heard the knock, the shock had worn off. In slow motion, I walked towards the door, placed one hand on the knob then the other over it. It literally felt like an out of body experience as I forced one hand to control the other. Hank had played with my life for over thirty-eight years and for that, he had to die.

The door opened slowly, and I stepped back to take it all in. The man that I was married to now looked totally different, but I immediately

WHEN I KILL HIM, JESUS CAN HAVE HIM

recognized those eyes and there wasn't an ounce of remorse in them.

I was suddenly paralyzed, and my eyes became the only viable part of me at that moment. I faintly remember hearing him say to Obie, "let's get this over with." Those were his choice words when he was agitated, and this wasn't a time for him to claim that emotion.

I launched out at him and wrapped my hands around his neck. I hadn't realized that I was holding my breath, probably with the same intensity that I squeezed at his throat. I wanted to break his windpipe or snap his neck and I probably could have, if I hadn't passed out.

## *Obediah*

Ro didn't help himself at all, walking into that hotel room with such a biggity attitude. I wasn't surprised by her reaction, I've seen that rage in her once before when we were younger. Seems to me she'd locked it away for just the right time.

I watched her small frame jump on my brother, wrapping her legs around his waist and her tiny fingers around his neck. She squeezed and growled like a feral animal and all I could do was watch the action. Ro fell to the ground, trying his best to unleash the dragon that was Elena but even with his strength, he couldn't loosen her clasp. The moment they hit the ground, with her on top, he hit his head on the edge of a table.

Elena had done exactly what she said she would. My brother had taken his last breath on that floor and I didn't feel an ounce of regret for what I had allowed her to do.

I picked her up off of him and laid her on the bed. She came too moments later and all I wanted to do was kiss the lips that I'd given to my undeserving brother over thirty years ago. I chose different. We had the rest of our lives to make up for time lost.

She looked at me underneath those long lashes of hers and asked,

"Is he dead?"

"Yes," I answered.

"Not a word about this," she whispered.

I shook my head and answered, "Not a single word, my dear."

# SWEET LIKE CANDY
## Yolanda Davis-McCullough

### Prologue

Lady Candice Sweet sits on the front row of First Baptist Church of Magnolia Park beaming with pride as she watches her husband deliver another dynamic sermon. She could not believe that after five years of marriage that she still felt a tingle deep in her belly every time her husband stood behind the podium. Who would have thought that she would be married to one of the most influential prominent men in the state? Not only was he a great expositor of the word, but he was also oh so fine. Candice began to daydream about what she would do with Rev. Rudolph Sweet when she got him home... As Candice slowly became aware that she was still in the church, she heard her husband inviting people to give their life to Christ. At first, she did not pay any attention to any of the people that came up to give the pastor their hand, and then she noticed something familiar about one of the new converts. Her mind raced, her heart started beating fast. No, it could not be him. Not after all of this time.

She shook her head to free it of the cobwebs and searched through her purse for her hanky to wipe the sweat from her forehead. As she looked up with the handkerchief in her hand, her eyes locked with the very last person she ever expected to see in First Baptist Church of Magnolia Park.

## *Part 1*

Flurries of snow whipped around in the morning light, as the sun peaked ever so slightly over the horizon. It was going to be a glorious winter day, a winter day where love stories are made. Candice shivered violently as another gust of wind blew over her on her five-mile walk into town. She quickly looked at her watch to see that her shift would begin in 10 minutes. At this rate, she would not make it to work in time to have breakfast before she had to begin serving. She pressed her hand against her grumbling stomach.

"I forgot that I did not have dinner last evening" Candice said out loud and quickened her pace, as she hurried towards Eat Em Up' Diner.

Candice was the oldest of five children and was essentially the guardian of her younger siblings since the death of her mother. They all lived with her grandmother, who did not have much to give but love. So, Candice took the job five miles away, not knowing how she would get to and from work, not knowing if her schedule would accommodate her continuing to attend the local college. All Candice knew is that they needed the money to survive. It wasn't just her she had to think about, she had to think about her younger brothers and sisters, she had to make sure that they were not a burden to her grandmother.

"Stop growling," said Candice as she patted her stomach, "I know you smell bacon, but if I don't hurry up, we will not get a chance to eat." She broke out into a walk-run so that she could get to the warmth of the diner and to a hot plate of food.

"Good Morning, everybody," Candice said as she walked into the homely decorated diner. She was greeted with several good mornings, grunts and other sounds of welcome. The diner's manager looked at her watch and then glanced at Candice. All it took was that look for thoughts of having breakfast to leave her mind. Candice hurried to the back to change into her work apron and shoes.

"That walk is too far for anyone to walk in this weather," mumbled Candice underneath her breath. She shook her head, rubbed her hands together to warm them and stepped back out into the dining area with a 100-watt smile.

Marquis was sitting in the corner of the diner, sipping coffee waiting on his waitress as he awaited word from the mechanic that his car was ready. Marquis could hear an occasional shout from the kitchen as he glanced around the room. Every conceivable decoration could be found on the wall. There were clocks, roosters, large wooden spoons. Marquis laughed quietly when he saw the wooden spoons. There clearly was no theme to the decorations, it just appeared to resemble an old country grandmother's home.

Marquis' attention was caught by the sweet voice of an angel. "Good Morning, may I help you? "Candice stood ready to take his order.

"You are so beautiful. How did Venus end up in Ashington, Georgia?" Candice clamped down her frustration with having another customer flirt with her and smiled brighter in return. A smile and a wink here and there helped to get good tips.

"Thank you, sir," Candice responded as she smiled brightly,

"Wow, your smile can light up a room," Marquis said as he took in all that was Candice. She was thick in all of the right places, with legs that seem to go on for days. She had a tiny waist, breasts that looked like they could fill a man's hands and a butt so round you could place a cup on it.

"Are you ready to order?"

"What do you recommend that I order?"

"Everything on the menu is good, sir. Mama Edna is the best cook in Southwest Georgia".

"Okay. That's good to know because I need something good to lighten up my mood", drawled Marquis. "My engine light came on in the car, so I pulled off at the Ashington exit to have the mechanic take a look at the car."

"I'm sorry to hear about your car. Do you need more time to think about what you would like to order?"

"No, I do not need more time. I'll take the pancakes and country ham steak. And can you dip your finger in my coffee since it needs more sweetener?" Marquis said as he winked at her devilishly.

Candice grit her teeth as she smiled a little wider at her customer. "Would you like anything else?" she drawled. Marquis nodded his head no and leaned back in his chair.

"I'll be back with your food shortly. Meanwhile, someone will come back around and fill up your coffee cup".

"Wow, she is really special," Marquis said to no one in particular. Marquis watched her walk away with a sashay that was mesmerizing to hand in his order. His eyes followed her around the diner; occasionally he would glance out the window looking at those wandering in and out. His smile grew bigger when he saw Candice heading his way again.

"Here are your pancakes and country ham, sir. Is there anything else that you need?"

"Call me Marquis, Candice." "How did you know my name?"

"Did you forget that you have on your name tag?" Marquis said with a soft laugh.

Candice smiled back at him genuinely for the first time all morning. "Okay, Marquis. Is there anything else that I can get you?"

Marquis shook his head no, as Candice's attention was caught by a customer two tables to the left. "I'll be back to check on you," she yelled over her shoulder weaving through the tables as she went to check on other customers.

The diner was bustling with every available table occupied. Marquis watched Candice as she glided amongst the tables. He watched her charm all of her customers including a little baby girl who had been crying. Marquis shook his head in wonder as he continued to eat his food.

"Man, this food is good," said Marquis.

"It's always good," said the patron behind him. "You should try her Sunday dinner special."

Before Marquis could reply, his phone began to vibrate. The mechanic was texting him that his car was ready for pickup.

"Candice," yelled Marquis as he flagged her over for the check.

"Yes, Marquis,"

"Beautiful, please bring me the check." Candice walked away to get his check, and Marquis smacked the table and nodded his head. Candice returned to the table and placed the check in Marquis' hand as another table flagged her for assistance. "I'll be right back Marquis". Marquis reached in his pocket and pulled out a $100 bill and left it on the table. He also wrote on the check, anytime you get tired of working in this diner and wish to make more money, you can work for me in Atlanta. He signed it with his name and phone number. Marquis, took one last sip of his coffee and one long look at Candice as he saluted her, smiled and walked out of the diner.

Candice returned to the table to see that Marquis had left her a generous tip for her service. As she was cleaning the table, she noticed that there was handwriting on the check. She folded it and placed it into her pocket and finished bussing the table. Candice worked long and hard the rest of the day, smiling, and charming all those that she came into contact with. When her shift ended, she went into the breakroom and began to get ready for the long walk back to her Grandmother's house. The good news was that the temperature had warmed up, so the walk home wouldn't be as bad, she just had to avoid the ice. Before leaving the breakroom, she remembered the check with the handwritten note that was in her apron pocket. She grabbed it and stuffed it into her coat pocket. As she was getting ready to leave the diner, the manager asked to speak to her briefly.

"Candice," said Ms. Ann, "I cannot continue to allow you to come in late every day. If you are late again, we will have to terminate you."

"But Ms. Ann, I am a hard worker, I don't take breaks, I do more than my share of the work."

"Here at Eat Em Up diner, we demand that our employees be punctual. If they are unable to be here at the scheduled time, then they cannot work here. So, I suggest that you get yourself together and plan on arriving on time if you want your job."

"Yes, ma'am."

## *Part 2*

Candice walked out of the diner, shoulders hunched, head down, kicking the ground periodically.

"I cannot lose my job. I need to figure out a way to get to work on time." Candice continued on her way home. "Argghh," she grimaced. "I forgot to eat," as she held her rumbling stomach. Candice stopped in her tracks and looked back the way she had come and decided that she would just continue walking home and hope to find something to eat there.

Candice was greeted by four little people as she walked through the door. Charles who was 12, Cynthia who was 10, Catherine who was 7 and little Craig who was 4. Charles didn't run up to her as the others did, because he thought he was too old to be happy to greet her when she came through the door.

"Candice, did you bring home anything from Eat Em Up?"

"Candice, how was your day?"

"Candice, did you remember to pick up the supplies I need for school?

"Candice, did you get my Legos?"

"Whooooa, one person at a time!" Candice laughed as she began removing her outer garments. "Let me see if I can answer those questions. No, I did not bring anything home from Eat Em Up. No, I did not get your school project supplies. Remember we have a stash of items in the bin, in the back room. Did you look there? And, we will get your Legos this weekend. I'll take you, that way you can pick out exactly what you want. Now did I answer everyone's questions? "

"No," yelled Charles, Cynthia, Catherine, and Craig.

"You did not answer my question," said Charles.

"And that was?"

"How was your day?"

Candice gave Charles the biggest hug that she could, her little brother was slowly growing into a man. And unlike the others, he only wanted to know how she was doing. "My day was great. Matter of fact, I made great tips today, enough that I can treat everyone to Legos this weekend!" Candice was cheered on by a chorus of "YAAAY!". She laughingly swatted them on the head and started towards the kitchen.

"Did Big Ma cook anything"?

Cynthia answered, "Yes, she made spaghetti."

"Okay. Thank God!" Candice said. "I am hungry enough to eat a whole horse!" It was a pleasant surprise that dinner was ready. It wasn't often that Big Ma cooked. Big Ma suffered from arthritis and some days it was difficult for her to get around, besides it wasn't always food in the house to cook. Times had been hard since her momma died and Candice was doing the best that she could, while still attending college. Candice stopped by the bathroom to wash up for dinner and yelled at her siblings to do the same.

Later that night as Candice was sitting at the dining room table going through the mail, she came across a letter from the college. She hurriedly opened it, hoping it was a letter congratulating her on receiving the presidential scholarship for which she had applied. Heart in mouth, Candice began to read the letter. Her smile slowly dimmed, and she let out a small cry.   It was not a letter of congratulations.

"Oh God," Candice cried, "how am I going to pay my tuition?" Tears slowly ran down her face "Tomorrow, I will ask Ms. Ann, if she could give me more hours at the diner."

"No, no, no" Candice continued the conversation with herself. "I will never make enough money before the spring semester to pay my tuition." She angrily pushed her chair back from the table

She angrily grabbed her coat and keys to head out the door for some fresh air.  Just before opening the door, she stuck her hand into her coat pocket and came into contact with the check from the diner that Marquis had written on.  She pulled out the receipt and read the message.  She grabbed her phone and called the number.  As the phone was ringing,

"This is crazy," said Candice as she put her finger on the disconnect button, as though she would hang the phone up.  "I made a promise to mama though."

So, she stayed on the phone and waited for Marquis to answer. The call went to voice mail.  Candice laid her head on the door, as her shoulders trembled from her silent tears

"What in the world am I going to do?  How will I be able to continue helping Big Ma and go to school like I promised mama?"  With a heavy sigh, Candice turned around, took off her coat and walked down the hall to begin preparing for bed.  "If I go to bed now, I'll be able to make it to work on time"

## Part 3

Candice awoke to another cold winter morning.  She quickly glanced out of the window to see what the weather was like.

"Charles, Cynthia, Catherine, and Craig, wake up and start getting ready for school." Her yell was met with grumbles and moans. Craig even buried himself further under the cover to try and hide from her. She quickly went into the kitchen to start breakfast for the kids all the while watching the clock so that she could leave home early enough as to not be late for work. She called the kids to the table for breakfast and gave each of them a kiss before leaving to go start getting ready for work.

As Candice walked into the diner and yelled a hearty good morning to everyone, she quickly glanced at the clock to see that she had made it to work with 10 minutes to spare. She gave a relieved smile to Ms. Ann on her way to the breakroom to change into her apron and work shoes. Candice's day at the diner did not go as well as the previous day. The customers were rude, and her tips suffered.

"You okay?" asked Paula, as she walked into the break room.

"Yes," Candice replied with no enthusiasm or certainty.

"Then why is your head down on the table?"

"My head is up now, is that better?"

"Have you been crying?"

That question caused more tears to run down Candice's cheeks. "Paula, did you know my mother?"

"Everyone knew and loved your mother. It was very sad to see such a lively vibrant spirit deteriorate over time."

"Cancer is such a beast. In the last days, I did everything in my power to make her happy. I would make her banana and mayonnaise sandwiches because that's what she always had a taste for." Candice laughed quietly. "I promised her that I would make sure that all of us stayed together. I promised her that I would finish college and marry a good man. But I don't know how I am going to finish school." Candice whined.

"Don't cry baby," said Paula as she comforted Candice. "I am sure that your mother knows that you are doing everything in your power to make good of your promises. Wash your face, smile and get back out to the floor. Don't worry – we'll cover you as much as we can around here."

For the rest of the day, she hustled to make good tips.

Candice's father had stolen her identity and that prevented her from qualifying for financial aid. He was always on the run, as he had made a career out of stealing identities.

Candice went to cash out at the end of the day and her tips totaled a whopping $22. She would have to dip into her tip monies from the day before that she had set aside to treat her siblings on Saturday so that she would be able to buy groceries for the remainder of the week.

Candice wiped away the tears as she walked home. Her shoulders trembled from all the effort of trying not to yell out in pain. She walked slowly towards home with her head hung low.   As she dug her hands deeper into her coat pocket in frustration, she came across the receipt again with Marquis' phone number. Before she could change her mind, she dialed the number.

"Hello," a male voice greeted her.

"May I speak to Marquis? This is Candice from Ashington, Georgia".

"Hello Candice, this is Marquis. I have been waiting to hear from you."

"You have been waiting to hear from me? Why?"

"You are very personable, and I believe you would be a great fit in my company. Are you calling about the job?"

"Yes. Yes, I am."

"This is great news. Are you able to get to Atlanta tomorrow for a job interview?"

Candice hesitated and Marquis repeated the question.  Before she could lose her cool, Candice answered, "Yes. I will come to Atlanta for an interview."

She listened closely as he gave her instructions on the time and location of the interview and asked him to also send her a text message with the information. Marquis asked Candice to send him a copy of her resume and they would be all set for her interview.

Candice walked in the house and went to Big Ma's room.

"Big Ma," she hesitated. "I have a job interview on tomorrow, however, it is in Atlanta".

"That sounds good child. What position will you be interviewing for and what is the name of the company? How did you hear about them?" Candice proceeded to update Big Ma about how she found out about the job and how she had met Marquis.

"Baby, you know I love you and I would do anything for you. But this sounds sketchy. If you go to that interview tomorrow, I believe you should take someone with you."

"I hear you Big Ma, but this could be the answer to our prayers. I could continue going to school. I would also have more money to help you out more with the kids."

"I hear you baby, but I don't feel right about this job in Atlanta. It sounds too good to be true," said Big Ma.

"I understand what you are saying, however, you are the one who constantly tells me that I have to have faith. I have prayed to God for an answer, and I believe this may be it." Candice pleaded.

"But have you heard from God? You should only follow through if you have heard from God."

Candice gave Big Ma a hug and a kiss on the cheek and went to her room. She stared at the ceiling contemplating what she would do on tomorrow and fell asleep still not knowing how to move forward.

## *Part 4*

Candice sat on the Greyhound bus looking out the window on her way to Atlanta for the job interview with Marquis,

"Oh mama, am I doing the right thing? You taught me that whatever

I ask of God, that He will give it to me. Mama, I am not sure that this is what God, wants me to do. Please send me a sign." Candice uttered softly underneath her breath.

Over the loudspeaker of the bus, she heard the driver announce

"Lotian Lakes next stop. Last stop before Atlanta with an estimated arrival time of 1:00pm."

Candice looked at her watch to see that it was 11:00am, she felt like she had been on the bus for days, not just hours. She decided that she would exit the bus in Lotian Lakes to use the restroom and get a snack. She hoped there was a decent bathroom at the Atlanta bus station so that she could change into her interview clothes. The Lotian Lakes bus stop was at the general store in town that did not have a lot of options for food. Candice paid for some peanut butter cookies and a bottle of water while she waited her turn for the restroom. She returned to the bus, took her seat and prepared to show her ticket to the driver. Soon thereafter the bus departed, and she begins to get drowsy.

"Ladies and gentlemen, we will be arriving at the Atlanta bus stop in 10 minutes. Please look around your area and make sure that you have gathered together all of your personal belongings," the bus driver advised.

Candice awoke with a shake of her body from the woman behind her. She wiped the sleep from her eyes and gathered her belongings. She took out her purse to make sure she remembered to bring the number for cabs in the area. As soon as they arrived at the Atlanta bus stop, Candice hurried to the restroom to change into her interview outfit and called a cab. When the cab arrived, she was smartly dressed in a crisp navy-blue skirt, with a silk white button down, and navy-blue tweed jacket. To complement the ensemble, she wore pantyhose and navy sling backs. She put on a touch of lip gloss, touched up her hair and greeted her cab driver. The driver took one look at her and let out a slow whistle.

"You are beautiful!" The driver nearly sang the compliment.

Candice flashed her 100-watt smile and demurely replied, "Thank You." The cab driver took a look at the address that Candice handed him and asked her if she was sure she had the correct address. Candice looked at the address she had written down from Marquis and confirmed the address was correct. "Are you sure?"

A little annoyed that the driver kept asking her if she had the correct address, Candice answered snappishly, "Yes, I am sure." She then sat back in the seat and pretended to do something in her agenda in order to halt any additional questions or conversation from the driver. Twenty-minutes later, the car stopped in front of a building that appeared to be a rooming house.

"We are at your destination."

"Are you sure?"

The driver snickered and said "Yes." Candice rolled her eyes at him and exited the vehicle.

She took one deep breath and entered the main door to the rooming house. There was a small area right off of the foyer which had a small desk with a computer, and chairs. Candice gave a small sigh of relief that the interior of the building did not match the exterior. Candice stood there for a few moments waiting to be greeted. She began to get antsy because she did not want it to appear as though she was late, as this was the first impression she would make. She was at odds as to what to do, should she say hello in a raised voice, or should she knock on the doors that she could see? Suddenly, Marquis came out of one of the doors.

"Candice, you are as beautiful as I remember. Please come in and have a seat." Candice followed Marquis into a room that appeared to be his office. The room was decorated elegantly. The walls were painted a muted green with the largest mahogany desk that she had ever seen sitting in the middle of the room. The seat behind the desk looked like it could fit two people and looked to be made of the softest leather.

"Please, sit down Candice. May I get you something to drink?"

"No, thank you."

"Okay, so tell me about you?" Marquis said as he took the seat behind the desk and steepled his hands together. Candice began to describe herself as a hard worker, who was a team player and possessed a willingness to learn anything. Hearing how Candice described herself bought a smile to Marquis' face. Candice seeing this smile, stopped short in her description of herself and asked Marquis, "What is the position that you had in mind for me?"

Carefully, Marquis began to describe the position. "I am looking for someone to head up my Business Development division. In this role, you would be responsible for obtaining potential clients and be instrumental in securing a contractual agreement. In addition to obtaining new clients, you would also be responsible for ensuring that existing clients maintain their business relationship with our company. You would also be responsible for ensuring that our relationships with our clients remain a positive experience. Does this sound like something you could do?"

Candice listened carefully to what Marquis had shared with her and replied, "I believe that I am capable of performing the tasks that you have outlined, after some initial training."

Marquis smile grew wider as he replied, "I am sure that you are more than capable; and I believe that you will excel in this position and I will personally handle your training."

"What type of business do you run?"

"I run a brothel."

"A brothel!" Candice choked! "As in ladies of the night? Prostitutes? You are a pimp?"

"Yes. And, with your looks and charm, the business will expand in no time."

Candice hurriedly got up from her seat and swiftly moved to the door. She could not believe that she had traveled all the way to Atlanta for this. To work as a Business Development partner for a brothel. A prostitute!

"Hear me out Candice," Marquis said before she could walk through the door. "I am offering you a guaranteed $5,000.00 a month to start with a $5,000.00 bonus payable after three months of employment. The position comes with room and board and a clothing allowance. "

Candice did not wait to hear any more, she raced out of the door and out of the rooming house, berating herself for thinking that this was going to be the way out. She hurriedly walked down the sidewalk, trying to get as far away from Marquis and his 'house' as possible. When she thought she was far enough away, she used her phone to order a cab back to the bus station.

## *Part 5*

"I cannot believe that I spent money to travel all of the way to Atlanta for this," huffed Candice as she stomped down the sidewalk. "This is crazy, he was crazy, wasn't his business illegal."

"Ma'am are you alright?" asked a passerby who looked as though she should be asking him the same question.

"Yes." Candice rolled her eyes as she realized that she had been talking to herself loudly.

"How can he offer $5,000.00 a month guaranteed for prostitution? What craziness would I have to do for that salary?" Candice ended her self conversation as she saw the cab pull up.

She heard the driver announce that they were approaching Lotian Lakes, the midway point between Atlanta and Ashington. She did not get off at this stop as she did when headed to Atlanta. She just wanted to get home and be surrounded by her family and be engulfed in a big hug by Big Ma.

She quickly changed out of her interview clothes and began the long walk from town back home. She wished they had more Uber drivers in Ashington, it would make her life easier.

"Well the good thing about me walking all of the time is that it keeps me fine. Fine enough to be considered to work in a brothel." She laughed hysterically and walked through the door of Big Ma's house. The house was in a complete uproar when she returned.

"What is going on?" Candice inquired.

"Big Ma, is in the room crying," said Cynthia. Candice ran to Big Ma's room and knocked on the door softly.

"Big Ma, it's Candice, may I come in?"

Big Ma replied with a muffled yes. "Baby," said Big Ma "Please tell me that you got that job. I received this letter in the mail today."

Candice reached for the paper that Big Ma was holding out to her and read the letter. As she quickly skimmed the letter, she noticed in bold letters that Big Ma was behind on paying the taxes for the property. They had given them so many days to bring the account current, or they would place a tax lien on the property and begin the process of selling to the highest bidder. Candice heart sunk.

"Well Big Ma, the job was not..."

Big Ma interrupted, "You took the job right Candice? I cannot lose this property, this property belonged to your great-great-grandfather. And has been in my family for generations. This property was meant for your mother and now you. We have to save it."

The tears started to roll down Big Ma's face. Candice did not know what to do, she had never seen Big Ma cry before. Candice's heart broke, and all she could do was give Big Ma a hug and tell her that everything would be alright.

## *Part 6*

Candice glanced out of the window of the Greyhound bus. She was on her way back to Atlanta to take the position that Marquis offered. He would be shocked. She had not called him to tell him that she would accept the job.

"Oh mama, how did it all come to this? Mama, you never prepared me for disappointments. How did you ever get involved with my father? You were such a good woman, what could you have seen in him? Oh mama, why did you have to die?" Candice cried softly. Candice wiped the tears from her eyes and tried to think of happy thoughts. Cynthia, Catherine, and Craig were happy and sad that she would be moving to Atlanta. She assured them that it would be a short stay and promised to bring them to visit soon. She also told them that she left Big Ma the money to take them shopping for Legos. Charles, on the other hand, was very somber. He gave her a big hug before she left and asked her to be careful. He touched her heart.

"Ladies, and gentleman, we will arrive at the Atlanta bus station in 10 minutes. Please look around you and gather up all of your belongings." said the bus driver.

Twenty-five minutes later Candice stood outside of what looked like a rooming house, took one long breath, said a prayer, grabbed all of her luggage and walked into the house.

## *Part 7*

As Marquis scanned the crowd at First Baptist Church of Magnolia Park, his eyes were caught by the second most beautiful young lady that he had seen. Then he realized, no, it was not the second most beautiful young lady that he had seen, but the first. He was staring at the one and only Candice from Ashington, Georgia.

" She is still as beautiful as I remember, no actually, she is even more beautiful." He mumbled. He gave her a huge smile and a wink when he caught her eye and smiled even brighter when he noticed how nervous she seemed. He couldn't wait until service was over so that he could speak to her. Marquis returned his attention to Rev. Sweet. He had been really touched by his sermon and felt a tug on his heart. He could not believe that he had walked into a church, let alone come up to the altar.

"My dear brother, would you like to give your life  to Christ?"

"Yes."

"Do you know that God loves you?"

"Yes."

"I want each of you to know that God is a forgiving God, He is a God that is loving and kind.  We would like to welcome each of you to the First Baptist Church of Magnolia Park. Please remain after service for a few moments for additional information."

Candice took a deep breath as she saw Marquis return to his seat. She did not know what she would do, after service.  Typically, she and Rudolph would personally welcome new members to First Baptist and exchange pleasantries prior to them meeting with the hospitality ministry.

"I  need an excuse," Candice said quietly to no one.  When Candice heard the benediction, she still had not come up with an excuse.  After the last amen, she turned towards the exit to try and get out of the sanctuary before Rudolph beckoned her to his side.  As she hurried towards the door, she saw Rudolph wave to her.

"Lady Sweet," said Mother Estile.

"Yes."

"Pastor would like for you to join him to welcome the new members. "

With a sigh of resignation, she walked towards Rudolph and their newest members.

Marquis stood in line behind all of the other new members and made sure that he would be last to greet the couple.  It came as a shock to him as he overheard Pastor Sweet introducing Candice as his wife. "Wow, Candice is married."  He laughed softly.  "Candice married, to not only one of the most influential men in the state, but a Pastor?"

Every now and then he glimpsed that smile that only Candice possessed as she greeted each of the newcomers.  She began to laugh nervously as he got closer to speaking to her and the Pastor

"Welcome Brother," said Pastor Sweet.

"Marquis, my name is Marquis Dhouse."

"Welcome Brother Dhouse to First Baptist Church of Magnolia Park. This is my lovely wife, Candice Sweet".

Marquis turned to Candice and smiled, "Hello Candy."

"No, my son, her name is Candice."

"I'm sorry, Pastor, I knew her as Candy, you see I knew her..."

Candy interrupted Marquis, "We knew each other in college Pastor. Some of my friends and acquaintances would refer to me as Candy."

"Oh, what a joy, one of your college friends. Welcome again my brother and we would love for you to be more involved with ministry activities. We are a family here and want you to know that we are here for you. The hospitality team will speak to you now and gather some additional information from you. We hope to see you Tuesday evening for New Member Orientation."

"Thank you, Pastor. I will see you on Tuesday," said Marquis as he walked away with hospitality. As he was walking out of the sanctuary he turned back and gave Candice another smile and a wink.

"Honey, how well did you know Brother Dhouse?" asked Rudolph.

"I did not know him well, I only knew him in passing."

"That's strange, he referred to you as Candy, I would think that is a nickname reserved for those who are close to you."

Candy shrugged and changed the topic. She grabbed her husband by the hand and began to head towards his office. She wanted to get him off of the property and home, before they ran into Marquis again.

## *Part 8*

Candice pulled into the church parking lot for another day of ministry, serving as a mentor to young ladies. She loved working with them and looked forward to Wednesday evening meetings. Candice stepped out of her car, smoothed her skirt down, and straightened her jacket. With a flick of her hair she closed and locked her car doors as she sashayed towards the church. She entered the administrative wing of the church and spoke to the parishioners and ministry team members as she walked towards her office. Being in her office always gave her joy. Candice placed her purse in the file cabinet as she sat down behind her desk. She leaned back in the chair and took a refreshing breath. She let her mind wander a bit, before she had to start preparing for the meeting with the young ladies. There was a knock at the door.

"Yes."

Sis. Townley stuck her head around the door. "Good afternoon Lady Sweet. There is a gentleman here to see you. His name is Brother Dhouse. He said to let you know that he would like to speak with you." Candice sat up in her seat hurriedly and went to interrupt Sis. Townley. Sis Townley smiled and put up her hand to stop her. "He also said that he could speak to Pastor Sweet if you prefer. "

"No, no, no Sis. Townley. Show him in." Candice sat at her desk with her shaking hands folded in front of her.

Marquis sauntered into the room and closed the door behind him ."Good Afternoon Candy."

"It's Candice."

"Candice." Marquis sat on the arm of one of the chairs.

"What do you want Marquis?" Candice posed as she stiffly got up from her desk and turned towards the window.

"What can you give me?"

Candice's spine straightened as she swiftly turned from the window and replied huffily ."I can offer you God."

"God? No Candy, I want something from you."

"Candice!"

"Candy Cane."

"It's Candice!" She emphasized each syllable of her name with a fist to her desk.

"Should I have this conversation with Pastor Sweet?"

"No," Candice answered with a resigned sigh as she sat back down in her chair. "How did you know I was here?"

"The ministry booklet that was given at New Members' Orientation. You know what Candy, because I like you so much, I am going to wait to let you know what I want from you. Have a good meeting with those impressionable young ladies."

Marquis left Candice's office with a smile and a wink. As he left, Candice placed her head in her hands "Oh mama, what am I going to do?"

## Part 9

The sun was bright, and a little breeze whipped through Magnolia Park. Candice hurriedly got into the car to keep the wind from blowing up her skirt. Rudolph climbed in next to her, reached over and squeezed her hand.

"Baby, what's wrong, you haven't been yourself lately. Wait, are you pregnant?"

"No, Rudolph, I don't think that I am. I just have a lot on my mind."

Candice used to look forward to Sundays, but since Marquis joined the church six weeks ago, all of her joy was gone. She never knew when he would show up or what he would say. Last month he interjected himself into a conversation she was having with a young lady, to say that she had worked hard to put herself through college. The young lady wanted to know what she did, and did she make enough money to live comfortably. She had to redirect the conversation and end it abruptly. Two weeks ago, he walked into choir rehearsal where she was preparing to sing and started singing underneath his breath "tastes like candy". And the kicker was last week, when he waved to her and Rudolph as they were leaving the church and shouted, "Bye Candy Cane".

She was on edge, it took all of her wits to be one step ahead. He seemed to always know where she was. Even crazier, he never returned to let her know what he wanted from her and her imagination was driving her crazy.

"Well Candice, I think you may be pregnant. You are moody, and you have been eating a lot lately."

"Tomorrow," Candice assured him. "I'll call the doctor's office and make an appointment."

Rudolph squeezed her hand as he parked the car and gave her a quick kiss. He walked around to her side of the car, opened the door, gave her a squeeze and a deep lingering kiss.

"Baby, do you know that I love you? I cannot believe how blessed I am to have met you. It is true that when a man findeth a wife, he findeth a good thing. You are my good thing."

Candice smiled at Rudolph as they held hands while walking into the sanctuary. Rudolph gave her hand another squeeze and a quick kiss on the cheek and walked to his office. Candice checked her watch and saw that she had a few moments before Sunday Church School started, so she walked to her office to check her mail. She walked into her office and before she could close the door behind her, Marquis walked in behind her.

"Well, well, well, if it isn't the Lady Candice Sweet. Tell me Candice do you still taste like Candy? Can you still do that trick that..."

"What do you want Marquis?" interrupted Candice.

"You know what I want."

"No, I do not know what you want. You have not made it clear."

"Candy," Marquis held up his hand to stop Candice from interrupting him. "Lady Sweet, you spent several years with me in Atlanta. You were closer to me than anyone else that I knew. I tutored you, trained you and taught you things that allowed you to make enough money to continue school and build your grandmother a bigger house. What do you think I want?"

"Marquis, stop playing with me and spell out what you want?"

"Lady Sweet when you stopped working for me as a Business Developer, my business suffered. Clients stopped using my firm because Candy had left."

"Marquis..."

"I'll tell you what I want, I want you. I want you back in my bed, I want you back at the firm."

"Marquis, I am a married woman who is in love with her husband."

"Does Pastor Sweet know that he married a whore?"

Candice slapped Marquis so hard he stumbled momentarily. "A minute ago, you said I was a Business Developer."

"I'll let you get by this time Candice but mark my words if I don't get what I want, not only will I tell Pastor Sweet about the tricks his wife used to do, I will run a full ad in the Magnolia Park Post with pictures describing your exploits." With that, Marquis turned to leave Candice's office before he closed the door behind him, he looked at Candice and with a smile and wink said, "Bye - Candy".

Candice sat in her chair and sent a message to Sis. Townly telling her to let Pastor know that she was not feeling well and would stay in her office through the service. Candice, locked the door, kicked off her shoes and paced. If Rudolph found out what she used to do for a living, he would be devastated. If the information was put into the paper, it would ruin Rudolph's ministry. "Mama, you always taught me to be honest. I don't understand why I never told Rudolph in the beginning? Mama, why had I thought that my past could be forgotten? What can I do? Candice began to clutch at her stomach and placed a hand over her mouth. She raced out of the door into the restroom to empty her stomach.

Rudolph walked into his wife's office after service to take her home. "My God, you have truly blessed me," said Rudolph as he stared down at his beautiful wife, His wife was a jewel, not only was she beautiful, she was intelligent and an awesome woman of God. "I remember the day that I met you. There you were on the side of the road in those slingbacks and pencil skirt trying to change the tire on your car." They both laughed at the memory. "You know what?" Rudolph was laughing so hard he could hardly speak. "I told my boys later on that what got my attention wasn't the tire but your derriere." Rudolph, while still chuckling, looked closer at Candice and noticed that she had dark circles under her eyes, and he recalled that she had not been sleeping well lately. He looked around her office and gathered her purse and gently picked her up in his arms. She restlessly requested that he put her down.

"Nonsense, my dear. You are tired and I'll just carry you to the car."

Rudolph placed her in the car, fastened her seatbelt and gave her a gentle kiss on the forehead. As he closed the passenger door to go around to the driver's side.

"Lord thank you for blessing me with the perfect helpmate for the ministry," Rudolph opened the driver side door, looked at his wife, smiled and began the drive home.


## *Part 10*


The Sweets were greeted with the pleasant aroma of dinner still in the air when they returned home. Candice had pulled a page from her Big Ma's book and had cooked a good old-fashioned Sunday Dinner before they had left for church. It felt good to be able to come home and relax after service. Rudolph and Candice removed their Sunday's finest and changed into something to lounge around the house. It wasn't often that Rudolph did not have ministerial duties after Sunday service, so today they had planned on taking advantage of a quiet afternoon.

"Candice, you sure did put your foot in those turnip greens. I am fit for nothing but sleep right now." Rudolph said with a slight laugh.

"Thank you baby, Big Ma taught me how to cook. I'll wash up the dishes and join you in the family room in a few moments. Would you like for me to bring you some banana pudding?"

"No, thank you. I'll have some later."

Rudolph hugged Candice and walked to the family room to his favorite spot. Candice could hear the TV as she loaded the dishwasher. She would give him about 15 minutes before she would hear light snoring. It always amused her at how fast that man could fall asleep. He once fell asleep at a traffic light because they had waited there for a long time. Candice continued with the happy thoughts as she tidied up the kitchen and began prepping for the next day. She didn't hear snoring, but she knew Rudolph was sleep. As she walked into the family room, Rudolph turned towards her and beckoned her to come sit with him in his Lazy Boy.

"Really?"

"Come sit next to me. The reason we have an oversized Lazy Boy is so that we can sit and cuddle."

"Why aren't you sleep?"

"The Lord is dealing with me right now, he is trying to tell me something, but I haven't yet figured out what the message is."

"Well, maybe I should leave you with the Lord and go to another room."

"No, baby, the Lord and I need you right here next to me."

Candice sat next to Rudolph with her phone in her lap and placed her head on his shoulder while they cuddled up nice and close to watch the basketball game. After a few moments, she began to feel his body relax as he began to take long even breaths. Soon thereafter, she heard light snoring. She chuckled, it never failed, and this man could not sit still for long without going to sleep. "Lord, I love this man." She was truly blessed to be married to him. Just then her phone vibrated.

Rudolph stirred in his sleep and asked drowsily "Who is that?"

Glancing at her phone quickly, Candice turned it faced down and replied, "No one, go back to sleep."

Rudolph drifted back to sleep as Candice sat there quietly. When Rudolph was sound asleep, she gently arose from the chair with her phone in her hand to head to another part of the house. She unlocked her phone and clicked on the message from Marquis. There on her phone screen was a picture of her and another man in an uncompromising position. Candice immediately deleted the picture from her phone and rushed to the bathroom to vomit. "Candice looked at herself in the mirror. "I look sick! "This cannot be my life. God, why now? Why would you have this happen to me right now? Lord, I repented, I have done everything that you have asked of me. Why would you ruin my life now?" Candice dropped to the floor of the bathroom rocking back and forth silently crying.

A soft knock came at the door. "Candice, are you alright?"

Candice dried her tears and answered in as normal of a voice as she could. "Yes, babe, I'm alright."

Candice could hear movement outside of the door and thought that Rudolph had walked away, so was surprised when she heard his voice again, this time from closer to where she was on the floor.

"Candice you know that I love you dearly. There isn't anything that I wouldn't do for you. I am not sure if I ever shared with you that the day that I met you, I was in a dark place with ministry. I had been pouring out my soul to the people of God. Giving my all, as God required of me, but wondering why weren't the people being changed? Why did it seem like the more I poured out, the emptier they and myself became? At that time, I thought that ministry would be a bed of roses, that every day would be Hallelujah. I asked God for a sign, I asked God to let me know if I should remain in the ministry and that is when I saw the cutest little derriere tooted up, attached to the longest legs that I have seen to a beautiful woman trying to change a flat tire." Rudolph laughed. "I stopped my car, got out and walked over to you and asked if you needed help. You turned to me and smiled. The Lord spoke to me and said, this is your wife. I am giving you a helpmate, to help fill you up and pray you up when ministry empties you."

"Rudolph, what if you did not find me by God's design?"

"Before asking for your hand in marriage, I sought God and asked if you were my good thing. I meditated day and night to make sure that this decision was of God. He answered me loud and clear to let me know that you were my wife. And since that time, the ministry has flourished, we have prospered, I have been strengthened. I do not know where I, or the ministry would be if it had not been for you."

"Rudolph, you sound so close."

"Open the door babe."

Candice reached up and opened the bathroom door, to find Rudolph sitting on the floor talking to her through the bathroom door.

"I love you Candice and I need you."

## *Part 11*

The next morning, Candice arose extra early to start preparing for their day. Mondays were usually a very lazy day as it was almost officially referred to as National Pastors' Day Off. Candice hummed a tune under her breath as she began to prepare breakfast. She really enjoyed cooking, it was something about being in the kitchen that gave her a calming feeling. As she was standing at the stove, she felt her husband behind her. He slowly hugged her and kissed her on the neck.

"Honey, you smell so good, and taste like Candy."

Candice tensed at this statement and tried to brush off how that comment made her feel. "Good morning honey."

"Good morning Lady Sweet. How did you rest?"

"I slept like a baby."

"Really, from my observation you did not rest well, plus you were up early this morning, and in the bathroom an awfully long time. Be sure to call the doctor today."

"Yes honey, I will give the doctor's office a call for an appointment. Now help me finish up breakfast so that we can eat."

The kitchen was filled with a comfortable silence as Rudolph and Candice continued preparing breakfast. Occasionally, Rudolph would glance at Candice and smile at her when he would catch her eye. Something was wrong, he could feel it in his bones. And it didn't have anything to do with her recent episodes of vomiting. He smiled to himself.

"Are you sure you are okay?"

"Yes babe, I am fine"

"I'm asking because you have been dealing with an upset stomach for a while."

He was waiting to hear her voice that she thought she may be pregnant. That was one of the things that got to him sometimes. Candice was such a closed book at times. She did not open up a lot about her past or even how she felt, and this frustrated him. He wanted to be her rock, her support, but it was difficult if she never showed any signs of weakness. He prayed to God daily to allow Candice to see that he was the husband that God had sent her. He often wondered what had happened in Candice's life to make her the way that she was. It was strange. Her siblings were very different from her, they were a loving bunch. Her Big Ma was open, loving and sweet. In time God will touch her heart and, in the meantime, he would just continue to love her as best he could.

"Rudolph, what do you have planned for the day?" Candice asked as they sat down to the breakfast table to eat.

"I'll probably laze about the house today. Maybe do some gardening. I don't have any real plans as I need to rest. How about you?"

"I am going to work on the curriculum for the girls mentoring today, and then send out letters to all of the local group homes letting them know about our girls' mentoring group."

"Didn't you forget something?"

"No."

"You are to call the doctor's office to schedule an appointment."

"Oh yes, that," Candice said with a nervous giggle.

They continued their breakfast exchanging small talk about their plans for the day. And cleaned up the kitchen together once finished.

"Well, I am going to go and pitter around in the garden, and you my darling need to call the doctor's office." Rudolph said as he swatted Candice on the derriere and headed out the door.

"This man never quits," said Candice as she headed to the family room to call the doctor's office.

A few moments later, Candice headed out to the garden "Rudolph, I got lucky, the doctor had a cancellation and said that if I could get there by 11am he could see me."

"What are you waiting for then, go start getting ready? Wait up, I am coming with you."

"You don't have to go with me, I am a big girl."

"I know, but I want to go with you. Now stop your arguing and procrastinating and let's get ready."

## Part 12

"Wow Candice, we are going to be parents. Can you believe this?"

Candice murmured a soft no.

"Are you happy about this Candice?"

"Yes Rudolph, just in shock. I never thought that I would be a mother. Wow, a mother, Candice. Mama." For the first time since learning of her impending motherhood, Candice broke out into that glowing smile she was known for. She turned around and gave Rudolph the biggest hug.

"Rudolph, we are going to be parents."

Rudolph took Candice in his arms, picked her up and swung her around in a circle, all the while both of them giggling like little kids on a playground.

"So, mama what would you like to do for the rest of the day?"

"Well, let's walk around for a bit, before heading to lunch. We also need to remember to pick up the prenatal vitamins from the pharmacy before heading home."

"Okay, let's head to the park."

"Pastor! Lady Sweet!" An all too familiar voice to Candice rang out. She cringed as she and Rudolph stopped in their steps and turned towards Marquis.

"Hello Brother Dhouse," said Rudolph.

"Hello Pastor, hello Lady Sweet. You all look very happy today."

"Yes, my brother, God has truly been good to us. How are you doing?"

"I am well Pastor. I flagged you all down, because I just received some wonderful news. I was able to contact several of my old business partners and clients from my firm and they have all confirmed that they will be in church on Sunday for our Family and Friends Day. Isn't this wonderful news Lady Sweet? I believe you may know some of them as they were acquaintances of mine from 'college'."

"That is great news Brother Dhouse. It is always a happy day in The Kingdom when you can spread the word of the gospel to others."

"Yes sir, ma'am. Also, Pastor I wanted you to know that I have joined the media ministry. They have begun orienting me with the equipment and I will be on duty this Sunday. I am excited to be working in the ministry."

"I am glad you are enthusiastic about working in The Kingdom."

"Well, I am going to say good day, you all have a wonderfully blessed day and see you on Sunday."

"Good day," beamed Rudolph.

"Bye," said Candice drily.

They continued on their way to the park, Candice with a little less pep in her step. She understood Marquis's cryptic message. He was inviting all of the former Johns to church. What excuse could she give to not attend church on Sunday? The pregnancy diagnosis had come just in time.

"Rudolph, do you think college we are having a boy or a girl? What would you prefer?"

"Honey, I hate to change the subject. I am as excited about becoming a parent as you are. There is something about Brother Dhouse, that just doesn't sit right with me. I don't know what it is, but I am on guard every time he comes around. What do you know about him?"

"Not much," stuttered Candice, "we had similar friends and would attend some of the same events during college," Candice whispered a silent prayer for forgiveness. She could not believe that she had sunk so low she was lying to her husband. Candice even crossed her eyes for good measure.

"Hmmm, strange. He seems to know a lot about you. And the way he looks at you..."

"I don't know," Candice said, shrugging her shoulders. "Let's change the subject, Monday is a no church business day."

"You are right" Rudolph said and laughed. "I am spending the day with my bestest girl."

## *Part 13*

Candice was still on cloud nine. She was now going to have a child of her own to love and care for. Maybe all of those years caring for Charles, Cynthia, Catherine and Craig would pay off. She couldn't wait to tell them the big news. Big Ma would be elated. As she continued to prepare for the mentoring group, she heard a knock on the door.

"Come in," Candice sang. She looked up from her paperwork and her bright moment dimmed when she saw who had just walked into her office. "Marquis. I would ask you to have a seat, but you are not going to be here that long."

"If it isn't Ms. Candy Cane. How are you?"

"What do you want Marquis?"

"I have told you already Candice, that I want you back in my bed and at the firm."

"Marquis, I would have thought that with you coming to Christ, that you would be a changed man."

"I am a changed man, years ago I would have just taken what I wanted. Now I ask."

"You call blackmailing me asking? That's funny. Leave my office please."

"I will, but I just wanted you to know that there is still time for you to avoid our friends coming to church on Sunday. All you have to do is agree to come back to me."

"Are you crazy, Marquis?"

"Maybe, and just remember if you decide not to come on Sunday, I'm working the audio video and may mistakenly upload one of your photos instead of the announcements. Bye Candy." Marquis growled leaving her office.

"Uggghhhh" moaned Candice. "This man is going to be the death of me and my dreams. I need a new plan. Maybe I should tell Rudolph? Oh mama, what should I do? Lord please guide me, I don't know what to do." At that moment the alarm went off on her phone. She glanced at the time and gathered her things and placed a smile on her face and headed to her young lady mentoring meeting.

\*\*\*

"Honey hurry up. We are going to be late for church."

"I'm coming, I am just finishing putting on the final touches to my makeup."

Candice walked out of the bathroom and Rudolph was startled. There stood his wife in the most hideous wig he had ever seen. She had on this voluminous dress that didn't touch any part of her body except her shoulders. The white pantyhose and prayer warrior 3 shoes she had on completed her ensemble. Rudolph started laughing hysterically.

"Really honey, you are pregnant, not dead. What are you trying to do? You look like you are trying to be incognito."

"No, I just thought, I would dress comfortably today."

"Well, you don't look comfortable, you look horrendous. Please change, for me, please."

"Well okay, but I am keeping on the wig."

Rudolph shrugged and gave up. At least she was changing some of the things.

As they were sitting in the car on the way to church Rudolph noticed how tense Candice was. He reached over and squeezed her hand and gave her a small sweet smile.

"Babe, loosen up, you are acting like you are going to the guillotine."

"Sorry, just feeling a little crazy. You know the hormones and stuff." She breathed heavily. "Rudolph, you know how I don't talk much about my past."

"Yes."

"Well, I would like to tell you..." the phone ringing interrupted Candice's confession.

"Hold that thought honey; it's the church. Yes, this is Pastor Sweet. Yes. Did you check the office next to the vestibule? Okay. And the camera system did not pick up anyone? Alright. I'll be there in a few; we are pulling into the parking lot. " Rudolph hung up the phone. "Honey can we wait to talk after church? It looks like someone may have tried to break in and security is reviewing the tape to see what might have happened."

When they arrived at the church, Rudolph jumped out the car, ran around to the passenger side, gave her a quick kiss, closed the door and jetted into the church. "Let me go get an update and I'll meet you in your office." He threw at her over her shoulders.

Candice slowly walked to her office tightly holding her purse. She placed her purse on the top of the desk instead of in its usual place in the file cabinet and went around the desk to stare out of the window. She heard the door opening and turned around expecting to see Rudolph and there standing in the door was Marquis.

"You were not invited in, you should really learn not to barge into someone's office without knocking."

"You are mine Candice, I do not need an invitation."

Candice glanced at her purse on top of her desk while responding to Marquis. "I do not belong to you!"

Marquis swiftly moved to the other side of the desk and grabbed Candice's arm.

"Let me go Marquis."

"Make me, agree to be mine again."

"I can never be yours. I was never yours to begin with."

"I was your first, I owned you. You did what I said, when I said and how I said it. Now tell me yes or I'll let your too good to be true husband know that he married a whore."

With those words, Candice stomped on Marquis' foot and spit in his face. Marquis grabbed her in a bear hug and started kissing her. Candice began to scream and struggle, yet her screams were muffled by Marquis's mouth. She started to cry, twist and hit at Marquis, but he wouldn't stop. He yanked her wig off and started ripping her clothes off with one hand while holding her arms and hands with his other hand. Candice began to fight even harder. He meant to force her, here in the church. Her office door crashed open.

"What the hell are you doing?" she heard Rudolph yell as he yanked Marquis off of her.

"I'm taking what's mine!"

"I was never yours," yelled Candice as her eyes lit upon her purse. She immediately jumped up, ran to her purse, yanked it open and grabbed the gun. As she turned, her tear-filled eyes met Rudolph's. The sound of the gun going off in the church elicited screams from all of those near. Candice opened her eyes and stared at the gun in her hand. "Oh God, what I have done? Mama, I just wanted to keep my promise"

All she could see were the two men on the floor and blood everywhere. Marquis looked at her, smiled and winked.

"You were always sweet like Candy, my Candy Cane," Marquis said with his last breath. She dropped the gun, and let out an earth-shattering scream, and fainted. Just as he promised to always do, Rudolph pulled her close and held her. Whatever would come of this, she was still his good and sweet thing from God.

# The Podium
## Stephanie Outten

### Chapter 1

"God, grant me the serenity to accept the things I cannot change, courage to change the things I can; and the wisdom to know the difference." The group of women recited the mantra in unison. They all exhaled a sigh of relief once it was over.

Sheila sat back in her seat. Waited for the bell to ring. Brrrrrriiiing...like clockwork.

"Line up!" The guard, Officer Sims, shouted out for the Alcoholics Anonymous (AA) group of fifteen to line up for count.

It had been five months, and Sheila mumbled to herself, "I can't believe my days and nights have been filled with bells that aren't school bells, guards telling me when to come and go." The place was filled with smelly 'she-hims' - women that looked like men - she had to protect herself from. Her family was now relegated to visiting her in this place - behind bars - for the crime she'd committed. The crime...

She chuckled - an angry chuckle that reverberated in her soul. Here she was, First Lady Sheila Davenport of The Potter & The Clay Ministries, remanded to a six-foot by eight-foot cell for at least the next five years. She stared at the pictures of her children and her father that she'd taped to the wall next to her cot.

Aggravated battery. Well, she was aggravated for sure. And, she did batter that trifling trick. Yep, she did that! She confessed, plus there were a few - more like a lot - of witnesses. Now, she had to be stripped of her freedom, her family, her life, all because her husband gave what was supposed to be all hers to someone else...

*** 

She shifted in her seat. Yes, HER seat! One of the blessings and curses of her position. She made a point to wear her fire red St. John dress with matching stilettos. Standing only five feet three inches, she needed the five-inch heels to get her close to her husband's six feet one-inch frame.

She swooped her jet-black weave over her shoulder and snarled at her husband as he took his place in front of the podium. That podium, with the big gold cross mounted to the front of it, had been his safe haven for the past two years. It was where he delivered his rousing, God-given sermons every single Sunday.

That podium was where he'd stood time and again as he called forth people out of their sinful state. It's where he stood to share the message of deliverance and resurrection right before turning around to enter the baptismal pool to baptize those who had been called by God to begin life anew.

That podium is where he broke the bread that represented Christ's body and drank the wine that represented our Savior's blood. And that podium, that same podium, was where Sheila found twenty-one-year-old Danithia Simmons bent over, dress hiked above her waist, panties down to her ankles, as Sheila's husband, the right Reverend Keith

Davenport, screwed Danithia's brains out like a wild rabbit in heat.

That podium is where he and Sheila's eyes locked as he gave Danithia one final thrust. She released the screams of a wild banshee as he screamed, "Oh my God! Sheila!" as Sheila ran toward them full throttle.

Sheila didn't fully remember everything that transpired after that. She blacked out somewhere between the punches to his stomach and chest, and her choking the mess out of Danithia. Somehow, with swollen knuckles, her knees and hands shaking like leaves, she'd driven herself home. Home? The pale-yellow Bungalow-style house with the white bench swing on the porch and the burgundy door. The house she and Keith shared for fifteen years with their three children.

She made her way inside the house and to her bathroom. As she stared at the reflection in the mirror - her mascara stained face, snot running down, disheveled hair - she didn't recognize herself. Sheila Davenport, the dazzling First Lady of The Potter & The Clay Ministries, was gone, replaced by a bitter, scorned wife who was ready to take her revenge.

She dug deep into the recesses of the cabinet under her bathroom sink. She felt for the cold, hard, long bottle that was once her only comfort. She pulled it out, caressed it as she closed her eyes. She was so familiar with the bottle she didn't even need to look at it to twist off the cap. When it opened, she was immediately intoxicated by the smell of the clear fluid that crept into her nostrils. It was like heaven on earth for Sheila as she brought the vodka to her lips, slipped her head back and moaned as the liquid slid down her throat. After gulping several times, she brought her head back to center, opened her eyes and stared, once again, at herself in the mirror and she remembered...

## *When Times Were Good...*

She remembered the day she met Keith like it was yesterday. She'd swung by her father's barber shop to get edged up. When she stepped in, she was instantly awestruck by the specimen that sat in her father's chair. He took her breath away.

"Hi Daddy!" She swung her hips a little harder than usual as she sashayed over to hug her father.

"Hey pumpkin!" He squeezed her tight, kissing her forehead as he pulled away. Since she was a child, Sheila remembered her dad calling her "pumpkin." His mother's pumpkin pie was one of his favorite things, so he nicknamed Sheila that to remind her she was one of his favorite things on earth.  At twenty-one years old, it never got old to her.

"I should have called to let you know I was coming. I just need to get edged up before I get my braids put in later."

"It's all good pumpkin! You know your daddy's got you." He smiled at her with such love. She knew her daddy loved her more than anything, but when he smiled at her, there was no doubt he would go to the ends of the earth for Sheila. He'd almost had to at one point in her life, the darkest time in her life, when only her father and the Father were able to bring her back to life.

"Hello! I'm Sheila!" She extended her hand to the stranger sitting in her dad's tattered barber's chair. That thing had so many rips and tears, the stuffing was falling out. But the clients never complained.

His head was tilted down as her dad shaped up the hair on the back of the man's head. He peeked up to look at her, extending his hand. "Keith Davenport. Nice to make your acquaintance, Sheila."

It was on from there. He asked Sheila's dad if it would be okay to give her his phone number. What a gentleman! Sheila's dad saw the cheesy grin on her face and gave Keith the okay. He felt comfortable because Keith had been in several times to get his hair cut, and drama never seemed to follow him.

Keith and Sheila dated for a year and a half before Keith asked her dad for Sheila's hand in marriage. For Sheila, life was sweet dating that man. Granted, he had women checking for him everywhere they went. But, when he was with her, he never looked their way.

They were engaged for six months before they got married on April 18, 2003. Her dad gifted them one of his rental properties - a pale-yellow four-bedroom, three and half bathroom Bungalow-style home in Seminole Heights, a revitalized community in central Tampa, Florida. Her dad had bought the property dirt cheap in 1998 when Seminole Heights was still gritty and far from gentrified. Sheila lived in the house during their engagement, and Keith moved in right after they were married. The neighborhood was now bustling with trendy restaurants, and colorful murals laced many of the older brick buildings.

Three years later, they welcomed their first son, Jacob. Their son, Malachi, came fifteen months later. And daughter, Sarai, the princess, was seven years old. They were the joy of Sheila's soul, her greatest accomplishment - other than being Keith's wife. They kept her mind stable and her heart at peace. Stability and peace. Two things she needed to keep her from going back to her dark place.

They lived a fun and non-stressful life. Keith was a store manager at Publix. He'd worked for the grocery store chain since he was fifteen years old. Started as a bagger and worked his way up. When he went off to college, the Publix leadership told him he would always have a role with them. Once he graduated, he went back to Publix and eventually got his own store.

She was a high school guidance counselor and found fulfillment helping teens figure out their next course in life. Lord knew she struggled at times to figure out her own life, but at thirty-eight years old, she'd finally come to grips with some of her past issues - some things she'd never even shared with Keith. Her parents' divorce, the rape, the weed and alcohol addiction. They still haunted her during her insomnia-filled nights.

Keith, the kids, and Sheila were totally immersed in their church. The kids loved children's church, and Keith and Sheila were active in several ministries - to include the marriage ministry.

Five years prior, Keith felt the move of God over His life and told Sheila the Lord was calling him to preach. Now, she'd seen him speak at the ministry meetings and lead them in Bible study. But preaching! That was a whole new level for Keith.

Sheila became the dutiful wife helping him study as he went back to school to study divinity. It was tough for her at first, especially since she never saw herself as a preacher's wife. There was a point in her life that she lost all faith in God and worked so hard to find her way back to Him. But, being a preacher's wife was something she wasn't sure she was fit for.

They left their home church for Keith to take an associate Pastor position at another church. He flourished. Three years later, he decided to start his own church.

"Babe, my life has been totally transformed since I took on the associate Pastor role." Keith sat in front of Sheila, taking both her hands in his.

"I see that, honey! I'm so grateful you've found your calling and feel so fulfilled." She was truly happy for Keith. Being a leader in the church helped him become a better husband and father.

"God is calling me to a new dimension now. It's time for our own church." Keith looked her dead in the eyes.

She flinched, hoping he didn't say what she thought he'd said. "Come again! What'd you say?" She was dumbfounded. Never in a million years did she think Keith would want his own church. And never in her life did she think she would become a First Lady. All the First Ladies she knew had too much stress in their life. Stress wasn't good for Sheila, so Keith's announcement was about to be the setback she didn't need in her life.

"The spirit is so strong in me about this, babe. It's time!" He was so convicted.

Sheila couldn't stand in the way of God. And just like that, Keith had scoped out space for their new church. In two years, they had built The Potter & the Clay Ministries, in the heart of historic Ybor City, to over one thousand members.

Sheila was proud of what God did with their ministry. Keith was a phenomenal Pastor, and she made a darn good First Lady. Having an assistant helped Sheila maintain her stress level so that she didn't go too far off the deep edge. Together, in ministry, they seemed unstoppable. A year ago, though, she began noticing a change in Keith. He was spending more and more late nights at the church.

"First Lady, I'm not sure if you realize this, so I figured I'd give you a call to let you know Pastor Keith has been having quite a few after-five meetings with that sweet new member, Ms. Danithia Simmons," Ms. Evelyn whispered.

"Ms. Evelyn, don't you start no mess over there." Sheila half-chuckled to keep Ms. Evelyn from hearing her disappointment.

Ms. Evelyn, Keith's administrative assistant was a sweet, mature woman who loved to tell stories. But this story carried some weight to it.

Sheila shivered, like a chill had run down her spine. She put it out of her mind. Didn't think anything of it after that. Danithia was a young woman who seemed like she had a good head on her shoulders. And Keith knew better. He knew what he had waiting at home. He came home every night; made love to Sheila like he did when they'd met all those years ago. There was no way he was doing anything or anyone other than her.

A few months prior to the day that changed First Lady Sheila's life forever, things drastically shifted in their marriage. They'd been married for fifteen years, and Keith suddenly seemed disinterested in Sheila. No more nightly talks. No more cuddling. No more four times a week hour-long love making sessions. Just a kiss on the cheek and a faint, "Good night," was all she got from him.

"Keith, we need to talk about us." She cornered him at nine thirty in the evening when he'd come home from the church. It was January, a little brisk outside, so she felt the cold air come into the house with him. She soon realized it wasn't just the cold air from the outside, but the coldness of his heart that she was sensing.

It was a Tuesday evening, so she knew they didn't have anything on the church calendar. She walked in front of him as he tried to walk away from the conversation.

"Keith, what is going on with you? I haven't done anything to make you treat me the way you are right now. So, what is it?" Sheila was in tears. She began fanning herself with both hands like she was on fire. If she didn't calm down soon, Keith would see the side of her she'd carefully hidden from him all those years. Keith had never mistreated her. Never dismissed her. Something was out of order.

"Sheila, please excuse me. I have work to get done." Keith squeezed by her to walk into his office. He closed the door to the office, closing the door on the conversation.

## *When Times Got Bad...*

Sheila had had enough. Keith knew better than to play with her. Early into their relationship, he almost had a slip up with an ex-girlfriend. Sheila caught him on the phone making plans to meet her at a hotel. She put an end to that crap really quick when she walked up behind him, snatched the phone out of his hand and raged on the woman on the other line. After she punched the hell out of him – because her daddy taught her how to fight - he never tried that mess again. And, Sheila tucked that side of her away - thinking it would be for good.

"I don't know who he thinks he is walking past me like I don't exist," Sheila mumbled under her breath as her daughter, Sarai, came into the living room.

"Mommy, who are you talking to?" For seven, she was inquisitive.

"Mommy's talking to God, baby. I was praying for safety and protection for someone." Sheila couldn't tell Sarai she was praying for God to protect her daddy from her if Sheila found out he was up to no good with Danithia.

"It's always good to talk to God. You and Daddy taught us that." Sarai looked at Sheila with her soft brown eyes that made her melt.

"That's right, baby! Talking to God makes it all better." Sheila knew that to be true, but at that moment she found herself choking on her own words.

"What's for dinner, Mom?" Jacob, the oldest, came barreling into the living room. Malachi wouldn't be too far behind him.

In the midst of what was going on with Sheila and Keith, she'd forgotten all about dinner. "You know what? Mommy's going to go out and bring us back something to eat. I have to make a few stops first, so eat some snacks in the meantime while I'm out."

She grabbed her purse and keys off the counter and headed to the garage. She wasn't fully sure where she was going. But she did know that she needed to get to the bottom of why Keith was treating her like a side-chick instead of a wife.

She headed south, but then turned her car around to head north to the church. It was after-hours, so she knew no one would be there. Since Keith had come home, she knew it would be empty. She walked in, turned off the alarm, and locked herself in. She walked into the sanctuary and went straight to the altar. She got down on her knees.

"God, I'm at a total loss. I need you right now. I know I can go to my earthly daddy when I'm hurting, but right now I need my heavenly Father to step in. It's taking everything in me not to go ballistic on Keith, not to hit the bottle and drown myself in sorrow. Ever since..." She let her voice fade away, not willing to speak the words that tore her life apart. She focused on why she was on her knees. "Keith and I have been great together for all these years. But this past year has been ridiculous. It's like he doesn't see me anymore...not like he used to." A single tear fell from her eye as she talked to God. She allowed her ears and spirit to be open to hearing from Him. On her knees, she felt her heart softening to the God she once blamed and lost trust in.

Once she'd received the revelation she needed, she knew what she needed to do. She went to her office and turned on her church computer.

She logged into the church database and filtered by last name until she saw it – Simmons. Sheila's nostrils flared, and her stomach churned at the sight of that name.

Sheila had never been the jealous type. She was a lot of other things, but jealous wasn't one of them. She rubbed her stomach. That gnawing feeling in the pit of her belly told her something wasn't right. After Keith's assistant told her about Keith and Danithia's late night meetings, she initially wasn't fazed. Now, with the way he'd been treating her, she needed to get to the bottom of it.

She tapped her nails across the glass desk as she stared at the picture of her, Keith and the kids on their last family vacation to the San Diego Zoo. The kids were so excited when their parents surprised them with the trip. They got a suite at the Westgate Hotel, which allowed the kids to have their own room and Keith and Sheila to have theirs. It was one of their best trips. Ms. Evelyn planned everything down to the detail. So meticulous. Sheila was glad she had hired Ms. Evelyn. She knew that having a more mature assistant, one experienced with working for head pastors, would be good for Keith as the head of his own church.

"That's why I know Ms. Evelyn is telling me the truth about Keith and Danithia. She pays attention to everything." She stopped talking to herself and did what she had gone there to do. Her hands shook. Before she dialed the numbers, she reached inside her bottom drawer and pulled out a tiny flask she kept in case of emergencies. She took a quick swig of the warm drink letting it slowly flow down her throat and settle into her chest. She moaned slowly and made the call.

"Heyyyy baby! I thought you already left the church," Danithia's voice oozed with sexiness...for Sheila's husband.

"I'm about to jump through the damn phone on this heifer," Sheila mumbled through clenched teeth, careful to hold the phone away from her mouth so Danithia couldn't hear her. She needed to play it cool. She still had a reputation to uphold as the First Lady of The Potter & the Clay Ministries. She couldn't come out of her skin like she would have back in the day. "Lord help me!" She breathed deeply.

"Ms. Simmons, this is First Lady Sheila Davenport calling. By your phone greeting, I'm guessing you thought my husband was calling. Would that be accurate?" Sheila made sure to emphasize her title and that Keith was hers, no matter what mess Danithia was trying to start. Sheila needed Danithia to know she may have started, but she definitely wouldn't be finishing.

"Um, um, um, First Lady!" Danithia stuttered like a spouse caught cheating – except she was the one cheating with Sheila's spouse. "Forgive me. How are you?"

"One thing I don't do is play games or mince words, so let's cut the bullshit now." It had been years since Sheila cursed. But let's not forget, she hadn't always been a First Lady. "What do you and my husband, your Pastor, have going on outside his pastoral duties to you?" She couldn't believe how dignified, yet 'skanktified' she could be.

Her stuttering ceased, and twenty-one-year-old Danithia came for Sheila. "Well, First Lady, if you insist on knowing what your husband and I have going on, you should probably ask him." She got bold, like her chest puffed out. "Now, unless you have church business to discuss with me, I suggest you not call my home again, Sheila.

Sheila took another drink, rose up from her chair, stared at the phone like Danithia was in her face. She pointed at the phone wanting to ram her fist down Danithia's throat. "Let me tell you something, you little..." Sheila had to hold her tongue before she called this chick outside her name. "Don't come for me unless I send for you. You hear me?" Her nerves were on edge. This was the piece of her she desperately tried to suppress. She spoke slowly through gritted teeth. "If you think you're going to come between me and my husband, the father of my kids... please think again."

Danithia let out a laugh that cut through Sheila's skin like a razor blade. "Well, since Keith sent for me, then I'll keep on coming, whether you like it or not." She paused.

"Little girl! When I kill him, you and Jesus can have him...but not before. Watch yourself! You don't want none of this. Trust me!" Sheila threw the church phone across the room and watched it shatter to pieces. She fell to the floor, into the heap of broken plastic resembling her heart, and hollered out to the Lord.

"Oh God! I can't even believe this is happening. Why? Seriously! Almost seventeen years with this man, and he does this to me? To our kids? Our family? I don't understand. I've been faithful, kind, better than good to him. I birthed our children, even when it was freaking hard. I've been an amazing wife and mother. I've been his best friend. I've even kept my emotions under control. What the hell?"

Suddenly, the bile rose from Sheila's stomach to her throat. She wouldn't make it to the bathroom in time. She grabbed the trash can and let all the pain, sadness, betrayal flow freely into the can. When it was all out, she realized her cell phone was ringing. She couldn't get herself off the floor. She sat against the wall with her body slumped over. She continued to sit and stare at her white and turquoise décor in the office, until she heard the phone ringing again. She crawled to the chair by her desk and pulled herself up.

"Hi sweetie!" Sheila perked up when she heard her daughter's voice.

"Mommy, you said you were bringing us something to eat. You've been gone a long time. I was worried," Sarai was on the verge of crying.

"I know! Mommy had to handle something first. Remember?" She looked to the sky asking herself, "Didn't I tell the kids I had something to take care of?" But with the state she was in, it was likely she couldn't remember how she got to the church much less food for the kids. "Where's your dad? Does he know I'm not there? Does he know to feed you all?"

"Malachi just went and told him. We weren't going to since his door was closed, but we're hungry now, Mom!" Jacob had gotten on the phone.

"Okay, Jay-Jay – the nickname for their first born – I'm heading to get food now. Tell your dad I'll be back in about fifteen minutes." She hung up and headed to grab a pizza and salad.

"I wish I had time to get another drink. I need one." Sheila scratched her throat as she drove to get the pizza. She would always rub or scratch her throat when she was itching for a drink. But she needed to get her kids fed more than anything else.

## Chapter 2

In all of their time together, Sheila had never dreaded seeing Keith. This day was different. This day confirmed he'd broken their marriage vows and her heart. This day changed the trajectory of Keith and Sheila Davenport forever. This day would take Sheila back to the part of herself she long ago tried to part with.

All she wanted to do was run to her daddy to tell him what happened. She knew he would set Keith straight if he knew. But, one thing he told Sheila and Keith when they got engaged was that they didn't need to invite anyone else but God into their relationship. As a wedding gift, he'd given them a plaque engraved with their names and wedding date right below the scripture Ecclesiastes 4:12, "Though one may be overpowered, two can defend themselves. A cord of three strands is not quickly broken."

They used to meditate on that scripture day and night. Keith and Sheila would actually repeat it together every night before bed...until they stopped. She couldn't even remember when that was. In the absence of their nightly ritual, one of them had been overpowered – Keith. Now was the time for them to come together to "defend themselves" against the trick of the enemy – Danithia. They would need that third strand, God, to help them get through this. Or, Sheila would use that third strand to choke Keith to death. Only time would tell.

## *Nothing Left to Say...*

"Yes! Mom's home! Dinner time." Malachi had this little "dinner time dance" he would do when he was really hungry. He would rub his tummy, wiggle his body, and shuffle his feet like James Brown. He was so cute.

"Finally! My stomach was about to fall out, Mommy," Sarai washed her hands in the bathroom off the kitchen.

"Where's your father?" Sheila asked Jacob, as she walked to the sink to wash her hands, too.

"He's still in the office. I think he's on the phone. He got really loud at one point, like he was mad at the person on the other line." Jacob was a "Mama's Boy" at his core. He would do anything to make sure Sheila was okay.

Sensing her son was feeling her angst, she told him to go get his siblings settled for dinner while she went to get their dad. He gave her a look that said he knew something odd was happening, but he did as she asked without question.

Sheila made what felt like the longest walk to Keith's office, even though it was only two doors down from where she was. She gently tapped on the door and went to turn the knob right as he opened it. His eyes were wet with tears. He pulled her into the office and closed the door. Once inside, she stared into his eyes that told her he knew that she knew. He must have been talking to that witch, which is what Jacob must have overheard.

He fixed his mouth to say something, but before he could, Sheila hauled off and slapped the hell out of him. "Don't say a damn word to me you lying, cheating, piece of shit!"

"Baby, please!" He rubbed the side of his face, visibly shaken by how hard she'd slapped him. "Please let me explain." He held the sides of her arms to keep her from hitting him again or running out of the room.

"Explain! Oh, you want to explain now? A couple of hours ago, you walked past me like I didn't exist, and now you want to explain." Sheila guffawed. Keith had the nerve to want to talk to her now.

She'd never done him wrong. Never cheated on him. Never cursed him - except in her thoughts. Never looked sideways at him. Yet, he popped off a side-chick and decided she was no longer good enough to talk to. Like she was invisible standing right in front of him. There wasn't anything he could say to make all of this go away.

She wanted her daddy so bad. It would break him to know Keith had done this to her. Her dad was a prideful man, and when he gave Keith Sheila's hand in marriage, he had stipulations. One of those being Keith would never dishonor his daughter. Clearly Keith had broken that promise.

Her mom and dad got divorced when Sheila was sixteen. That's when the anger overtook her - when she no longer had their marriage to focus on. Drinking and smoking weed became her best friends. Vodka and Cranberry Juice provided the comfort she needed when her parents divorced. The weed dulled her, made her drift...forget. Forget the time she was sexually violated by one of the ministers of their church - right behind the old podium in the storage room of the church. Forget the time God turned his back on her and allowed something so callous to happen to a fourteen-year-old girl. She kept it from her parents for two years, never allowing herself to fully break. She knew at fourteen that if she broke, she'd be broken the rest of her life. She wasn't about to let that happen. Pretending became her modus operandi. Then she discovered her other close friends - angry outbursts, vodka and weed.

Because she was old enough to think for herself, her parents let her decide who she wanted to live with. There was no question she would pick her dad. Most girls that age would want to be with their mother, but not Sheila. Her mom was a good woman, but she wasn't a good mother. Most of the time growing up, Sheila's dad played both roles in her life. He gave her baths, washed and combed her hair, took her to school and picked her up. He could do all that because he worked for himself all of Sheila's life.

Sheila's mom worked for a bank and loved work more than home.

She ended up meeting another man while working at the bank. She had a longstanding affair with him that Sheila's dad eventually found out about. When he confronted her, she didn't deny it. After more than twenty years together, Sheila's dad, Ron, and her mother, Diane, divorced. It was the only period in time Sheila ever saw her father defeated.

"Ron, I'm sorry I didn't tell you sooner. Honestly, I didn't want to hurt you or Sheila." Her mom sat on the couch wringing her hands together with her head down.

"How long has this been going on?" Ron's voice weakened with every word.

Sheila sat at the bottom of the staircase eavesdropping, watching them through the railing. She stayed quiet, so they wouldn't know she was there. She listened as her mom told her dad she wanted a divorce to go be with a man she barely knew. Diane moved out the same week, and Sheila and her daddy had to figure out how to move forward without her.

Even though Diane wasn't a great mother, Sheila still enjoyed having her around. When she was gone, it only increased Sheila's anger and other negative behaviors. Ron had a time keeping her under control, but he never gave up on his pumpkin. He got Sheila into therapy when she was seventeen. Therapy allowed her to be open with her parents. Tell them what happened to her at fourteen. Tell them about the drinking and weed smoking. It nearly killed her father to know she'd been violated. He was even more angry that she wouldn't tell him who did it. She knew if she did, her father would be in prison to this day. She kept that secret knowing she would take it to her grave. Only she, the minister, and God knew about it.

It was tough remembering that time in her life. It served as a reminder of why she couldn't tell her dad. It would bring up too many painful memories for him, especially since Sheila's mom left him for someone she only stayed with for a year after their divorce. She'd dated several men after that, never finding what she had with Ron. She never remarried.

Sheila's drinking and weed smoking continued even after therapy and all through college. She became a functioning alcoholic and a master at keeping the smell of alcohol and weed off her breath.

"Sheila!?" Keith gently shook Sheila out of her thoughts. "Please listen to me. This thing with Danithia was a big mistake." He stared at her with tears welling up in his eyes.

"Wait! What? A mistake?" She shook her head. "How long has this 'mistake' been going on? And, don't lie to me Keith." Sheila used all of her energy to break free from his grip. She began to scan the room looking for something to hit him with. Her eyes settled on the Prayer of Jabez stone he used as a paper weight. She rubbed her throat as she stared at it.

"Uh, uh, uh..." He stuttered, looking over to see what she was staring at.

"Uh, uh, uh, what? A mistake happens once, Keith. If you're stupid enough, it may even happen twice. So, how the hell long has this been going on, Keith?"

"It's been a year," he spoke firmly this time.

The wind had been knocked out of her. Sheila was done. She flung the office door open and rushed out of the room.

"Mom are you okay?" Jacob ran after her. He wasn't fast enough. She had gotten to her bedroom and slammed the door before he could get to her. He lightly knocked on the door. "Mom, can I come in?"

Sheila loved and adored all of her children. There was a special connection, though, that she had with Jacob. As her firstborn, he received the first love she could ever give to a child. The Bible talks about how God knitted us together in our mother's womb, and that's exactly what Sheila would say about Jacob. Not only was he knitted in her womb, he was also knitted in her heart.

"Jacob, Mom needs a little time to herself, okay?" Sheila fought back tears as she struggled to keep her voice calm. She'd managed to get to her bathroom to dig under the cabinet for her bottle of refuge. She took a swig, basked in the soft burn, then put it away. She did a quick swish with mouthwash and sat back down.

"Mom, what did Dad do to you?" He was resilient and wasn't about to give up. He always stood up for Sheila, no matter what the situation.

She didn't want this issue to come between Jacob and his father, so she let him in. "Honey sit with me for a sec." Sheila led him to the chaise lounge in front of the bed. "Mom and Dad had a disagreement. I shouldn't have gotten as upset as I did. I just have a lot on my mind." She hated lying to her kids, but she couldn't tell him the truth - that his Dad was a lying, cheating bastard.

"Okay, are you sure? I mean, if you need me to talk to Dad too, I will." He put his arm around her back and lay his head on her shoulder.

Sheila wiped the tears that were coming. She didn't want Jacob to know how much the situation bothered her.

Before Jacob had come into the room, Sheila spoke to God. "If I could take another ride, get in my car, with my kids, and drive away from Keith's ridiculousness..." Sheila loved her husband though. She wasn't ready to fight a trick for him. That was a job for God, and she needed to leave it in His hands to see what would come of this. She kissed Jacob on the head, asked him to get his brother and sister ready for bed, and then get to bed himself.

\*\*\*

"Is it over?" Sheila said to Keith when he walked into their bedroom at two o'clock in the morning. She'd sat on that chaise lounge crying so much her eyes were burning and puffy. She was partially drunk and tried desperately to keep Keith from noticing.

He must have been crying too because he looked like Sheila felt... broken. "Yes! I promise you. I talked to her today and told her we are through." He knelt down in front of Sheila. "I don't know how I let her possess me into getting into this mess with her in the first place."

"Let her possess you?" Sheila was pissed all over again. "Keith don't put this whole thing on her. She's almost half your age, and you're married for God's sake. You know better!" Her words slurred, but Keith didn't seem to notice.

"I didn't mean it that way." He slammed his fist into the floor. He was angry with himself for getting wrapped up in something like this. "I mean...it's like...I don't know," he stuttered.

"Because I'm tired, we'll have to table this until tomorrow. Your stuttering is aggravating me, and I don't have the energy to try to figure out what you want to say. You can sleep here," she patted the chaise. "Or, you can sleep in the guest room. Whatever you do, please keep your ass away from me until tomorrow. I can't even breathe with you in front of me right now." She pushed him out of the way. He fell to the floor. She didn't look back as she crawled in the bed, turned out the lights and closed her eyes. Sheila prayed sleep would invade her quickly as she heard the bedroom door close gently. By how Keith silently exited, he must have thought the guest room would be safer. He was right.

## Games People Play...

All throughout the week their home phone would ring and the person on the other end would hang up when any of them answered. They called three times every hour on the hour all through the night. Sheila told Keith it had to be Danithia. It was going to take an act of God for her not to strangle the hell out of that girl if she had the audacity to show up at church on Sunday, which was six days away.

It had been cold and rainy the past couple of days. January weather in Florida could be so fickle. Hot one day, cold and raining the next. Sheila got up early to run to the store before everyone woke up. She couldn't sleep. She'd been awakened by the hard rain that fell in the middle of the night. When she was upset, she liked to cook to take her mind off things. She knew she couldn't indulge in a drink, so she decided to make pancakes for the kids before they went off to school, but they were out of pancake mix. She hopped in her car and clicked the garage door opener. The garage door opened slightly and then slammed back down. She tried it again thinking she didn't click it hard enough. Same thing. The third time had to be a charm, but the garage door slightly raised then slammed shut again. What the hell is going on? She got out the car and went back inside to go through the front door. In her haste, she stepped out the door without looking. She felt something squish under her feet. What the flip? She took a few steps forward scrapping her shoe off in the process. When she looked back, she was mortified.

A mutilated animal, blood everywhere, lay in front of the door. She screamed bloody murder and threw up all over the planter on the porch. She ran away from the door screaming at the top of her lungs. She stumbled backward into the grass and was able to see that the garage door had somehow been tied down. In red paint, or maybe it was animal blood, read "He's Mine!" Sheila stared at the words as Keith came running out the front door and into the same bloody mess she'd just stepped in. He seemed oblivious to it as he came to pick her up out of the grass.

"What happened?" He grabbed her up. "Sheila are you okay?"

It was her turn to stutter. "Loo..loo..look!" She pointed at the front door first then the garage door. The neighbors were also out staring at the craziness that had become their morning.

"Oh my God! Sheila, get inside and call the police." Keith was livid.

She kicked off her shoes, ran inside the house careful to jump over the dead animal at the door. She saw the kids coming down the staircase. Her screams must have woken up the whole neighborhood. She rushed the kids back upstairs. She couldn't have them see what was outside. They all loved animals too much and would have been in shock if they saw it.

The fact that someone would do this to their family pissed Sheila off. "I know this was Danithia," but she didn't want to rush to judgement. Rather than allow her blood to boil, she called the police like her husband told her to and waited for them to come. They were going to have to bare their marital woes in front of the police since Sheila planned to tell them everything about Keith and Danithia's affair. He got them into this mess, and he was going to get them out...otherwise, Sheila would.

When she heard the doorbell, she assumed it was the police. Imagine her shock when her dad came charging through the door. "Dad, what are you doing here?"

"Ms. Elliot called and told me she saw you fall out screaming in the yard. Told me someone spray painted some mess on your garage. What the hell is going on here?" Ron was as angry as Sheila was. Crap! Now he would be there when the police came. He would hear about Keith and Danithia.

The doorbell rang just as she was about to sit down with her dad. Keith was in his office hollering like a mad man. Obviously, he was doing an investigation of his own. Sheila opened the door to see a male and a female officer. "Come in, please."

She had them go inside the living room and asked her dad to go upstairs with the kids to keep them company while Keith and Sheila talked with the police. Thank God he did without question. Sheila went to get Keith from his office, but he was already on his way out to the living room.

They told the police the whole sordid story. Told them about their suspicions that Danithia had a hand in this. Told them about the constant hang ups on their home line. Keith was able to give them her address for them to go and question her. Sheila looked at him with disgust, infuriated that he knew the address by heart. She wanted to punch him in the face but knew it would be a bad idea in front of the cops. They went outside to take pictures, and they left to head to the trick's house.

A couple days went by. The hang ups continued. Obviously, the police hadn't resolved things. On Wednesday, on her way home from Bible Study, Sheila got a flat tire. She called Keith to meet her but got no answer. She called for a cab to take her back to the church where she knew Keith would still be.

When she walked in, she saw them. Keith and Danithia entangled in each other so much so, that they didn't even notice her walk up to the podium - that podium with the gold cross shining brightly. When Keith's eyes locked with hers, he knew it was going to get ugly. Everything that happened next was a blur.

When Sheila got home and buried herself in the bottle, she was overcome with rage. She was ready to pop off. Her target - Danithia Simmons.

The kids stayed with their granddad every Wednesday, so she didn't have to worry about the kids. She dragged herself to the car. She'd learned a long time ago how to function as an alcoholic. Driving slow enough not to get pulled over, but fast enough not to seem suspicious. She passed Keith's car as she drove down the street. He didn't seem to notice because he kept driving. In ten minutes, she was in front of Danithia's apartment banging on the door like a maniac.

The neighborhood was quiet. Sheila looked to her right and left. It felt eerie that Danithia lived that close to the church in a small apartment complex near Downtown Tampa. She must have been a trust-fund baby, or she made a lot of money on her job to live in those fancy apartments.

"You hear me out here, heifer! Open the damn door before I kick it down." Sheila screamed at the tops of her lungs. "I'll wake up your whole damn neighborhood if you don't open the door. You got all day to screw my husband, but you can't open the..."

"What the hell do you want?" Danithia answered the door with a huff. "Get out of here before I call the cops. I'm sick of you." She was pissed having to stand at the door looking at this madwoman standing in the cold.

"You're sick of me? You're sick of me? Is that right?" Sheila was in Danithia's face. "Let me tell you something. If you think you can come between me and my husband and break up my family, you got another thing coming."

"Get your drunk ass out of my face," she pushed Sheila. "I do what I please and what pleases your husband, as you saw. Clearly something you're not doing, or he wouldn't be running up through here every day."

No more words were exchanged. Only fists and blows as Sheila swung on Danithia like Muhammad Ali against Joe Frazier in the famous "Fight of the Century" boxing match of 1971. She gut-punched her, hooked Danithia in the face with her right fist then left. Sheila elbowed Danithia in the chin trying to land her, but Danithia wouldn't go down without getting in a few punches on Sheila. The two fought for what seemed like an hour before Danithia's neighbor came to break up the fight.

The scene was chaotic. Danithia's busted lip, swollen eyes, ripped clothes, and the gash in her cheek proved that Sheila still had it in her. She whooped Danithia like she stole something...like she stole Keith.

Danithia's neighbor tried holding both women back, but Sheila was able to break free. "You haven't seen the last of me you homewrecking slut!" Sheila spit at Danithia on the way out the door, slamming it shut behind her. Walking back to her car as the brisk January wind slapped her in the face. She could now hear the trees rustling - a sign that a shifting was coming.

Sheila heard Danithia say, "Your husband hasn't either, wench!" That comment almost made her turn on her heels and run back to the house to tear Danithia a new one. She reserved herself instead. Got in the car. Drove off...straight to the nearest bar to soothe her pain.

It was three o'clock in the morning when she pulled into the garage. Before she could open her car door, there was Keith standing in the doorway leading from the garage into the house.

It took every ounce of her strength to get out of the car. Danithia had gotten a few punches in, and Sheila felt the throbbing. "Keith, get out of my way," she pushed passed him. "I'm dr..rr..unk, tired, and sore from b..b..beating your trick down. I'm ready to do the same to you."

He threw his hands up to concede. "Please forgive me baby. I'm through with her. I promise!" He was begging hard. "I've already told her to leave me...I mean us, alone. I'm so sorry baby!"

Sheila stumbled passed him and up the stairs. He followed behind her wanting to talk. She didn't want to. Out of respect for her kids, she didn't push Keith down the stairs with all intent to break his neck. All she had energy for was to plan her revenge.

### *Revenge is Bittersweet...*

From Wednesday to Sunday morning, Sheila barely spoke two words to Keith. Her drinking increased, and it became noticeable in the home. Sunday morning was different. She didn't drink on Sunday. She wanted to be sober to see that trick, Danithia, stumble into the church pews. Instead, Danithia pranced in like the number one stunner ready to take Sheila's First Lady title.

Sheila shifted in her seat, pulling on the bottom of her fire-red St. John dress. Her matching stilettos swelling around her feet. When Danithia walked up to Sheila and tried to take the seat next to her in the front row, Sheila didn't need liquid courage to pounce on Danithia like a hungry cheetah. Her jet-black weave swung everywhere as she gave Danithia a beat down worse than the first. She yanked off her stilettos and stomped Danithia into the ground as Keith looked on in horror from the pulpit. There he stood at the same podium where Sheila had discovered his dirty deeds.

The church was in an uproar. The ushers pulled on Sheila trying to get her off Danithia, but she was too strong for them. Her anger made her stronger than ten men. With one kick too many to Danithia's ribs, Sheila saw blood dripping from Danithia's mouth. She stumbled backward in a daze as she saw Keith coming down from the podium - that damn podium that started all this mess to begin with. She threw her stilettos at Keith's head, missing him by an inch.

Sheila heard the sirens. She fell to the floor as a few of the church mothers attended to Danithia while Keith pulled her into his arms, remorse all over his face as the police took her from his arms, handcuffed her and led her out to their squad car as the congregation watched Sheila Davenport, their First Lady, dismantled.

## *Epilogue*

The trial was short. Sheila was convicted of aggravated battery after several of the church members testified against her in court. They had to tell the truth about what they saw - their First Lady attacked "poor Danithia" for no reason, or so they thought.

Keith was ousted from his position when the congregation and Board found out about his affair with Danithia. They shamed him for how he destroyed his family and the church's reputation. The media publicly humiliated him throughout the trial, which brought him great distress. He cracked under the weight of it all and ended up seeking treatment for depression. He had to get back on his feet to take care of the kids in the absence of their mother - an absence the kids and her dad blamed him for daily.

So, for the next five years Sheila would live in her cell knowing she'd broken five of Danithia's ribs and one of her arms, caused her a head injury that kept her in a coma for a month, and embarrassed herself in front of the congregation. Worst of all, she would be separated from her kids, her father, and the Keith she once loved. If she had let God handle it like she said she would, she wouldn't have to lie in that six-foot by eight-foot cell on a cot in the corner looking at pictures of her family instead of being with them.

She would have taken it all back to reclaim her time with her family. Instead, she would work to erase the memories of Keith and Danithia at the podium that fateful day. She would focus on God's forgiveness in her life, make peace with her past, and prepare for her comeback. The Potter & the Clay Ministries hadn't seen the last of First Lady Sheila Davenport...

# RAVEN'S ALTAR

## L. MELISSA SMITH

"Where are you going?" Phoebe Dawson asked her younger stepmother who was dressed in a skimpy outfit, looking more like a hooker rather than a preacher's wife.

"Out!" Raven was really getting tired of being questioned every time she went out of the house.

"Again?" Phoebe was exasperated. "You don't ever stay home!"

Raven replied sarcastically, "And your point would be?"

"My father needs you here and church members are wondering where their first lady is," Phoebe replied. "You obviously aren't going to the church, so where do you go?"

"I don't have to explain myself to you, the church folks or even to your precious daddy," Raven retorted angrily. "Leland hasn't been in the pulpit since he fractured his spine in that car accident two months ago, so if he's not there, I'm not there either."

"You're still the first lady, and the congregation expects you to be there, not raking around town, doing who knows what," Phoebe said, her teeth clenched.

"Maybe that's what your mama would have done, but my name is not Mavis. Raven is not one to deal with sick folks. I married your daddy so he could take care of me, not the other way around."

"Nobody expects you to be like my mother, but you could do better, Raven," Phoebe admonished. "Daddy has to be on bedrest so that his back can heal, and Lord willing, he can soon be back to normal. Because he's sixty-two, it's taking him a little longer to mend, but his health is going to be restored. You don't even try to sit with your husband for five minutes. Come on now!"

"Like I said, I don't do sick people," Raven replied unapologetically. "I've told you and your sister where your father needs to be, but you want to keep him here at home. He probably would heal quicker if he was at the nursing home."

"He can get all the care he needs here," Phoebe said indignantly. "The home health aides come when we need them, and Portia and I are covering the shifts to be here. Lamar is a big help too. He loves his daddy so much!"

"It's not good for him to be sitting and looking at Leland every chance he gets," said Raven. "He needs to be out playing and having fun with other kids his age."

"Since when did you become so concerned about Lamar? He has always been around Daddy. Why should he stop now?" Phoebe asked, annoyed.

Phoebe did have a point, not that Raven would acknowledge it. Raven was young, gorgeous and barely twenty years old when she was compelled by her mother and grandmother to marry the handsome, widowed 50-year-old senior pastor of Brighter Days Christian Fellowship in the town of Barnhill in eastern North Carolina. The elder women told Raven that she was very fortunate to marry their pastor. Her status as first lady was something to really be proud of (especially for them). They added that because of his age, Leland was more settled and financially, she would want for nothing.

Although she wasn't crazy about the idea of marrying a man thirty years her senior, Raven went along with everything to please her mother, her grandmother and even Leland, whose main reason for marrying her was to father a son that he always wanted. Leland loved his daughters dearly, but he had always hoped he would have a son one day.

At first, married life was fine for the new couple. Raven became pregnant on their wedding night. Leland's desire to have a son finally manifested itself when Lamar was born twelve years ago.

Raven suffered through gestational diabetes and endometriosis following Lamar's birth. Lamar would be her first and last child – a situation that didn't bother her in the least. She suffered from postpartum depression as well as her normal selfishness and wanted nothing to do with the child.

Leland happily did everything, from middle of the night feedings and changing diapers and making sure the baby went to his doctors' appointments. Lamar's doting big sisters were also available to help whenever needed. They were a tightly-bonded unit and Raven was an outsider, mostly of her own making.

Even though Lamar called her Mama and was respectful to her, she and Lamar had no loving mother/son connection. He was always respectful to his elders, even to strangers, and strangers were what Raven and Lamar were to each other.

Leland was a perfect, doting husband who did his best to please Raven, but it was never good enough. She wanted new furniture but got bored with the style after a year. She wanted a bigger diamond ring. She wanted a newer car. With Raven, there would always be new and expensive whim.

The congregation at Brighter Days never accepted Raven as their first lady either. Some members would always say or do something hurtful whenever Leland or her mother Cecelia or grandmother Geneva weren't around. If Raven had it to do all over again, she wouldn't have married so young and she wouldn't have married a man who was so much older than she.

Just because she had been raised up in the church didn't necessarily mean than Raven was a Christian. Yes, she knew all the Christian jargon and how to jump around and sing and shout, but she wasn't about to listen to other people's problems and serve on thankless committees and counsel about Christianity. Leland knew she wasn't a Bible scholar when he married her, or at least he should have known. Her name was not Mavis. His first wife was a good and proper first lady – a true Christian woman; something Raven was not.

At 32, Raven reasoned she was too young and vibrant to be sitting around nursing an old man. Petite at only five-foot-two, Raven had smooth, dark chocolate skin and arresting milk-chocolate brown eyes. She made it a point to stay in shape, working out at least five times a week. She had recently reconnected with an old high school friend, Monte Davenport. Monte was a little older than Raven at 35. Lean, tall, muscled and incredibly handsome, Monte was a licensed, professional plumber who sometimes dabbled in selling drugs. Raven tingled inside when she thought of having sex with Monte. She had to get out of here.

Raven growled, "What do you want from me, Phoebe?" Her stepdaughters tolerated Raven for their father's sake.

"I want you to show my daddy some compassion by spending some time with him," said Phoebe. "When was the last time you even looked in on him? You're his wife! He's always asking about you."

"Alright," Raven snapped. "I'll chat with him for a few minutes, and then I have to go. Ugh! Y'all want to act like that man is on his death bed."

"Thank you," said Phoebe sarcastically. "You're so kind."

Raven cautiously went into the master bedroom. Their marriage bed was temporarily replaced with a hospital bed where her husband now lay. She knew he had to be in a lot of pain, but as always, Leland had a beautiful smile on his face – a real smile; one that shone in his eyes. Sometimes Raven wished she could be full of hope and faith like Leland, but she wasn't like that.

"Hello Beautiful," he said, his voice barely above a whisper. "Good to see you."

Raven said nothing but stared at her husband awkwardly. Leland was nice, but he was hardly oozing with sex appeal. He was only 5-foot-9, and he was shaped like a barrel. He wasn't an ugly man. In fact, he was handsome in an average kind of way. Their son Lamar was just like his daddy – boring!

Leland pursed his thick lips and asked, "How's about a kiss?"

She grimaced but bent down to kiss him dutifully on the cheek, but he turned his head and kissed her fully on the lips. She jumped back as though she had been scalded.

"I've got to go!" Raven turned to quickly walk from the room.

"Don't go!" Leland's deep baritone voice found strength and was deep and authoritative as he ordered her to stop.

As though hypnotized, Raven walked back into the room and sat quietly by his bedside.

"Raven, the streets are talking about all the running around that you're doing. I know you're half my age and there are things you probably wanted to experience before you got married, but that's not your reality anymore sweetheart. I'm your husband and I love you. You have a son who loves you. You have stepdaughters who love you. You have a church family who loves you. Most importantly, you have a God who loves you. I can't physically stop you from leaving this house, but I'm asking you for the sake of our marriage, don't go! Please, don't go! When you go outside of God's will, you go outside of His protection."

Raven pouted, "I'm not doing anything wrong, Leland! I'm just having fun."

"The orthopedic doctor says to relieve the vertebral compression fracture from the accident and get me back to normal I qualify for a procedure called kyphoplasty. Just give me a little more time to heal and we can have some fun together," Leland said eagerly. "We can go wherever you want to go and do whatever you want to do – just the two of us."

"That sounds nice, Leland but ..."

"Baby, please don't go. Don't walk out that door. Don't leave me," he pleaded.

"I'm sorry, Leland but I have to go."

"I love you, baby. Always remember that."

"Toodles," she said as she turned and walked out of the door.

"You barely spent five minutes with Daddy," said Phoebe when Raven swiftly came downstairs after seeing Leland.

"What of it?" Raven snarled. "I went to see him."

Something in Phoebe, a fitness instructor snapped, and she jumped on her stepmother and began pummeling the younger woman.

"Get off me! Get off me!" Raven cried, her hands going up in a defensive mode to protect her face.

"What's going on?" Leland, hearing the commotion, yelled from upstairs.

Phoebe ceased her attack on Raven and yelled, "Everything is fine, Daddy! There's nothing to be concerned about."

"You get out of my house," Raven said fiercely.

"Make me," Phoebe challenged. "I'll be here in this house when I want, anytime I want to take care of my daddy and my brother since you refuse to do it."

"Big mistake, Phoebe," Raven warned. "Big mistake!"

Raven left the house to spend time with her lover, Monte. They spent a night out on the town at the trendy nightclub called the Blues Temple. The Blues Temple featured live music from popular blues music artists. It also had a restaurant that served the best soul food in town.

When they returned to Monte's place, he and Raven spent time having sex, watching porn and smoking marijuana.

"If you put your old man in the nursing home, you would be able to take over his house, his money and everything," Monte said. "I know he's got paper. He buys you anything you want. When have you ever had to work?"

"I work dealing with those witches and goblins at the church. I get so tired of hearing, 'when Mavis was first lady, she did this and when Mavis was first lady, she did that.' She was so perfect. I can't live up to her standards."

"Bump them," said Monte. "I bet your husband takes up for you when they start putting you down."

"Well, you bet wrong. Maybe he did at first, but not now. Leland and his daughters also think Mavis wrote the book on how to be a perfect first lady."

"Well, you don't have to take this mess from his daughter," said Monte. "This is about the second or third time since we've gotten together that you said that heifer jumped you."

"I know, but I need her there to take care of her father and Lamar. If she wasn't there, I wouldn't be able to see you," Raven cried. "Plus, his daughters and Lamar don't want him in the nursing home; even if it's temporary," said Raven.

"The daughters ain't the wife," said Monte. "You're the one with the say, not them! You could also put that boy in boarding school once the old man is in the nursing home, and then you could have the house all to yourself. Changing the locks and putting in a security system will nip those daughters in the bud. That's what you want, isn't it?"

"I don't know," said Raven, hesitantly.

"You just need a plan girl," he said. "I'll help you." Monte was thinking more about himself than he was of Raven. Having a crib on her side of town would help to elevate his plumbing business and he could get out of pushing and become a legitimate businessman. He was tired of the police sweating him; a new, prestigious address was what he needed.

*** 

Raven had coveted Mavis and Leland's house since she was a little girl. When she was eight or nine years old, Mavis had a tea party for some of the little girls at her home. Dressed in frilly dresses and black or white patent leathered shoes, twelve little girls used their best manners and drank from beautifully delicate floral teacups and ate finger sandwiches and petit fours.

Although Raven's family did not live in poverty, Raven had never been to a home quite as beautiful as Mavis's home. The house was cheerful, neat and modern. Other than on television, Raven had never seen a home so beautiful.

Raven had admired the miniature ballerina music box that was located on the table full of knick-knacks. She reasoned that with so many knick-knacks, one little trinket would not be missed; she grabbed it and slipped it in her dress pocket.

Mavis, seeing Raven steal the trinket, was deeply angered. "Empty your pockets!" Mavis yelled at the little girl.

Raven complied and pulled the ballerina from her pocket. The other little girls gasped in dismay.

"If there's one thing I can't stand, it's a sticky hand thief!" The high-yellow woman with fierce green eyes, tightened her thin lips, then raised her hand to strike Raven across the face. The little girl's cheek stung with the assault, but she was more embarrassed by the looks, giggles and knowing glances of the other girls.

"You're right Monte," said Raven, bringing her thoughts back to the present. "It's my house and it's time to take what's mine."

Portia, Raven's other stepdaughter, was at the house when Raven returned the next day from her rendezvous with Monte. Portia was married with two children and treated Raven more nicely and respectfully than her hot-headed sister Phoebe.

"Paul and I are taking the kids to the amusement park next weekend, and want to take Lamar with us," Portia said. "Would that be alright with you?"

"Yes, that would be good for him," said Raven. "Thank you for asking."

"Phoebe has to attend a workshop next weekend, so she can't be here to care for Daddy," Portia said hesitantly.

"I'll take care of him," said Raven. "He is after all, my husband."

"Yes, he is," Portia conceded.

Raven and Lamar argued before she put her foot down and told her son he was going to spend time that weekend having fun with his niece and nephew at the amusement park. Even though their relationship was not close, Raven knew it was unhealthy for the boy to spend so much time with Leland and not enough time with children closer to his own age. Portia and Paul would pick Lamar up after school on Friday, and since it was a holiday weekend, they wouldn't bring Lamar back home until Monday afternoon. With Phoebe gone too, she and Leland would have the house to themselves.

"I'll have the house to myself tomorrow, except for Leland," Raven whispered to Monte on her cell phone. "Phoebe's going out of town and when I take Lamar to school tomorrow, Portia and her husband will have him for the long weekend."

"I'll come over tomorrow night and we'll put our plan in action," Monte said.

"I'm still not sure about this," Raven said. "What if everything falls apart?"

"It won't," Monte assured her. "You want your house, don't you?"

"Yes. You know I do," Raven said.

"Then trust me," said Monte. "Do as I say, and everything will work out fine."

***

Leland was upstairs sound asleep after Raven gave him lunch and his pain medications. Raven spent the afternoon going through the house, taking down every picture of Mavis and ridding the house of anything Mavis had ever purchased and throwing those things in the garbage. Raven picked up the miniature ballerina music box and smashed the offending trinket into the fireplace, reveling as it shattered into pieces. She haphazardly threw the other porcelain knick-knacks in a box, not caring that they smashed to smithereens. Raven just wanted her house to be Mavis-free. She should have cleaned the house of Mavis's things years ago.

She didn't worry about Leland waking up again. Earlier that evening, the associate pastors and a few other officers and members had dropped by unannounced to visit with Leland. They told Leland how much he was missed and wondered when he would be able to come back into the pulpit. Although it was a good visit, Leland was worn out and in extreme pain by the time his visitors decided to leave. Raven gave her husband his pain medications and he fell quickly asleep.

Monte used Uber to drop him at Raven's home close to midnight. Raven opened the door and threw her arms around her lover. Monte looked around nervously, wondering if it was wise for him to be in the other man's home.

Monte didn't feel comfortable at all being in Leland's home. He and Raven shared some blunts but even that couldn't quell the uneasiness he felt at being there. He called for an Uber ride and went back to his place. Disappointed, Raven did the rest of the drugs Monte left behind.

***

"I don't like you," said Raven, holding a knife against her husband's throat.

Leland lay perfectly still as his young wife berated him while holding the point of the razor-sharp steel against his neck. The slightest move and he would be dead. Then who would care for Lamar?

"You're nothing! Your make my skin crawl," Raven scoffed. "I saved my virginity for your old ass, but you suck in bed," she taunted. "And you were married before with two daughters. I guess it didn't take much to please your perfect Mavis!"

Raven took the knife from his throat but kept it near.

"You know what? I'm going to help you spice up your sex life," she declared. "Today, you're going to watch some porn."

She turned on the TV, flipping to channels until she found what she was looking for.

"Today is Saturday," he finally whispered hoarsely.

She spun around quickly and forcefully slapped him across the face bringing tears to his eyes.

"Who told you to speak? I know what day it is," she barked.

"I have to finish my sermon for tomorrow," he explained.

"No, you don't!" Raven sent him a quelling look. "You're not going to church tomorrow. That's why you have associate pastors. They will handle it. Right now, you're going to watch how spicy sex can be." She turned on an adult channel.

"Where is Lamar?" Leland asked.

"See how senile you  are," Raven taunted. "Lamar is not here. He's away for the weekend so it's just you and me.  If you want to get really kinky and have a threesome," she jeered. "I can ask my lover Monte Davenport.  She laughed, flaunting her sexual dalliance with Monte in her husband's face. "Monte could teach you a thing or two about being a man. A real man," she taunted.

The sunlight glared through the guest bedroom window, as Raven heard the tinkling of a bell – Leland's bell.  The fog cleared her mind. It was all a crazy dream.  She had to leave drugs alone.  She went into Leland to see what he wanted.

***

Leland had awakened around midnight when he heard the doorbell rang.  He knew that his wife opened the door and allowed another man, her lover, to come into his home. Although Leland was tired and in pain from the unexpected company from earlier that evening, he had been weaning himself from the medications and was taking half of the dosage or none at all, preferring to endure the pain rather than constantly be in a drug-infused sleep.

Leland noticed that the other man didn't stay long and was glad when the younger man left. It was apparent that he and Raven had plotted to do some sort of evil towards him, but God saw fit to upset their scheme. Although he had been in denial about it, Leland and nearly everyone with eyes could see that Raven was cheating on him.

The smell of pot permeated the air even several hours after Leland heard his stoned wife stumble into the guest bedroom to sleep. The fact that Raven felt bold enough to bring her lover to his house, their home, gave Leland a lot to think about. Raven's actions, not just tonight, showed that she didn't care about him or their marriage.

Leland wondered how the seemingly sweet young woman he had married had turned into such an evil twisted woman. Maybe it was always there, but he hadn't seen the signs, but it seemed the moment she gave birth to Lamar, the innocent young woman Leland thought he knew suddenly became a sophisticated conniving abuser who did her best to humiliate him.

At first, Raven verbally abused him. Next, she started throwing objects like plates and once, she even threw a heavy paperweight that narrowly missed him. He excused it all, reasoning it to be postpartum depression. He tried his best to get her to seek counseling, but she refused and seemed to resent him all the more for suggesting it. That was the first time she physically assaulted him.

"Are you trying to say I'm crazy," Raven asked Leland in disbelief.

Raven hurled herself toward Leland's unsuspecting back as he walked away from her. The force of her momentum knocked him to the floor, making him fall hard on his right knee. While he was hugging his knee, Raven slugged him hard on the left side of his face. His teeth clattered with the impact of her fist.

"I'm not crazy," she said vehemently as she watched him roll in pain on the floor. "I'm out of here!" She turned and walked quickly from the room.

Leland tried to speak but couldn't. The pain he was experiencing physically and emotionally was excruciating.

Raven tugged on the wheels of her traveling bag which she had obviously already packed.

"Where are you going," Leland managed to strangle out. "Where is Lamar?"

"Where I'm going is none of your damn business," she shouted with disdain.

"What's wrong with you Raven? I'm your husband! I have a right to know," said Leland. "What has happened to you?"

She looked at him with disgust. Suddenly she kicked him with all her might in his lower stomach although she was probably aiming for his groin.

"Shut up! Just shut up," she yelled. "I don't need to tell you anything. I'll be back when I get ready. That damn baby you wanted is crying," she scoffed before turning to walk out the door.

Leland could hear the unmistakable wailing of his baby boy through the intercom of the baby monitor. By God's grace, he stood shakily, went to the refrigerator to retrieve some infant formula, and warmed it to take to his son. After the battering Leland had received from the hands of his wife, climbing the stairs to get to Lamar was indeed an act of faith. "I'm coming son. I'm coming," he said, wincing with each painful step.

For most of his married life to Raven, Leland had been the victim of domestic violence. He couldn't understand the depth of cruelty and evil in his wife. He knew he was a good husband to her. Like his mother-in-law and grandmother-in-law had predicted, he made sure that his young wife wanted for nothing. But nothing Leland did was ever good enough.

After his first wife died, Leland wasn't trying to look for a bride. He had two grown 20-something daughters and their welfare was uppermost in his mind. He had a good wife in Mavis. She wasn't the most physically beautiful woman, but she loved the Lord. She loved her husband and their children, and she loved people. She was anointed to serve, encourage and support.

Nobody could touch Mavis's famous homemade chicken and dumplings. Their home was clean and filled with joy and laughter. Leland would rush home just to be with Mavis and their children. In their bedroom, she was a more than satisfying lover.

Even though Leland knew that when Mavis died of ovarian cancer, she was in the bosom of Jesus in heaven, he greatly missed her. Soon after Mavis passed on, women of all ages threw themselves at him. Leland was shocked and dismayed at some of the indecent and profane things that these professing Christian women said and did.

He didn't rush to marry again. He waited until 10 years after the death of his beloved Mavis before he once again entered into matrimony. He had fallen in love with a seemingly innocent young woman from a "good family" in his congregation. Her parents and grandparents were faithful members of his congregation and had been for many years. He had baptized Raven when she was a child. But he had never looked at her like a lecherous old man. Perhaps on the periphery Leland had taken note of Raven, but the year before they married Raven was suddenly everywhere and in nearly every event that the church had.

Leland knew now that this whole "romance" between he and Raven had been orchestrated by her mother Cecilia and her grandmother Geneva. The older Randolph women pushed Raven into wanting the affections of a man old enough to be her father. If she didn't want that too, Raven initially showed no sign of it.

Pride comes before the fall. Leland reasoned that his ego ruined him, thinking that an enticing young woman like Raven could be in love with him.

He was so entranced with Raven that his prayer life was virtually nonexistent. At the church, he preached the sermons and conducted church business, but he was absolutely enthralled with the young woman and he truly believed the feeling was mutual. The feeling probably was mutual. His for love and marriage and hers for every selfish reason one could think of.

For Raven, it was all about her and once they made their marriage vows, she made sure that Leland catered to her every whim—that he worshipped daily at the altar of Raven. Leland should also have looked more thoroughly at Raven's family rather than focusing on her. But then Cecelia and Geneva were both skillful in teaching their willing pupil the tricks of the trade of "training the man."

Everyone in the congregation, including Leland, knew that father and son Charles (Cecelia's husband) and Jasper (Geneva's husband) Randolph were henpecked. Cecelia and Geneva did all the talking and if either Charles or Jasper would dare to speak, the two men were glared at and immediately silenced. And how many times during Leland's tenure at the church had the Randolph men come to the church with a black eye, a split lip, unexplained burns or on crutches?

Leland suddenly realized that the Randolph men had been silently crying out. Their lumps and bruises were on display for the world to see, but Leland and so many others had let these men down. Men like him and the Randolph men weren't wife beaters. Striking a woman went against everything decent they had been taught about how a man treats a woman. Besides the Randolph men, Leland could think of several other men who were laughed at and called henpecked and emasculated as men. Along with the physical abuse, Leland unfortunately now knew firsthand that the endless verbal and emotional abuse was just as destructive as the physical abuse.

When Leland awoke the next morning, he knew what he had to do. There was no way he was going to stay married to his cheating, abusive wife. As he lay in his bed last night, he prayed fervently, drawing closer to God in the midst of his physical and emotional pain. He made up his mind that he was divorcing Raven and he would find ways to help other men to cope and escape from this humiliating, life-threatening abuse. He would also help his son and other children who also suffered directly and indirectly from domestic violence in the home.

***

"I don't know what happened to us Raven," said Leland when she walked into the room.

"What are you talking about?" Raven wasn't fully awake. She was still groggy from smoking all that pot last night.

"Why did you allow that man, your lover, to come into my home last night?" Leland asked angrily.

"You must be hallucinating," Raven said. "Nobody else was here last night. It was just you and me."

"Stop the lying, Raven!"

"I'm not lying," she said, suddenly annoyed with Leland. "What's wrong with you?"

"I want you out of my house," he said.

"I'm not going anywhere," said Raven. "This is my house now."

"I want you out, today," Leland persisted.

"Who's going to make me go, Old Man?" Raven scoffed. She easily knocked Leland to the floor and began to pound him mercilessly.

Lamar liked spending time with his niece and nephew, who at the ages of seven and nine were more like his sister and brother. He loved them and enjoyed them, but he wanted to be at home to protect his father from his mother's violent outbursts.

Lamar didn't like his mother much. At only eleven-years-old, he knew how pretentious and manipulative Raven was. She was constantly threatening that she was going to take him away from his dad, and there was nothing Leland could do about it. Lamar knew that Leland took the abuse so that he could always be near his one and only son. Lamar knew beyond a shadow of a doubt that his dad loved him, but both felt helpless when it came to Raven. She was a consummate and convincing actress who could make the police, the courts and everyone believe that she was a victim, not an evil abuser.

Because of thunderstorms in the area, Portia and her husband Paul decided to be safe and cut their family fun short at the amusement park. That suited Lamar fine. He wanted to go home to see his dad whom he had not seen since before school on Friday.

Portia, Paul and Lamar walked into the house to find Leland brutally beaten and Raven nowhere in sight.

Raven was arrested at Monte's place when he turned her in after she bragged to him about what she had done to the pastor.

After a brief stay in the hospital, Rev. Dr. Leland Maxwell was rejuvenated. He knew he could no longer stay in his house—the house that was once a home when he was married to Mavis. A house where they raised their two daughters, spent time with their neighbors and were an active part of their community. Now it was a house of painful memories of the time he shared with Raven.

The only good things to come from his marriage to Raven were his son Lamar, lessons learned and God's protection, mercy and loving-kindness.

Leland put matters in motion to concentrate on building a new ministry to help mainly male victims of domestic violence. He contacted a pastor friend of his in Australia who had for years wanted him to help in his men's ministry.

While Raven was seething in jail, Leland instructed his lawyers to immediately file for a petition of divorce. He handed in his resignation from his church of more than 30 years effective immediately. Leland also closed all of his social media and financial accounts and then created new ones. He gave his son and daughters powers of attorney over his finances and health should he become incapacitated in any way.

After she finally made it back to her home after her parents posted the bail, Raven stormed into the house angrily, ready to tear into Leland for not coming to get her out of jail, and to insist that he drop the ridiculous domestic violence charges.

When Raven walked into the house, everything looked the same, but the house was different -- empty and lifeless. A note was waiting on the kitchen counter for her.

"I'm keeping the deed to the house. You are free to live here for the rest of your life," Leland wrote. "Don't try to find or bother me or Lamar unless you want it broadcasted to everyone just how nasty and evil you are. My lawyer has drawn up a fair plan where you will receive a monthly stipend to help with your living costs. If you get a job, you can live quite comfortably. I am praying that the evil and violence that consumes you will go away someday. It's so unfortunate that someone so young and beautiful can be so old and ugly."

# HEX AND HAIR GREASE
## Craig Stafford

Two days after her husband, Pastor Henry Hendrix died, Lady Mape Hendrix, popular owner of Luxe Beauty, gave birth to a baby girl, in the alley, right behind her hair salon. She was dumping the trash when her water broke. Falling to the ground from the sharp pains. She could not muster enough strength to crawl into the shop to call the medics.

She sat in a puddle of garbage can discarded water, rotting meat and food from the surrounding cafes and a baby crowning. The death of her husband may have been accidental but having her baby four months early was destined. It was foretold in a bibliomancy session by her grandmother Maple, where she gets her nickname. Her real name is Mapleton Hendrix. Grandma Maple would open the Bible to a random scripture and tell of its meaning. Lady Mape's meaning had come some 33 years ago at the request of her mother, Connie.

Connie wanted to know what type of child she would have. Grandma Maple grabbed the white, dingy, oversized Bible with gold lettering, placed it on the floor and had

Connie Joe to place her hands on it. After a few moments, she motioned for her to move her hands and she immediately opened it casting her eyes on Luke chapter 12, verse 53 and read aloud, "They will be divided, father against son and son against father, mother against daughter and daughter against mother, mother-in-law against her daughter-in-law and daughter-in-law against mother-in-law". Grandma Maple looked at Connie Joe and said, "joy is added unto you, but your child's child will usher in five generations of family division. So says verse 52 "For from now on in one house there will be five divided, three against two and two against three."

Connie Joe was most happy, but suddenly overcome with sadness after realizing what would befall the bloodline. Her mother nor her grandmother ever told Lady Mape of her certain misfortune. Connie Joe thought she could change the family's fate by teaching her daughter the sacred ways of redeeming curses according to the work of Ephesians chapter 5, verse 16: "Redeeming the time, because the days are evil." But mastering the redeeming of time is only half the art. You have to also redeem the soul according to the work of Psalm chapter 49, verse 15 "God will redeem my soul from the power of the grave."

## DON'T ASK, DON'T TELL

Henry Hendrix, or Henny as his beloved called him; loved being the one to get up and cook breakfast. He got joy out of fixing heavy butter, heavy grease meals for he and his wife; especially with their bundle of joy on the way. A Southern boy by birth and by heart, he would tell Lady Mape he wanted a plump and full child. The kitchen was also where he practiced his sermonic delivery. Bible and butter. Theology and toast. Pneumatology and peanut butter.

While Henny made breakfast, Mape would fiddle around in what she called her workroom. She had one at home and one in the salon.

She was always brewing a root, a leaf, or creating butters for hair and skin and injuries. Henny didn't understand everything his wife did; but he would often pray about the stirrings she came up with in the workroom. Although in conversation, and some downright fights, he would beg her to assure him she wasn't doing anything that could be considered witchcraft. She would always resent what he was saying; but in seven years of marriage, she had never denied it.

"Henny, how you feel this morning, my preaching pipe-man?"

"Girl, I am feeling like new money wrapped in old money coming up with mo' money! And you're going to feel that good too. I found that spicy Georgia sausage you like."

"Well, put the sausage on the plate, Mister. How'd it go last night?"

Henny's actions slowed. Mape raised her eyebrows as she watched him slide the sausage on the plate. When he reached for the plate of waffles, she stretched her eyes. Strangely, it seemed to jolt him, and he dropped into the chair in front of her.

"Mape. It's like this entire association has relegated me to a low-level pastor. They aren't taking my request to be named pastor of Mount Pisgah seriously. We may be one of the smaller churches numbers wise and income wise, but we are by far more advanced technologically and when it comes to street outreach." Henny dropped his head. The weight of his frustration pushed his shoulders down as well.

"Pick your head up pastor. The association is driven by the two things you just mentioned – numbers and money. But the last shall be first. You will get the votes. I know it with everything in me."

Henny rose and walked over to the side of the table where his wife sat. Kneeling before her, he softly kissed her belly and then her lips.

"You are my Eve – bone of my bone, flesh of my flesh."

Mape laughed, "Yes, I am - and when you get this new pastor's position, don't you forget that."

He grabbed a slice of sausage from her plate as he continued. "Forgot to tell you. Bishop Wemer was rushed to the hospital right before the meeting. How do you eat this sausage? It's too hot."

"I didn't tell you to eat it." Henny didn't notice Mape's unconcerned face about his news. She did try to put some concern in her voice. "What happened to him?"

"They say he had some kind of seizure. Mape. It's not looking good. By the end of our meeting, we got a call saying he was on life support."

"Well, then we'll put him on the altar. Yes? I have to get to the shop. It's my day to host the First Ladies Council – so I'm having brunch catered in there."

With that she kissed him as though she needed to remind him that he was still a man. Then she ran out the door. Henny looked after her. His face full of questioning and concern. All he could do was turn to face the door to her workroom. A room he didn't have a key to.

## IN THIS PLACE

Lady Mape pulled into the parking lot of her salon. Every newspaper and magazine in Lemon City had written about how fabulous the place is. Luxe Beauty was her dream come true. She descended from a long line of women who do hair and women who do hoodoo. Hoodoo wrapped in the bible. Mape was a powerfully creative student of both.

She didn't tell Henny she had visited the Wemer's the day before the meeting. She baked bread pudding with raisins for the choir and remembered that Pas. Wemer loved it. She also knew that with his wife out of town, he likely was grabbing food from here or there. So, she also took him a healthy, hot meal from The Bistro.

Pulling out her phone, she put a check mark next to a list of names on her notes app. As she glanced up at two women exiting the shop, she touched a bright red key on her keychain and inhaled deeply.

Sukie, Lady Mape's right hand at the shop, had everything buzzing. Latte and espresso cups were in several hands. Cold teas and other beverages in others. Three under the dryer, four at the shampoo bowls. Business was buzzing.

"Good morning Lady Mape. The tables are dressed and set up in the back. Sharon's Tapa Bar will bring brunch over and I did call First Lady Stocks and told her that she could bring her own meal to enjoy with everyone else." Mape embraced her and pulled a smock from a gold hanger, preparing to get to work.

"You are tight work, little diva. I appreciate you. I'll take Lady Jeeks. Good morning! How are you? How'd that conditioner feel on your hair?"

For the next few minutes the ladies talked about everything from the new line of church hats in the Ashro catalog to the latest on who got caught with whom; and what happened on Greenleaf, The Haves and Have Nots and Queen Sugar.

"Now, remember Lady Jeeks. You are going to apply the hair butter every three nights to stimulate hair growth. Do the cross down the middle of your head while you speak Matthew chapter 10, verse 30 "The very hairs on your head are numbered", massage it in and then massage the ends of your hair. Then brush and wrap. And no more cotton scarves. Use the satin caps. The ones I gave you are comfortable, and stylish. Agreed?"

Before she could answer, the staff from Sharon's Tapa Bar entered to set up, and several of the other pastors' wives were behind them. Mape took the smock off, gave Sukie some instructions and entered the back room to assure everything was straight. She smelled the flowers. Looked at the serving utensils. Adjusted the lighting.

"Creating the atmosphere to convince the women that the illustrious Pastor Hendrix should have Mount Pisgah, are you?" Bridgette Stocks did not like Mape, and she did not try to hide it. Mape returned the dislike even though she did not really know Lady Stocks. Their spirits clashed. Their energies were always at war.

"Lady Bridgette. I do love that purple on you. Royalty – pure royalty."

"Are we starting now?" She moved a set of dishes and silverware from one of the seats and opened a black carryout container in its place.

The other ladies entered, interestingly not surprised that Lady Stocks was not eating the same thing they were. She had declined to do that when at one meeting Mape made a comment about her mother cooking chicken feet and Bridgette proclaimed loudly, "the tricks of her trade and yours as well, I presume."

With brunch served and eaten, Lady Stocks rushed the conversation. "Ladies, we know this is not a meeting to discuss a fashion show or anything pretty and trivial like that. This is about Mount Pisgah and whose husband should get it. Bishop Stocks holds three voting blocks in this election, and I can tell you – he is leaning in a couple of directions."

Her eyes locked on Mape's face. Mape did not look up. She simply smiled. The other ladies moved their eyes between the two of them like a heated tennis match was in play.

"Well," interjected Lady Roberta Still. "I'm certain my husband is withdrawing his bid for the position. We had hoped his mother would be with his sister; but that suddenly changed, and we are re-arranging everything to bring her to live with us."

Bridgette watched Mape. Mape kept picking at the fruit left on the platter.

"Bishop Wemer is out of the voting. The vote is a week away and as of a few moments ago, he was on life support. His votes will go to Bishop Stocks." Lady Charlotte Clout seemed to be reading from a charter or similar document.

"Life support?" Mape seemed overcome with sadness. "I didn't know. Henny told me he had a seizure. How horrible!"

"Horrible? Or expected?" Bridgette strutted out the door; throwing a comment to the ladies before she did. "You can count on this, Bishop will have the deciding votes, and nothing will stop that!"

The ladies assured each other and Mape that it was just a bad day for Lady Stocks. Within moments, the room was clear. Mape busied herself with clearing dishes, blowing out candles and other things. She picked up a bible from the head of the table, and turned to Psalms 91, and read aloud.

"He that dwelleth in the secret place of the Most High shall abide under the shadow of the Almighty. I will say of the LORD, He is my refuge and my fortress: my God; in him will I trust. Surely, he shall deliver thee from the snare of the fowler, and from the noisome pestilence. He shall cover thee with his feathers, and under his wings shalt thou trust: his truth shall be thy shield and buckler. Thou shalt not be afraid for the terror by night; nor for the arrow that flieth by day; Nor for the pestilence that walketh in darkness; nor for the destruction that wasteth at noonday. A thousand shall fall at thy side, and ten thousand at thy right hand; but it shall not come nigh thee. Only with thine eyes shalt thou behold and see the reward of the wicked. Because thou hast made the LORD, which is my refuge, even the Most High, thy habitation; There shall no evil befall thee, neither shall any plague come nigh thy dwelling."

She didn't hear Henny walk in. Him reciting the next verses made her smile. "For he shall give his angels charge over thee, to keep thee in all thy ways. They shall bear thee up in their hands, lest thou dash thy foot against a stone. Thou shalt tread upon the lion and adder: the young lion and the dragon shalt thou trample under feet. Because he hath set his love upon me, therefore will I deliver him: I will set him on high, because he hath known my name." Who are you protecting yourself from?" He rubbed his stomach as he approached her and kissed her lightly on the forehead.

"Your stomach still bothering you?"

"Yeah. I can't eat that spicy stuff like you. Plus, I think this pastor vying has got my ulcers acting up."

Mape rubbed his stomach, commanding it to behave and to cease from all its troubles. She then recited Matthew chapter 15, verse 17 "Do not ye yet understand, that whatsoever entered in at the mouth get into the belly, and is cast out." Henny kissed her praying hand as she yelled out into the salon. "Sukie, bring me a cup of hot ginger tea. There are some prepared pouches in the can in the refrigerator."

Henny sat on the folding table and nibbled on the leftovers watching Mape. He noticed the door to her workroom and the strong lock on it.

"Mape. Did you know about Wemer before I said something?"

She did not answer. But reached for the cup of tea from Sukie and handed it to her husband.

"Drink it slowly."

"Did you know about Wemer? Did you know about Pas. Still? Do you know that Pas. Roosevelt is going to announce his resignation because of some indiscretions?"

"You told me about Wemer. Roberta told us about Still. Roosevelt should have resigned before the 16-year-old boy. What are you asking me?"

"What do you do in those workrooms?"

"I mix butters. I mix creams. I play with herbs and roots and make teas. For me it's like a photographer's dark room. It's my she-room. My secret place. I guess you can call it my mixing room. What do you think I'm doing? And be very careful how you answer."

"I'll see you at home." He stopped, breathed deeply. "My mom used to say some of us like to dance with the devil, thinking we're leading the dance, but his sway is deadly."

Henny's word left Mape's body trembling.


## *READ BEFORE YOU DRINK*

Two days passed and Henny and Mape were being very careful around each other. Mape didn't know Henny had a locksmith come to the house about opening her workroom. He came, but Henny couldn't go through with it. Mape would cook. They would eat. Henny would study. They would watch TV. They would do everything but talk and be husband and wife together.

Mape broke the ice on the third day, "People would tell me my great great grandmothers and even my grandmothers were and are root workers. Maybe that's how I learned to love stirring up things and praying and worshipping while I do. That's what happens in my mixing room. Do I see things sometimes? Yes. But I see things like people who dream. You deserve that pastorate baby; and while this may sound harsh, if God is moving people to raise you up – then – HALLELUJAH!"

"It does sound harsh. But if you tell me you had nothing to do with any of those incidents, then I believe you." For the first time in days, he held his wife and held her for quite a while.

Returning the embrace, she took his hand and led him to the couch, reassured him the baby would be fine; and reminded him that she is his Eve.

Fast asleep, Mape suddenly and violently began to toss and turn. She seemed to be trying to rise but couldn't. Her eyes flew open and she yelled, "FOR HE SHALL GIVE ANGELS CHARGE OVER THEE!" And started speaking in tongues. Her words filled the room. As did the sound of crashing downstairs. Looking over to the left where Henny always laid, she realized it must have been him. She ran down the stairs and there he was writhing and convulsing on the floor. His heart beating so profound she could see it through his chest. She pounded on his chest, a trickle of blood dripped from his lips. She grabbed the phone from the counter, noticed the opened jar and hoped it would all be well.

## *WHAT DID I DO?*

Lady Mape knocked on Grandma Maple's door like a mad woman. When Grandma Maple came to the door with shot-gun cocked and loaded. Lady Mape bellowed a haunting screech and screamed, "I killed him! I killed him! I killed my Henny! Grandma I didn't mean to. I forgot to label the stuff and he drank ... he drank ... it shouldn't have been enough ... it couldn't ... I killed him!"

Grandma Maple shook her. "Calm down child. You gone mess around and scare our ancestors the way you carrying on. Calm down and tell me what happened."

Lady Mape calmed down just enough to get the words out where Grandma Maple could understand. "He drunk the sour root I was brewing based on the work in Job chapter 20, verse 14 "his food will turn sour in his stomach; it will become the venom of serpents within him" for the special coffee instead of the mint oil for his stomach. He was supposed to take the sour root coffee to Bishop Stocks. Henny was supposed to give to his secretary for her to brew him a cup, like she always does. Just enough to make him sick, so he wouldn't be able to host the Regional Church of Holiness Gala. And so, he wouldn't be able to vote on the new pastor appointment."

Henny, as the vice-president would automatically assume the honor and obtain his voting rights. With Bishop Stocks and the other two out the way, Pas. Hendrix would have the majority votes needed, he would become the new pastor of the historic Mount Pisgah Church of Holiness, and the money collected in the offering would go to him to merge his current church with The Mount – as it is affectionately called.

"I didn't know we were concocting our own death sentence. What went wrong grandma, what went wrong?"

Grandma took a handful of pages of the Bible and flipped them backwards as is custom with bibliomancy. Flipping pages forward foretell what's to come. Flipping backward tells what happened. She turns the page to Ecclesiastes chapter 10, verse 1 and loudly whispers "Dead flies cause the oil of the perfumer to send forth an evil odor; so doth a little folly outweighs wisdom and honor."

Grandma Maple looked Lady Mape in the eye with a look of disappointment, "it was foolish of the two of you to think the Stock family wasn't working roots of their own. First Lady Bridgette Stocks is a Seer. She was born with what the old folk call "a veil over your eyes". The scripture speaks of a mix of anointing oil and dead flies with evil intent of death sent Henny's way. Granddaughter, you've been outwitted." Grandma Maple raised her voice a bit. "You should have went after the First Lady. Always go for the woman. A woman is a man's weakness. A man truly loves a woman or trying to hide what he truly loves. Whichever way you flip it, a woman is involved somehow. Mrs. Stocks is good, but I'm better. No one messes with my family and goes un-hexed. Go look under my bed. You'll see a wooden box. Grab it and bring it to me."

"What's in the box? Lady Mape inquired.

"My mama's root book. It's full of hexes. No one messed with my mama. She was a tough, fair skinned, red haired woman with freckles. Her daddy was an Irishman and her mama was French creole," reminisced Grandma Maple. She then went on to say there's a bottle of hair grease in there too.

"Hair grease? What for?" Lady Mape was puzzled.

"The grease is used like a glue. Keeps your target stuck and unable to remove the curse. A heap of dirt and a little water will do just fine too. We call that black mud root," exclaimed Grandma Maple.

"It makes sense now. Now I know why I'm so drawn to homemade hair care products. It's my heritage. My birthright," gleamed Lady Mape. "What next?"

"You write the hex on a piece of brown paper bag and stick it inside the grease," replied Grandma Maple.

"Why a brown paper bag?"

"Back in the day, us root workers had to use whatever we could get our hands on. Money was scarce and the market was a long way off, so we made do with what we had. Hair grease reminded them of the nut butter and clay mixture back in Africa. That's where the black mud root come from. The brown paper bag is just something us Black folks been using for a while now for all sorts of stuff. Carrying our food, ridding ourselves of the hiccups and patching up clothes. Go and get the box like I say child."

Lady Mape hurried to her grandmother's room, hurried back to the kitchen table, and placed the box in front of Grandma Maple. "My mama always told me Psalms 18 is one of the most powerful scriptures you can use against your enemies. Sit down at this table and jot down the words from the first page of my mama's book and when you finish read it out loud." Grandma Maple commanded.

Lady Mape jotted down what she was told and when she finished, she started to read it.

Grandma Maple stopped her right away. She said, "Mapleton, you just can't read it. You have to feel it and speak it from the pit of your belly. Start over, but don't say another word until you can do that. You hear me child?"

"Yes." She took a deep breath, waited a few seconds and then began to read. Her voice trembling initially became stern and compelling.

Hex to vex in secret First Lady Bridgette Stocks

He made darkness his secret place; his pavilion round about him were dark waters and thick clouds of the skies.

Hex to vex

I have pursued mine enemies and overtaken them: neither did I turn again till they were consumed.

Hex to vex

I have wounded them that they were not able to rise: they are fallen under my feet.

Hex to vex

For thou hast girded me with strength unto the battle: thou hast subdued under me those that rose up against me.

Hex to vex

Thou hast also given me the necks of mine enemies; that I might destroy them that hate me.

Hex to vex

They cried, but there was none to save them: even unto the LORD, but he answered them not.

Hex to vex

Then did I beat them small as the dust before the wind: I did cast them out as the dirt in the streets.

Hex to vex in secret First Lady Bridgette Stocks

When Lady Mape finished reading, Grandma Maple stood up and declared, "That's a girl. That's how you hex a Seer. Soon enough we'll get word about Bridgette's mishap. In the meantime, go lay down and get some rest."

## THE BABY IS COMING

Lady Mape is in the alley, leaned against a trash dump, sitting in sewage and bleeding like the Red Sea in the dead of winter. It is 45 degrees outside and drizzling in an area the parishioners call Swamp River Orleans. She has lost complete control of her bodily functions and finds herself covered in her own feces.

She began to sense the presence of evil. She had sensed it before, but not like this. Everything was different. The evil wasn't around her. It was much closer. Way closer than should be. What she felt was from within. Her own baby was trying to kill her. She became extremely hot all over as if she was on fire from the inside out. She felt as if her whole body was being smothered. She started hyperventilating and gasping for breath.

In an attempt to cool her body, she struggles to remove her dress. Finally, she managed to get the dress off and tear her panties. Her face grimaced at the pain, and her body heaved with each breath.

"God, please help me. Whatever curse this is – please help me. Don't let my work take my child." Naked, filthy, alone and struggling to breathe she yelled out. "God send me my redeemer!"

She blacked out, her head hitting a pile of discarded boxes. Just as she did Sukie ran through the back door to find her face down in a puddle of vile. Mape's body hovered over the scene, as she stood crying, she could see her dead great grandmother, Kattie Lee. Kattie's bare hands were cupped and extended fresh water to her. The water was seeping through her fingers, yet her hands remained full. Her grandmother hovered over her body placing her hands over her mouth. The dripping water strengthening her weakened state.

Her grandmother encouraged her, "You must scream child. Scream now or you'll die." Lady Mape began to scream herself into consciousness. Sukie at her side and the paramedics rushing from their emergency vehicle. She screamed that she felt like her spine was being torn apart. She screamed that it felt like the baby was coming out sideways. She screamed that no evil would befall her. Then she stopped screaming.

When she came to in the Intensive Care Unit, it was five days later. She had been in critical condition. She'd lost so much blood they had to give her a transfusion. It was something she was not happy about. She had not been able to rebuke any evil from entering through another person's blood. The only thing she did remember was her great grandmother giving her water to drink. What she didn't know as she was screaming, she was pushing, and she gave birth to her baby girl, four weeks early, while she was in and out of consciousness.

She rose and looked at the flowers and balloons around her room. Sukie had left a note telling her she would keep the shop going until she told her otherwise. Bishop Stocks stopped by while visiting his wife. The note said she was involved in a bad accident. Her note also said that her grandmother had come by and left something for her in the drawer. Mape opened the drawer and there was a deep purple rope tied around the prettiest amethyst she had ever seen. It came with instructions.

"Wave this over your baby once in the morning and once in the evening. If you can lay it between her heart and her belly, even better."

Mape read the instructions and fell over into tears. She called the nurse and asked if she could see her baby finally. They wheeled the baby in. She was still in an incubator. She was big, to Mape, for a premature baby. But Henny made sure he fed her well. Mape pulled the incubator to the bed, put her hands through the gloves and touched her little girl all over.

"You still need to give her a name. Your grandmother nor your assistant knew what you wanted." The nurse made notes in the computer while she spoke.

"Constance Henryetta – H.e.n.r.y.e.t.t.a Hendrix. I'll call her Henny."

The nurse scribbled the name on a piece of paper and left the two alone. Mape pulled out the stone and held it up to wave over the baby. Then suddenly put it back in the drawer. Tears flooded her face. She laid her head on the incubator, her tears flowing over it and breathed deeply.

"My angel. No hexes. No vexes – just forgiveness Little Henny. Forgive your mama. I wish you could know how good your daddy was. Henny, my dear pastor, please forgive me." She stroked Constance's face. She touched her heart and cried. "Lord, the very thing I have feared has come upon me according to Job chapter three. You said in Second Chronicles chapter seven, verse 14, "If my people, which are called by my name, shall humble themselves, and pray, and seek my face, and turn from their wicked ways; then will I hear from heaven, and will forgive their sin, and will heal their land." God, please hear me, forgive me and heal my family. I never meant to sow wickedness. Teach me, to be rooted and grounded in You. Amen."

Constance kicked her feet and seemed to giggle; and so, her mother smiled and cooed.

# Don't Tell Me Nothing About My Pastor!

### Margarette Joyner

I'd been out of fellowship for several years before my spirit let me know that it was time to find a church home. This was a little daunting to me because when I left the last church I attended, I vowed I'd never join another one. It was a holiness church and I had gone through the tarrying at the altar until I spoke in tongues, surrounded by all the saints who were prodding and pushing me to "call on the name of Jesus, Betty, call him."

When I'd received salvation, according to the saints, I was deemed "saved." Within six months, I found out all about the Pastor's past, the devilish deacons and the stanking saints, all by way of the First Lady - who was just as messy as those she talked about.

There seems to be something about me and First Ladies. They endear themselves to me. Maybe it's the air of wisdom and no non-sense that I give off. Yet, they always seem to find something about me that enrages them. One First Lady didn't want me in the choir – voice too rich and sultry. Another didn't want me on the Pastor's Esteem Board – "we don't know you!" Yet another said, "So what if older women in the church love you?" She deduced that I could be conning them out of their Social Security checks. Messy women in pretty suits and big hats need to know that Betty doesn't want their suits, their position, and most certainly don't want their husbands. I just want to go to church and get The Word. Now - tarry on that!

I hopped around for several months, then one day I spotted a fairly large church sitting on a corner not four blocks from my home. One Sunday I decided to go in and see what they had to offer. I pulled my little gold pickup truck into the graveled parking lot and watched the joyful people go into the white, stained glassed building and I instantly felt a sense of warmth. I thought, maybe this was where I belonged.

I got out of the truck and made my way to the front door as best I could, trying to find balance between the rocks and my three-inch pumps. I'd decided to dress my thick frame in one of my cutest, black dresses, and donned a purple head dress with matching wooden, drop earrings to give them the full effect of me. As I walked in, I was greeted with warmness, smiles, holy hugs and greetings that made me feel right at home.

The sanctuary was just large enough not to be mega and small enough to feel like family. I sat on the back pew as I always do at any church I visited, so that I could have a bird's eye view of everything and everyone. The praise and worship part of the service began, and it was an old fashioned, down home, foot stomping good time that had me remembering my days in the holiness church back home. I was having myself a good time!

Then the choir took their turn singing and although they weren't the greatest choir I'd ever heard, they had heart and conviction and I loved it so much that I joined them from my seat in the rear. This brought attention to me of course because God saw fit to bless me with a rich and powerful voice that could fill up a church like that without a microphone. Just before the end of the song, the man of God took the stage and the song; the church was on fire! I could tell this man, as short as he was, was going to be a huge presence and a terror with The Word and he did not disappoint. The Holy Spirit was so high in there I thought I could see it!

I continued to attend the church with the little preacher just to make sure I'd actually experienced what I did. One Sunday as the man of God preached the church into a frenzy, a woman jumped up and started running around the pews. I thought she was filled with the Holy Spirit until I heard her growling over and over again, "I gotta get out! Let me out!"

The man of God continued to preach and the spirit in the room continued to rise and the more intense it got, the more her desperation became. She took off running around the pews and finally reached the front door where I was sitting, which for some reason seemed to be locked or she just couldn't get it together enough to open it. I swiftly moved to the other end of my pew being sure not to be in arms reach of whatever was happening to her. She hit that door with such force, I just knew she had knocked herself out. Instead she turned to face the congregation and her back seemed to be pinned to the door.

Her eyes were glazed over, and I literally saw her hair stand on ends. Several of the saints surrounded her, shouting "Help her Lord Jesus! He's in the house, Lord!"

Other's shouted, "I'm not scared of you! Get thee behind me!"

By now the preacher had come down from out of the pulpit as he often did. As he made his way down the center aisle wrapping up his sermon with, "Ain't He alright! Won't He do it," he now stood face to face with her or it. The possessed woman slid down the door and began moving like a snake slithering up the aisle. Sister Butler, who sang in the choir and was the one who took care of Pastor's needs by handing him his handkerchief when he needed to wipe his face and gave him water when he was thirsty, reached down to lay hands on the thrusting body of the woman.

The preacher warned, "Don't you touch her, you ain't strong enough!" He then went back up to the podium and retrieved some holy oil. He returned and stood over the body of this poor soul and began to sprinkle the oil on her. One would have thought she was being shot as each drop hit her body and interrupted her sporadic pace. Saints were praising, musicians were playing, and the Pastor was praying. The Holy Ghost was in the house and so was His opponent!

Suddenly, the woman jumped straight up off the floor and took off running around the circle of speaking in tongue saints. She found an opening amongst them and ran out of the building still gurgling, "I gotta get out! Let me out!"

I joined the church the following Sunday. While I was greeted and welcomed by most of the people in the sanctuary, the one that Pastor had warned during the possession episode, Sister Butler, didn't seem to take too kindly to a newcomer who could out sing her. I'd overheard Sister Jackson tell her, "Sister Butler, you need to stop being so insecure. You can't keep running good folks out of this church."

"Sister Jackson I am not insecure, I just don't want anybody coming in here thinking they're going to get between me and Pastor!" She retorted.

Her jealousy was instant, painfully obvious and I thought to myself, "Oh Lord, here we go, First Lady troubles already."

When they realized I was in ear shot, Sister Butler changed her tune. "Oh, you know you're right, Sister Jackson, I'm a work in progress, just pray for me."

Not long after joining, the preacher, Pastor Marcus Winter and I engaged in several conversations and I liked him because he kept it real. I could tell from our talks and the way he carried himself that he was a rough neck brother from the hood who had found and given his life to God. That resonated with me because I had been brought up in the projects and had given my life to the Lord after I realized that a relationship with God had nothing to do with rituals or religion but was spiritual and personal. I especially enjoyed how proudly he wore his gold tooth and signature Kangol cap.

One day, we were having one of our conversations and he asked if I would create a drama ministry. I agreed and asked, "is your wife going to be okay with me doing that?"

He seemed confused and taken aback by the question, "What do you mean?"

"I asked because ever since I got here, she's been giving me the side eye. She seems to hate it when I sing, makes sure she interrupts our conversations and always disagrees with anything I have to say in Bible study."

He responded, "That doesn't sound like her at all."

"Well, for instance when you asked me to lead the bible study lesson in your absence and we were talking about treating all people with love and respect, she flat out disagreed with my teaching and expressed that she did not think anyone could be capable of loving everybody. She went on to say that she couldn't love and respect a drug addict because they chose to live that kind of lifestyle. I reminded her of who Jesus hung out with and loved. I told her that no one addiction is any worse than the other. In fact, I mentioned that I happen to know she was addicted to chocolate, even though doctors have told her not to have it because of diabetes, but that doesn't stop her from eating it. Man, she got very angry. Neck and eyes rolling and all and yelled - 'I'm not an addict! I can quit any time I want to!'"

The preacher couldn't help but smile and tried hard not to laugh, but he didn't succeed. He then informed me, "The woman you're speaking of is not my wife. She's a member that has been infatuated with me ever since I got here, and I just haven't figured out how to deal with her."

I then asked the obvious question, "well you're wearing a ring so who's your wife and why is Sister Butler acting like she is?" He seemed genuinely apologetic and promised to introduce her to me on Sunday. I did note that he gave no response about Sister Butler's behavior.

His sermon the following Sunday was just as powerful as it usually was, only this time for some reason I noticed how he preached. What I saw was that whenever he got into the climax of his whoop and holler, his preaching would come from his groin. With every "Ain't He alright" his pelvis would thrust forward and then back again in between breathes. I could see this because he didn't wear a robe (as most preachers don't anymore). What I also noticed was with every thrust, several of the women were caught up in an ungodly way, especially Sister Butler who always sat or stood directly behind him in the choir stand.

After the service was over, the preacher came down out of the pulpit and greeted his congregation as he always did. Then he motioned for me to come up front and I complied. He tapped the shoulder of a short woman who was immaculately dressed. It was communion Sunday, so her frame was dressed in an all-white suit that seemed to be tailor made for her. She donned an appropriately embellished, white hat that was strategically cocked to one side. The white, ankle strapped, high heeled shoes she wore were what afforded her the right to say she was five feet tall. Her makeup was meticulously placed on the cutest face I'd seen in the congregation. Her brown skin was flawless, her small eyes that sat just above a small nose glistened and her smile was bright, even infectious as we matched delight in meeting one another.

Pastor offered, "Sister Betty, this is my wife, Silvie Winter." I extended my hand and as she returned the gesture, I thought the rock on her finger would blind me. What a lovely woman she was.

First Lady Winter and I quickly became very close at Butternut Baptist Church. This well-educated woman had a beautiful spirit and was one of the most attractive women I'd ever seen. Her milk and honey skin was as smooth as silk. She had long, curly hair that was just shy of blonde which cascaded in waves on her shoulder. One could have melted in her soft, chestnut, doe eyes which were warm with just a hint of sadness and the smile that came from her full lips revealed a perfect set of pearly white teeth. Her hourglass figure, though tiny, was the envy of many and the dream of others. Her very presence would light up a room and every time we were together, she revealed more about her husband, my Pastor. And the more she talked, the more I wondered why she was still with him.

The first time she and I hung out, we visited the newly opened, black owned "Organic Tea Spot" and she began. "I was only 14 when Arthur and I met. I was back home in Adaline, Georgia and we had just been let out of school for the summer. On my way home, I noticed a young man noticing me as he leaned against a spanking brand new, gold Buick. The dust from the red dirt road covered the shine of it but I could tell it was his pride and joy. He smiled at me, still maintaining the toothpick that rested between two gold crowns on the left side of his top and bottom teeth as my friends and I walked by. He had the blackest skin I'd ever seen which made the gold in his mouth that matched his car glisten even more. His eyes were intense and seemed to be carving his name in my heart. He was a short man, I could tell because his head barely extended the top of the car, but his body was muscular and strong. Girl, I tell you something rose up in me that I had never imagined and although it scared me, I liked it. I knew he was much older than me, but I didn't realize the difference was as vast as it was until much later. He was 20-years old; six years my senior."

I continued to half listen to her because my mind was trying to wrap itself around the legality of fourteen and twenty. She continued, "It wasn't long after that my mama and daddy had to give him permission to marry me because after the second time I gave myself to him I got pregnant. After that, every time he took me it felt like he was devouring my veins! And to tell you the truth, it got more penetrating with every passing year." She laughed loudly because she couldn't believe she'd just told me all that. I smiled uncomfortably because I now knew my Pastor was a beast in bed.

All I could say was, "Wow!"

She went on, "That's why I look at females like Sister Butler and feel sorry for her because she thinks she can take my husband, but there is no way she or any other woman can compete with the rhythm me and this man have perfected."

I knew she was talking about Sister Butler, but I couldn't help but think that it was a warning to me as well, just in case the thought had run across my mind. I did absolutely pay attention to the way she paused with her teacup midair and looked me directly in the eyes as she lingered at "no way she or any other woman can compete with the rhythm me and this man have perfected."

I sipped and assured, "I hear you First Lady. Cover home."

That Wednesday after Bible study, the Pastor asked me to stay back, he had something he wanted to talk to me about. We sat down with a cup of coffee and he explained how he and his wife had discussed what she and I had talked about. I thought, "Oh Lord, I'm in trouble now." But I wasn't in trouble at all. Instead he thanked me for making them aware that I'd been confused as to who his wife was because I never saw them show any affection toward one another. I'd never heard him refer to her and the only woman showing him the attention a wife would was Sister Butler.

He confessed that she had spoken to him about it, but he just thought she was being jealous and that he'd been taking her feelings for granted. "But I do want to let you know that my wife can sometimes be a little too revealing with the information she shares. And I'd like to ask you to please take what she says with a grain of salt, if you know what I mean."

"No problem Pastor and I'm glad I could help."

"There is one thing I don't quite understand though," he went on. "What's the deal with me needing to wear a robe?"

Being me, I broke it down for him, letting him know about his groin preaching. Although he was clearly uncomfortable or something, he accepted my observation and said that he would fix it. He then gave me a hug thanking me for my input. The hug lasted a little longer than it should have, and I broke the embrace with "God bless you and your wife, Pastor."

He smiled, gave me a wink of his eye and thanked me again, this time cupping my hand in his.

When First Lady Winter invited me to their home for dinner, I was surprised. They live in an elegant, brick home which sat on a slight hill. It was surrounded by a white picket fence that encased a perfectly manicured lawn. When we graced the etched glass front door and entered in, the warmth of the décor enveloped me in its soft, pastel tones. She offered me a seat at the large, beige dining room table and turned on the chandelier while removing her shoes and slipping into a pair of dainty house shoes. She first brought out two glasses and a bottle of Moscato wine and then a cheese and cracker platter for us to nibble on while she prepared our dinner. Pastor was away at a conference, so we had the house to ourselves.

"Girl, what in hell's kitchen was that guest preacher talking about this morning?" She asked.

I answered laughing, "I don't know. He had me for about ten minutes and then I just kept looking at him wondering what he had taken or smoked. And when he came down out of the pulpit into the aisles and buckled his knees looking like he was doing the wobble I was through! You tell Pastor I said, if he ever let that man guest preach at our church again, we are having words."

We laughed loud but my mouth reminded me that a few days before, my front tooth decided it didn't want to remain in my mouth and politely dislodged itself while I was asleep. I'd just gotten a temporary tooth, so my gums were a little tender.

"Now you know can't nobody tell your Pastor nothing and I doubt he really cares," she said. My eyebrows went up in the air and before I could stop her, she reminded me. "Look at how he approached you in Bible Study about the pledge you didn't make. Girl, between me, you and the wine, that man is all about that money."

I thought about that for a moment and recalled our conversation on a Wednesday evening, Pastor Winter stood in front of me, with all his hood posture swag, asking why I hadn't pledged the $500 he requested from each of his tithing members. It was the first time I came dangerously close to disrespecting him. There I was standing in front of this man with my front tooth gone, self-esteem under my shoe, spitting and drooling with each word I tried to speak. I sounded like a kinsman of Elmer Fud and he wanted to know where his money was.

He even had the nerve to tell me he could put me on a layaway plan if I needed him to. I took a cleansing breath and carefully responded with grace, "the five hundred dollars I have is going toward fixing my tooth sir," and I walked away. What the unsaved me wanted to say was, "Sir, you can go f*** yourself with your pledge and your layaway plan because clearly you don't give a damn about me!"

Then the First Lady went on to tell me, "The congregation has no idea what Pastor is doing with the money because he says the Lord hasn't given him the word to reveal to them where it's going. But I can tell you this, we don't live like this," as she waved her hands Vanna White style, "from his salary from work! So, girl, you were right, take care of you because Pastor is going to take care of us." Dinner was fantastic that evening, but the more wine she drank, the more painful truths she revealed about the pastor's calling and all of the financial and sexual perks it afforded him. It seemed like she enjoyed most of it as much, if not more, than he did. I drove home wondering why she was so forthcoming with me. Was she lonely? Bored? Posturing?

First Lady and I became almost inseparable. I liked her company – until I was privy to the latest – what pastor is really up to news. We worked side by side on many projects, including the church's first dramatic production with the children as the performers. She encouraged me and provided me with all the assistance I needed. That also meant that we were spending even more time with one another and the more that happened, the more comfortable she got with her opinions. That's when things began to get a little different.

As we discussed who I'd cast in the show, she looked at me and said pointedly, "I don't think you should keep Bobby in the role of Jesus, I mean anybody with an eye can see that boy is sweet. And really, what kind of message will we be sending if we act as though it's okay to have somebody like that in a play about Jesus?"

Until this point, I'd been accepting of her and her gossiping spirit because her information had mostly been about her husband, but this time she'd gone too far. "First of all, sister, we don't know what that young man's personal preference is and even if we did, we have no right to stand in judgement of him. All I see is a beautiful spirit who is willing and able to participate and has not only done everything I've asked him to do but has gone above and beyond. And the message we'll be sending is that we are obeying Jesus' greatest law and that is to love everybody."

Nearly offended, she quipped, "I hear you, but..."

"No ma'am, there is no "but" and I stand by the decision I've made."

She could see that I was not having it and politely excused herself from the project. But my standing my ground had rubbed her the wrong way; especially because I did so in the presence of others. Problem.

Initially it wasn't obvious. I thought everything was fine. She was heading the church anniversary committee and asked me to be a part of it. She said she was going to handle the pastoral portions of the anniversary and she asked me to put together a grand church anniversary event. The event would be in one of the largest theatre spaces in the city. I was excited and honored that she had asked.

"I want it big!" She said as she spread her arms wide as though she was envisioning it.

I pulled her aside after the meeting and said thanks but advised that "big" costs money.

She smiled, looked me in the eyes and said, "Sister don't worry about the money, just draw everything up and I'll handle the rest."

On that note, I pulled out all the stops and created a spectacular affair. A play that included mini sermons, gospel songs, praise dancers, musicians and a storyline to boot. This was going to be a show that would put all "chit'lin' circuit" plays to shame. I was so excited to share what I'd created and was ready to give my presentation. Before going into the meeting with the Event, Trustee, Missionary and Pastor's Aid Boards, I said to First Lady Winter point blank, "You know, and I know these people still don't really like me or know me, please don't let them attack me."

"I got you girl! Don't worry," she reassured.

The minute I walked into the room I knew I was in trouble when I saw some of the members – including Sister Butler - looking me up and down with those fake holy smiles. Something was going on and clearly, I was the only one in the dark. The timid handshakes that only link at the fingertips told me that the women were not interested in connecting with me or my ideas. The men, on the other hand, whose contact reached all the way up my arm and sometimes at the small of my back wanted very much to connect, but it didn't have anything to do with the business at hand.

I passed out my proposal and as they looked over it, I could hear the scoffs, the sighs and saw the slight shaking of heads or the looks of disbelief. I gave them a few minutes to digest it all and to give me time to gather my own thoughts. Every now and then I would look to First Lady for comfort. She in turn made sure to avert my eyes. I began my pitch and by the time I'd gotten to the fifth sentence or there about, one of the members threw up her diamond encrusted wrist and hand and stated bluntly, "Let me stop you right here sister, where do you think we're going to get the money to pay for all this?"

I again looked to First Lady for rescue and again she sustained her focus on the proposal and said nothing. I explained to them that the extent of my responsibility was to create the vision and put the proposal together.

Another chimed in, "And I see here that you expect us to pay you for coordinating and directing this. Why would we do that when as a member you should be doing it out of the goodness of your heart for the benefit of the church?"

By then I was getting a little heated and was trying to be diplomatic by reminding them that this is what I did for a living. I also tried to make him understand that I would not expect him to come and do my taxes for free just because he was a member since that's what he did for a living. "And besides that, if you're paid for the work you do in maintaining the upkeep of the building, why do you think I wouldn't deserve compensation for what I do?"

This back and forth went on for what seemed like hours but was more than likely about thirty minutes or so. The First Lady, the one I'd shared wine and intimate secrets with, the one who promised "I got you sister, don't worry," sat there the whole time in silence as these people, one by one and sometimes two by two, belittled what I'd created. I allowed them to make me feel unworthy and every time I looked to her for refuge, she said nothing until she saw that I was about to lay my religion down.

Then she quipped, "I think maybe we should table this and come back to it another time."

I gave her – and them – the project and went back to worshipping quietly, not intruding in their world. Then comes an apologetic phone call from First Lady. She asked me to meet her for lunch because she wanted to talk with me. In hind sight I should have declined, but I didn't and met her as requested.

"I want to ask you something," she started. "I'm having a little bit of trouble with some of the women in the church; one in particular, and I'm not quite sure how to handle it. I've tried talking to my husband about it, but he just thinks I'm overreacting and being jealous. I've also tried to talk to Sister Butler, but she is bound and determined that she is going to have my husband. I'm at my wits end and I just need somebody to talk to that I can trust."

I wanted to jump up and run screaming from the restaurant, "I gotta get out! Let me out!" She wanted me to give her advice on dealing with the same Sister Butler that weeks ago was part of her gang-up on Betty committee. I should have used every curse word running through my head. But I didn't, instead I told her that it might be helpful if she and her husband made it known that they were happily married.

"I attended this church for well over a month and never knew who you were. I never heard him refer to you, I never saw you taking care of his needs and I've never seen either of you show any affection for one another. I thought Sister Butler was his wife. She is the one publicly paying attention to him." She was stunned for a moment but thought about it and agreed that I was right. "And your husband still needs to wear a robe when he preaches. You've got women problems in part because he keeps advertising his part of the rhythm you say no other woman can handle." She sipped her tea and nibbled on her salad. I bit into a healthy portion of my fish tacos.

The Sunday of Valentine's Day weekend, Pastor preached from the Song of Solomon, Chapter 4 and yes, he was wearing a robe. When he got to the passages he was referencing, he dropped his voice into its lower register and spoke softly as if he were on stage at an open mic night.

"How beautiful you are, my darling! Oh, you are beautiful! Your eyes behind your veil are like doves. Your hair is like a flock of goats streaming down Mount Gilead. Your teeth are white like newly sheared sheep just coming from their bath. Each one has a twin, and none of them is missing." Solomon 4:1-2.

Sister Butler could not control her lust and began getting lost in the moment. She sat in the choir stand and looked like she was being bathed by every word he spoke. She had laid back in her seat with her eyes closed.

Pastor went on, "Your lips are like red silk thread, and your mouth is lovely. Your cheeks behind your veil are like slices of a pomegranate. Your neck is like David's tower, built with rows of stones." Solomon 4:3-4. Sister Butler breathed heavily with one hand clutching her seat while the other held on tightly to her leg. As he continued, "Your breasts are like two fawns, like twins of a gazelle, feeding among the lilies." Solomon 4:5. "My darling, everything about you is beautiful, and there is nothing at all wrong with you." Solomon 4:7. By now Pastor had turned to his wife as he spoke. "My sister, my bride, you have thrilled my heart with a glance of your eyes, with one sparkle from your necklace. Your love is so sweet, my sister, my bride. Your love is better than wine and your perfume smells better than any spice." Solomon 4:9-10.

While everyone cooled themselves with programs and funeral fans watching Pastor as he walked toward his beaming wife, I watched Sister Butler looking like she was close to having an orgasm as her legs slowly began to spread.

Pastor forged on, "My bride, your lips drip honey; honey and mild are under your tongue. Your clothes smell like the cedars of Lebanon. My sister, my bride, you are like a garden locked up like a walled-in spring, a closed-up fountain." Solomon 4:11-12. One of the other choir members saw the disbelief on my face and I pointed to Sister Butler who was lost in her fantasy. When the choir member turned and saw what I'd seen, she grabbed her chest, her mouth fell open and her whole body shook as though she'd been hit with a stun gun. She immediately shook the woman back to reality. I don't know if anyone else saw what I saw but I was disgusted and intrigued at the same time. I wanted to look away but for some reason I couldn't. Pastor took his bride's hand, kissed it and made his way back to the pulpit.

"You are like a garden fountain – a well of fresh water flowing down from the mountains of Lebanon." Solomon 4:15. He wrapped up by talking about how we as a people need to go back to the values of old. "We need to go back to our vows and remember why we fell in love in the first place." By now he was sweating, only this time instead of reaching for the hankie that was dangling behind him from the choir stand, he looked toward his wife and came back to the edge of the stage on the side where she was sitting. First Lady stood, looking straight at

Sister Butler and flashing her with a smile that said, I saw you. She met Pastor at the edge of the stage, turned to face the congregation and whipped out a monogrammed handkerchief that matched her husband's monogrammed robe. Sister Butler was livid! The hatred that overtook Butler was so prevalent that it distorted her face and she didn't even try to hide it. She sat back in her seat, glared at the First Lady and shoved the handkerchief back in her purse.

When Pastor closed out the service, First Lady walked up to the podium and handed him a bottle of sparkling water. Again, she was dressed to the nines. This time she wore a red skirt suit with a beige hat, beige keen toed shoes that matched her beige purse that was lying on the pew where she'd sat. She was draped in pearls and grinned broadly when her husband took the water and held her hand indicating that he wanted her to stay.

"Well I'm here to let anybody that wants to know, that I love my wife dearly. She's my rock and without her I wouldn't be where I am today. She's the one that listens to me when I need someone to talk to. She's the one that takes care of me when I'm not at church. She's the one that prays with me when I wake up in the middle of the night and she's the one that pushes me to be better." He then turned to his wife and pronounced, "I love you baby and I thank you for everything you do for me."

All I could think was, Lord I wish I had some popcorn because this is the best movie ever!

After service was over, Sister Butler asked First Lady if she could meet with her in private. First Lady looked at me and I shook my head for her not to do it, but the woman was insistent on it. They went into one of the back offices and after just a few moments their voices began to raise. Then we heard First Lady scream, "bitch you're crazy!"

Pastor and a few of us ran to the office door and flung it open. Desk accessories were strewn about the floor, lamps were turned over and papers were everywhere.

First Lady continued, "you are not going to keep disrespecting me! That man out there is my husband and you need to accept that and get your own man!"

Sister Butler gurgled her inaudible anger, picked up a bible from the desk and flung it at First Lady. It missed her and flew just past the Pastor's head. Sister Butler grabbed First Lady and pinned her against the wall choking her. I looked at Pastor to see if he was going to stop it, but he seemed frozen in disbelief or was enjoying it, I couldn't quite tell. Before any of us could react, First Lady grabbed Butler by the face and dug her fingernails into her eyes. Butler released her hold and First Lady was able to get away and ran to the other side of the room. Sister Butler recovered quickly and was right on First Lady's heels.

Butler towered over her by at least a foot and was every bit of 190 pounds as compared to First Lady who was all but 100 pounds soaking wet with an overcoat. But First Lady was scraping like she was in the boxing ring and I was quite proud of her. Butler tried to grab First Lady by the hair, but she was quick and shook her with a basketball move that would have made Michael Jordan proud, rendering Butler off balance.

First Lady got around to the back of her and when the woman turned to face her, First Lady jumped up and clocked her in the face so hard she broke her own hand. Butler screamed and fell right into the Pastor's arms who had finally decided to step in and stop it. He quickly past her off to one of the deacons and went to comfort his wife. As they drug the hysterical Butler and her bleeding face out of the room, she berated First Lady with every vile word she could think of.

The next Sunday, First Lady was there, dressed to kill as usual. That day she draped herself in a black, form fitted, couture dress with gold accessories and donned a gold, crystal encrusted hand cast. Sister Butler was in the choir stand with her bandaged nose, singing the Lord's praises as if nothing had happened.

After service, First Lady came to me and expressed how disappointed she was to see Sister Butler up there. "I can't believe this negro let this woman back in the choir stand!" I had to admit that I was a little confused by that as well. She said she asked him to put Butler out of the church, but Pastor insisted, "we can't turn our backs on her, she needs prayer." I just shook my head because I really didn't know what to say to her. She then looked at me bluntly stating, "I don't know why these women are so desperate to get at him anyway, he can't keep it up any more long enough to satisfy anybody!"

I was done! I knew right then and there that it was time for me to move on. Just as I was about to tell her "Don't tell me nothing else about my Pastor," the church door flung open and a giant of a man walked in wanting to know where the preacher was.

Someone pointed to the Pastor and the man briskly walked over to him and knocked him down. Standing over him, "Next time you want to be sexting somebody, you better make sure they ain't married to me! Clara Butler is my wife and if you ever send her some nasty pictures like that again, I'll kill you where you stand! Let's go Clara! I'll deal with you at home and don't think you ever coming back here again! I can't believe I got to go through this again!"

Sister Butler looked as if she could have crawled under a rock and quickly got her things and left with her husband. Everyone in the room just stood there frozen for a moment. Then we turned around and Lady Winter had walked over to where her husband lay, pulled out a handkerchief and was tending to his bleeding face. I gathered my belongings, quickly made my way down the middle aisle and headed out the door.

The next Sunday I sat in my usual pew and looked around this church I'd joined. I looked at First Lady with her casted hand and Pastor preaching up a storm and they looked as happy as they could be. I tried not to think of all I knew about him and watched him methodically climb to his climax as sweat poured from his dark, dusty face and I thought to myself, "what an awful human being you are."

And then I glanced at First Lady and saw that she seemed to be glowing with pride as she was fixated on him. As Pastor was about the close out his sermon, I noticed a new lady sitting behind him in the seat Sister Butler used to occupy in the choir stand, dangling a handkerchief which he gladly retrieved.

After church was over, she came to me, "I'm so sorry you had to witness all that," she chuckled, "just another day at Butternut Baptist Church."

I looked at her like she was crazy and could only gift her with a barrage of questions. "You really think this is funny? Is this what normal looks like to you? Is this how you all are representing God? What is wrong with you?"

She looked at me innocently and said, "I don't understand why you're so upset?" I thought about this man of God who I now knew as a user, cheater, a man who would indeed rob God; thought of his unstable First Lady and breathed a breath of relief as I made my exit out of the church vowing never to join another one again. But more importantly, I vowed never to get that close to another First Lady.

Now, whenever I visit a church on more than one occasion and someone insists on me meeting the First Lady, my first thought is "I gotta get out! Let me out!"

# I KNOW WHAT YOU DID
## LASHAWN HEWLETT-WILSON

### July 10, 2016

The butt of my 380-handgun slammed against the right side of her face with so much force that it sent her reeling backwards onto the floor. She touched the side of her face with her hands, blood oozing from her mouth as she struggled to get up.

"Stay down bitch! I'm not going to ask you again," I said through clenched teeth. "Where is the rest of my money?"

"I-I don't have it." The poor woman whimpered.

I kneeled down and grabbed a lock of her disheveled cinnamon colored hair. She grimaced in pain. I sent another blow to her face and blood spewed from her lips and splattered onto my dress.

"Look at what you've done. You got blood all on my dress." The droplets of crimson looked like polka dots on my pretty navy-blue Chanel.

"I should slap your ass again for ruining my dress. Instead, I'll just add how much it cost to the money you stole from me." Pointing the gun to her temple, I could see the fear gleaming from her big, brown eyes. "Now...let's try this again. Where is my money? And be careful how you answer me this time?"

Struggling to get the words out, she finally broke under duress. "S-Ste-Steve has it. I gave it to him. I'm supposed to meet him at the airport."

"So... you two think you were going to run off with my money. Give me one good reason why I shouldn't kill you?"

"P-Please...no...don't," she pleaded through sobs. Even with a badly bruised face mixed with snot and blood, she was still a pretty yellow bone.

I reached inside my dress and removed a white handkerchief that was tucked inside my bra and wiped off the butt of my gun. Turning towards Bruno, I said, "Tie this bitch up. You know what to do afterwards."

"No! No. Please!" she cried out.

Bruno snatched her up from the floor and threw her down in the chair. In savagely quick movements, he tied her hands and feet with thick nylon rope to the chair, and applied duct tape to her mouth.

"When you came to work for me, the rule was never bite the hand that feeds you. Loyalty and respect. You chose to betray me. Therefore, you must die, and I will make you suffer."

I turned to walk away, but before exiting the room, I took one look back. The fear mixed with tears in her eyes held a sympathetic plea. One that did not phase me a bit.

Bruno covered her head with a bag full of rodents that would have their way and feast on her flesh. Many considered me ruthless. Running my type of business, I had to be.

As a lump formed into my throat, I turned to leave the warehouse. Was not going to give her the satisfaction of seeing me shed a tear. The hissing from the rats commingled with muffled screams faded into the background.

The sound of an inmate crying out, broke me from my memory. Rolling over from my side and onto my back, I stared up at the bunk over top of me. Geneva was sound asleep. Her light snoring gave indication.

Tomorrow was going to be different. I would no longer have to deal with the restrictions of prison. Nothing about this place I was going to miss. Although, I'd developed rather a great rapport with some of the other inmates and prison guards, I was never coming back. After enduring the idiosyncrasies and incongruities of prison life, I wouldn't wish this type of environment on my worst enemy.

***

Being on the outside assured me that the surreal situation was really happening. The lingering, pungent, malodorous smell of prison was un-akin to the outside air that permeated underneath my nostrils. Prison harbored a hideous smell, but it was one I grew all-too-intimate with over the years, and it somehow became my strange comfort.

Even with being released, the smell of prison still lingered beneath my fingernails and hair. I frowned and uttered, "God I can't wait to take a shower and rid this smell from my body."

I squinted and covered my eyes as the sun shined across my face. Momentarily disoriented, I looked around my surroundings, anxiously waiting for my sister to arrive.

"Hey baby, what's your name?" A dingy, snag-a-tooth brother asked, as he approached.

"Beat it asshole. Not interested."

"Excuse me momma. No need to be rude. I was just trying to have a friendly conversation."

"If you don't---" A sleek, brandy-wine Cadillac Convertible pulled along the side of the curb, cutting my words short. A loud honk blared from the old school automobile.

"Are you going to stand there, or get your butt in this car? The window to the passenger side rolled down and my sister's face appeared.

Excited to see Sylvia, I rushed over to her car and hopped inside. She leaned over and gave me a huge hug. Tear drops rolled down past my lashes and down my cheeks. We rocked back and forth not wanting to let go. Releasing from our embrace, I shouted, "Let's get the hell away from this place. I don't want to ever see another jail cell in my entire life!"

Sylvia pressed the gas pedal and sped off towards I-69. The Federal Detention Center faded into the background. I leaned my head back onto the headrest and closed my eyes, and all I could think of was... *I'm finally a free woman.*

## *Two years later...*

It was a Saturday evening and Brian Washington sat across from me in a lovely private booth framed within a large wooden arch at Ruth's Chris in Atlanta, Buckhead. The aura of richness permeated the restaurant, from its atmospheric lightning and smooth, dark wood tones.

The waitress topped off our water glasses then sat the water pitcher in the center of the table before walking off. *God, I love this man.* I smiled at my handsome husband.

We met two years ago at the Ruth's Chris in Houston, TX. I was there celebrating my release from prison with my sister, and he was having dinner there as part of a church convention.

Knowing he could have any woman he desired, he chose me to become his wife. Perhaps it's because our relationship started off as a lie. If he knew the amplitude of my secrets, I wouldn't be so lucky.

Basking in the romantic ambience, Brian placed his large hand over mine. "You look amazing tonight," he said and smiled.

"Thank you, darling. You look handsome as well."

I took a quick glance around the restaurant and observed other couples staring into each other eyes, displaying affectionate smiles and engaging in intimate conversations. I assumed they too were there celebrating a special moment and in love with one another just as much as I was in love with Brian.

Removing his hand from mine, he picked up the half-filled wine glass and raised it to his sexy, thick lips and took a long gulp. His collared shirt was opened three buttons down, exposing a crisp white Tee underneath that hid the innermost area of his black- and gray-haired sprinkled chest. As I dwelled in my intimate imagination as if he was nude, I became moist between my thighs.

Fifty-two looked good on his six-foot three-inch frame. His black, wavy hair was gray along the sides, complimenting his smooth chocolate complexion.

Sitting the wine glass on the table, his hazel eyes stared at me with an intensity. He reached for my hand and intertwined his long fingers with mine, gently kissing the back of my hand. "I love you Maxine Washington."

I blushed crimson.

"I love you more."

As he continued to hold my hand, I tried to focus on his neatly trimmed, clean fingernails, but the strange, disturbing notes I've been receiving for the past month took an impromptu invasion of my mind.

One Saturday afternoon after an outing with the church's administrative secretary, Mya, I returned home only to discover a white plain envelope in front of my doorsteps. As I opened up the envelope and removed a piece of paper, an uneasy feeling slithered down my spine, giving me a split-second warning before those words printed on the page jumped out at me.

## I KNOW WHAT YOU DID. THERE WILL BE RETRIBU-TION!!!

Since then, I'd received four more notes. Each note more threatening than the last. Trying to wreck my brain as to who was behind the encrypted messages were pointless. I had no clue except for the person behind the notes was someone I shared a personal connection with. It had to be someone from my past. But who?

"Is everything okay, dear?"

I released Brian's hand. Felt the perspiration on the palms of my hands and rubbed them against my dress.

"I'm fine, dear. Why do you ask?" I nervously licked my dry lips. Picked up my glass of wine and took a long sip.

"You have this pensive look on our face. Are you sure?"

I nodded. "I'm sure." I sat my glass down.

"I'm going to hate being away from you for the next four days. Not waking up to your beautiful face is going to drive me insane."

"The feeling is mutual." I blushed crimson.

"What? Why are you smiling like that?" A devilish smile dangled from his lips.

"Baby, that red dress is doing something to me?"

I was unable to bear the intensity of his stare without blushing.

"I wanted to wear something really special for you. I'm glad you like it."

"I don't just like it, I love it. I can't wait to get you home and take it off you."

"We haven't even ordered dessert yet."

He chuckled. "I don't need to order dessert when I got what I need right in front of me." He winked.

I flashed him a sultry smile.

Brian's grin widened and he threw his hand up, signaling for the waitress. "Check please."

***

Clothes and shoes made a trail from the front door to the bedroom. Brian's hands were all over me, exploring every inch of my body. He kissed me fervently as if I've never been kissed before. Then he stopped and looked me into my eyes. "You are the best thing that has happened to me in a long time. I'm so happy to have you in my life."

His affectionate sentiment began to whirl and drown in my transgressions blazing inside me. I was afraid he would release me, and my demons would reveal their true selves and ruin the happiness in my grasp.

This was meant to be. This is real. I told myself. This man, this glorious, magical moment swept my guilty conscious aside. I had to pull it together and not ruin the moment. My mouth parted and I crushed my lips over his.

Feeling my body melt against his, I yielded to submission, no longer my own person. I'm completely his. His tongue danced inside my mouth and he held me so tight that I gasped. If he wasn't holding me so tight, my knees would have given way. As his lips traveled my entire face planting soft gentle kisses on my cheek, lids, chin, forehead; he murmured soft words that felt sweeter than the touch of his lips. I became weak and my eyes became moist with tears. Brian saw the sweep of emotions run across my face. A look of tenderness filled his eyes as he laid me on the bed.

He laid on top of me and kissed me with more passion than ever before. He slowly slid himself inside of me and we made sweet love and held each other until we fell asleep.

I awoke in the middle of the night in a panic from a bad dream crying. Brian had left me. Looking over and seeing that he was next to me sound asleep, a sigh of relief escaped my lips. With an aching need to urinate, I climbed out of bed to use the bathroom. As I climbed back into bed, a plethora of thoughts ran through my mind.

Dismissing all of them, I turned and put my arm around my husband's waist, snuggling against his warm body. Brian moved a little, but not enough to wake him. Good. Didn't want him asking me a lot of questions as to why I was up at 3:00 in the morning. When he sensed something wrong, his intuition was always dead on.

It wasn't that long ago we made sweet passionate love. I closed my eyes, thinking about the romantic and beautiful evening we had just shared. I wanted to hold on to this feeling forever. Didn't want it to end. But you know what they say, 'all good things must come to an end.'

## A Day I'd Rather Forget

It was a Monday morning and I arrived at the church at 9:30a.m. It was the senior and associate's pastor's day off. Brian left for Detroit that morning. I normally came into the church on Fridays. Tuesday through Thursday, I devoted my time at the group home, Second Chances, I owned and operated for young teenage mothers. Since the building was fairly quiet on Mondays, I decided it was a good day for me to get some work done without too many distractions.

I made my way to my office humming "Take me to the King", while carrying a bag with a Starbuck's blueberry muffin and caramel Frappuccino in my hand, when I saw our administrative assistant coming out of Jeffrey's office.

"Hello, Mya. I'm surprised to see you here. What are you doing here? You don't work on Mondays."

"Good morning, Mrs. Washington. Mr. Washington and I were going over the bookkeeping."

"Where is Evelyn? Doesn't she sit in on those meetings too?"

"Ummm...yes...but she couldn't make it in today. Something about her grand-daughter," she said, and hunched her shoulders with a sense of uncertainty.

Giving her the side eye, my gaze shifted with suspicion. I don't know why. It just did. Mya was young and extremely attractive. Her beautiful chocolate skin complexion, long, straight hair, tall slim frame and gorgeous smile kept the men of the church staring. I sensed Jeffrey was smitten with her the moment she walked inside this church. Every time I stared at her, she reminded me of someone, but I could never quite put my finger on it.

"Do you need anything before I leave?" she asked.

"No. I'm fine. I'll see you Friday. Don't forget we have to work on the program for the women's revival. I need you here 8:00 sharp."

"Yes, Lady Washington," she smiled, then turned to walk away.

Watching her walk away, I thought to myself, *yeah, something's going on between those two.* I shook my head, quickly dismissing the thought. I hope I'm wrong. He's old enough to be her father.

I entered into my office, sat my bag and Frappuccino down on the desk and sat in my leather chair. I pulled out my cell phone and sent a quick text message to my sister. Then I powered on my computer and spoke into my Echo Dot. "Alexa, play Kirk Franklin in Pandora music." Alexa spoke back, "Playing Kirk Franklin in Pandora music."

The sound of gospel filled my office, giving me a calm and relaxing atmosphere.

For the first fifteen minutes I was deep into reading my emails when a knock sounded at my door and Jeffrey Washington strolled in, shutting the door behind him.

"Good morning, Lady Washington. Surprised to see you here." Jeffrey was Brian's brother and the Associate Pastor. He assisted Brian with ministerial and support needs as they arise. He was handsome and a tad bit shorter than Brian. He was light skin with a goatee that accentuated his clean-shaven head, and deep-set eyes.

"I should say the same about you. Seems like today is full of surprises."

He chuckled. "Is that supposed to mean something?"

"Never mind. What can I do for you, Jeffrey?"

"I'm actually glad you're here. In fact, this couldn't be a better time," he said, as he walked towards me carrying a yellow envelope.

The manner in which he spoke sent an eerie chill down my spine. I gazed down at his hand incredulously.

Crossing his right leg over his left, he settled into a comfortable position in the leather chair in front of my desk and said, "I have a proposition for you."

The way he looked at me was unnerving. I cleared my throat, shifted in my seat. "Excuse me."

He leaned forward and handed me the yellow envelope.

I hesitantly took it and opened it up, pulling out several pieces of paper stapled together. I ran my eyes eagerly through the papers. Fear surged and snatched my heart straight out my chest. A clammy sweat broke out over my body. I looked up and our eyes locked.

A sinister grin dangled from his lips.

"Wh-wh...what...how...." My throat tightened, choking off the rest of my question.

Jeffrey chuckled. "Somebody's been a naughty girl?"

"Where the hell did you get this?" I asked through clenched teeth.

"Does it matter?" he sounded nonchalant.

"What do you want?"

"Now you're speaking my language. I want you to have sex with me and I want $500, 000 in exchange for my silence."

I was horrified by his request. "You've lost your damn mind!" You can forget it. I will never! I would rip your heart out and shove it down your throat before I..."

He held up his hand in protest. "Hold up. There is no need for violence."

"You clearly don't know who I am and what I'm capable of." I had to reassure him.

"I'm aware of who you are, and yes, I know how you deal with people you want to get rid of."

I folded my arms and rested my elbows on the edge of the desk, "In that case, you should know I would never submit to your demand. I'm not scared of you."

He chuckled as if I said something funny. "I don't expect you to be scared of me. You are feisty and I love it." He licked his lips. "Keep going, it's turning me on."

If I wasn't a changed woman, his brains would be splattered across this office by now. "You're disgusting. What kind of pastor are you?"

"Me being a pastor has nothing to do with this." He uncrossed his legs. "I'm only asking for one week. Me as your client. That's not too much to ask for, is it?"

"Go to hell."

He chuckled. "If you want your dirty little secret kept that – secret - you'll do as I ask."

I wanted to regurgitate my muffin and drink in his face.

"Look, I don't know what sick, twisted game you're trying to play, but I'm no longer that person. I've put that part of my life behind me. I'm not going to go along with these shenanigans you're playing. Now if you don't mind, I have a lot of work I need to get done. You can see your way out of my office."

He just sat there, motionlessly.

My sense of foreboding grew as I noticed his cold, callous glare.

After an intense silence that brewed between us, Jeffrey spoke, "Do you want this to get out to the church. I'm certain you don't want Brian to find out. You'll lose everything. Your big house, lavish lifestyle, luxury cars, and all the perks of being First Lady will come to a screeching end."

I gaped at him in horror. "Why are you trying to blackmail me?"

Jeffrey smiled narrowly. "Don't look at this way. I feel blackmail is such an ugly word. Think of this as a business transaction that is mutually beneficial."

"Silence for pleasure and money. You call that a mutual agreement. You're sick." I shook my head. "No, I can't. Only you're getting something out of this. I will end up on the losing end."

He shook his head. "That's not true. If you cooperate, I won't disclose your dirty little secret."

"What if I don't do it?"

"Trust me...you will," he said with certainty.

"What makes you so sure I will?"

If my brother knew about your past, he wouldn't look at you the same. The church members will never look at you the same. Brian hates scandal. Most of all, he hates liars. The church would swear up and down he knew about your lifestyle and chose to marry you anyway. This would hurt him, and he would hate you. How long you think it would be before he kicks you to the curb. You can forget about being First Lady. He would get rid of you so fast that your head would spin. So, what should I call you when we're having our experience: Maxine or Veronica?" He paused and leaned forward. "I mean your real name is Veronica, correct?"

I could not believe this was happening.

"This is insane. You can't make me do anything."

"You're right I can't, but what other choice do you have."

"Why the hell are you doing this to me? What have I ever done to you?"

"This isn't about you?"

My eyes narrowed. "Oh, my God. You hate your brother that much?"

According to Brian, the brothers never had a good relationship growing up. They never saw eye to eye. All they did was argue. He said if Jeffrey didn't get his way, he was impossible to deal with. Their mom believed it was their dad's favoritism towards Brian that led to Jeffrey's insecurities and failed attempts to compete with him.

"Hate is such a harsh word." he smiled coyly. "Time is ticking. I'll give you twenty-four hours to consider. I think that's a fair offer."

I gritted my teeth, felt the muscles of my jaw tighten, as I glared at him. "Get out of my office, now."

He smiled, revealing his straight, pretty white teeth, then rose to his feet.

He rounded my desk and came towards me, and I hurriedly laid my eyes on the letter opener, wondering if I had enough time to grab it and stab him straight through his heart. My split decision was too late because he was already mere inches in my face.

His lust filled eyes traveled down to my chest, burning a hole through my cleavage like hot candle wax. "Milk sure does the body good," he smirked, licking his lips.

His innuendo made me feel even dirtier. I leaned back and quickly folded my arms across my chest. As I averted my eyes, Jeffrey leaned in closer, his warm breath fanning my cheeks. "You have twenty-four hours to consider my offer." he whispered in my ear. "Don't disappoint me. If you do, I promise you'll regret it."

I swallowed hard and was shaking like a leaf. When I opened my eyes he was gone, like a thief in the night. "This can't be happening," I whispered. My cell phone alerted me of an incoming call. I looked down at the screen. It was Brian. As much as I wanted to answer it, I just couldn't. Not with Jeffrey Washington's shocking ultimatum.

## *Enjoying Her Like I Do*

I didn't think it would be that easy. It was like taking candy from a baby. For the past three days, I've had the pleasure of having my way with my brother's wife. To think, all I had to do was threaten to expose her secrets that would surely rip her world apart.

I was standing on the 14th floor balcony of my condo, staring out at the intriguing view of the lively and energetic heart of Midtown. Even the view couldn't distract me from the plethora of thoughts that ran through my mind: from my resentment towards my brother; my wife Monica leaving me for her lover, to my estranged relationship with my two kids.

As I took another sip of my cognac on ice, I raised my right arm to check the time on my Rolex watch. It was fifteen minutes pass ten. About five minutes later, my doorbell rang. I departed from my balcony and headed to the door to answer it. I pressed my eye against the peephole. The image was distorted but I could see the person behind the door was turned away. I knew who it was without even asking, so I opened the door.

She turned around inspecting me from head to toe, then flashed me a sexy smile.

I took a few steps back and to the side to let her in. I peeked my head out into the hallway. Seeing that the area was deserted I closed the door.

I followed her to my bedroom. She wasted no time, standing next to my king size bed with her trench coat wide open, revealing a red silk thong, matching bra, and red stiletto heels. Her D-cup size breasts, tiny waist, and curvy hips made her body resemble an hour glass. Her melatonin was glowing, and long, jet black hair made her look like a Nubian queen. Thirteen years my junior, Mya Jones was beautiful, sexy, and confident. She was the tender-roni that had my nose wide open, and I didn't foresee that ever changing.

A few hours after we made love, she was on her elbows with her head resting in the palm of her right hand staring up at me. "When this is all over, we should leave for Jamaica. I've always wanted to go there."

Sitting up with my back to the headboard, I took a long drag of my Newport. "You'll love it there. Beautiful island, great food, sexy women."

Swatting me playfully and laughing she replied, "Hey, hey. I'm the only sexy woman you should be looking at." She giggled.

I turned and stared into her light brown eyes. "You sure are beautiful. How did I get so lucky?" I leaned over and stubbed my cigarette out in the ashtray on the nightstand.

She climbed on top of me and started nibbling on my earlobe, neck, and traveled a trail of kisses to my chest. Stopping, she looked up at me and said, "No, I'm the lucky one. Thanks to you, it is all about to come to an end."

I let out a hearty chuckle. "You don't know how long I waited to turn my brother's life into a living hell."

She displayed a wicked grin and said, "Well, it seems like we both have something in common."

## *Secrets Are Deadly*

The magnitude of my life has been measured by the secrets I have kept. I never imagined a different lifestyle from the one I lived seven years ago. Married to Atlanta's prominent and successful Pastor of Buckhead's mega church, New Beginnings; I was the First Lady and had big shoes to fill. There were over 3000 members that looked up to me. Only if they knew about my past. They wouldn't look at me the same.

I feared that one day my past would catch up with me, but I didn't know exactly how. I left Houston, Texas to distance myself from that part of my life that ended nine years ago when I had to do seven years in prison for tax invasion and pimping. No one was supposed to ever find out about me being a former call girl to running my own successful escort business. My network consisted of 50 beautiful young women that catered to my wealthy clientele of political figures, married men, athletes, rich businessmen, and elite socialites. I lost everything when I went to jail; my home, cars, clothes, jewelry, and my bank account was seized by the IRS.

When I met Brian, I went by my alias, Maxine Davenport. I changed my real name from Veronica Campbell because I needed a new name that would afford me protection and kept my real identity a secret. We dated long distance for six months before I decided to move to his hometown, Atlanta, GA. It was a no brainer. It was perfect. The chances of him finding out who I was...slim to none.

I don't think I'd ever be ready to unleash my sinful secrets. I'm not ready to bear my soul. The last thing I want to do is hurt my husband. He had been so good to me. He was everything I wanted and needed in a man.

Because no one knew me in Atlanta, for two years I developed a false sense of security my days as a call girl/Madame was behind me. Damn I was wrong.

I was leaving from the group home when I received a text message. I fetched my phone from my purse and read the text.

# YOU'RE LATE. NOW IS NOT THE TIME TO GET COLD FEET.

I was trying to avoid Jeffrey. I made up every excuse in the book not to be with him, but he wasn't buying anything I was telling him. Thank God Brian was still out of town because I don't know how I could get away with my betrayal. I climbed into my Mercedes Benz and threw my cell phone dow in the passenger seat and sped out of the parking lot like a bat out of hell and headed towards 1-85 to Midtown. Twenty minutes later I pulled up to The Windsor Over Peachtree, a 19-story high-rise located on Peachtree Street.

Once inside, I was greeted by Frank, the concierge. I didn't have to check in and be cleared. This would make my fourth time at this dreadful place. I boarded the elevator that took me up to the 14th floor.

The sound of my Manolo Blahnik heels clacking against the marble tile floor as I made my way to his unit, made my heart thump in my throat. When I reached Jeffrey's door, I closed my eyes, took a deep breath, and then let it go.

*Forgive me Lord for what I'm about to do again. I'm so sorry, Brian. If you were to ever find out, I hope you find it in your heart to forgive me.*

I've repeated this same prayer every day. *I will be glad when this madness is all over.* Reluctantly, I mustered up the courage and rang the doorbell.

Jeffrey opened the door wide, a devilish grin tugged at the corners of his mouth. His glanced at my appearance with his lust filled eyes looking me over from head to toe. I wanted to hightail it away from him, but I knew he'd have Brian on speed dial before I made it to my car.

I forced my way past him and stood in the foyer. He closed and locked the door behind him. Jeffrey wasted no time pulling me towards him, forcing my mouth open with his nicotine saturated tongue. He pulled away, his eyes were filled with amusement as he stared at me.

"This dress is fitting your body nicely." he smiled.

I refused to tell him thanks. Instead, I rolled my eyes upward.

He ran he slender hand in my razor cut, chin length bob. "I love what you've done to your hair."

I flinched.

"You're tense. Relax a bit. This will be all over soon."

"Please let's just end this. I can get you your money now."

He stared at me like I had lost my mind. "It's not going to happen so you may as well save your breath. Till then, you can hold on to my money. I'm confident you're not going to screw me. I have three more days to enjoy myself with you. After that, this will all be over. The fact you keep coming back tells me you're enjoying this as much as I am."

I frowned. "You're a very confident man. So, let me bust your bubble. I hate it. The only reason why I'm doing this is to keep you from telling your brother." I scowled.

He smiled crookedly. "Even when you're mad you still beautiful. But the way you sex me tells a different story."

He rendered me speechless. My mouth fell open.

"Now come."

He grabbed my hand and led me towards his bedroom.

"I need to use the restroom."

"While you're in there, take off your clothes. I expect you fully nude when you return."

I stood in front of the mirror and swallowed painfully as tears gushed from my eyes and poured down my face. "I'm so sorry," I whispered. I cut on the faucet of water and splashed the cold water on my face. After cleaning myself up, I slowly began to undress. As each piece of clothing came off, memories of me as a call girl came crashing down on my soul like a great weight.

When I emerged from the bathroom, Jeffrey was laying on his side in his boxers. My body froze and I stood at the doorway not wanting to move.

"Get your fine ass over here."

As I walked towards the bed he got up. "Bend over," he demanded, licking his lips.

I never felt dirty when a client asked me to get in certain positions because they were paying for an experience that I enjoyed providing, but Jeffrey on the other hand was a different story. He was taking advantage of me for his own personal gain.

"My brother sure is one lucky man."

*I hate this man.*

I bent over and my stomach churned with disgust.

He slid himself inside of me and started pounding into me fast, then slow, then fast again. It didn't matter how Jeffrey found out about my past. What mattered was that he was blackmailing me for money and sex in exchange for his silence. If I didn't give him what he wanted, he would go to Brian and I would lose everything I worked so hard for. In hindsight, I knew what would happen if I gave in to his demand, but if I could turn back the hands of time, I would have chosen to come clean to my husband. I couldn't be angry with anyone but myself. All I could do was pray that my husband would never find out. It would be a cold day in hell before I lose everything. If it came to that, I was not going down alone. I swear on my sweet, dear, Grandma Bertha's grave...I am going to kill Jeffrey.

## *You Make Me Sick*

The weekend was coming to an end. I've endured the longest, stressful  six days of my life. I couldn't wait for Jeffery to get his $500,000 dollars and leave me the hell alone.

The birds were chirping, and the sunlight peeked through the half open blinds pouring in warm sunshine over the bed. I could lay here forever, but I needed to get up and get ready for church.

The most handsome man emerged from the bathroom with a towel wrapped around his waist. For a senior, Brian was well toned. That's because he took care of himself by eating healthy and going to the gym. My body began to tingle all over.

He walked over to the bed and leaned over me. "Good morning, beautiful." He pressed his lips to mine.

"Good morning."

"Honey, is everything okay with you?"

His question caught me off guard. "What do you mean?"

"Last night you tossed and turned all night talking in your sleep."

I panicked and asked, "I didn't say anything crazy, did I?"

"You kept repeating, "I hate you...I'm going to kill you...I'm sorry. I tried to wake you, but it didn't work. Finally, you stopped and went back to sleep with a creepy grin on your face. Care to explain what that was all about?"

"I'm not sure, honestly. I don't remember what I was dreaming about. It could have something to do with that horror movie I watched last night before going to bed. Sounds like quite a nightmare, huh?"

"If you say so," he raised an eyebrow. "I didn't know you like horror movies."

"I don't, but it was nothing else on T.V. and it looked interesting."

He removed his towel and pulled on his boxer briefs. "You can't be watching that stuff that has the ability to taint your spirt. Isaiah 33:15 speaks on it, "Who stops his ears from hearing of bloodshed and shuts his eyes from seeing evil," avoids what wouldn't do him any good. You must filter what goes through your eyes and ears."

"You're right, dear. No more horror movies for me." I pulled the duvet from my warm body.

"I already called chef to make us egg benedicts, toast, bacon, grits, fresh fruit, and shrimp cocktail. Did I miss anything?"

My taste buds started doing summersaults inside my mouth. "No. I think you covered it. Everything sounds delicious. I better get out this bed, get showered and dressed."

Thirty minutes later, I joined Brian for breakfast.

"I have a surprise for you." he said, sipping his orange juice.

I spread some strawberry preserves on my toast. "You do. What is it?"

"I've arranged for us to fly out to Paris in two weeks."

My eyes lit up like a Christmas tree. Best news I've heard all week. "Honey, that's wonderful, but what about the church and the group home?"

"I'm arranging for Jeffrey to preach in my stead while I'm gone and I'm sure Beverly can handle things at the group home."

I smiled and said, "Sounds like were going to Paris."

***

I sat in the third-row pew listening to my husband deliver a powerful sermon on sins of the heart. Brian pulled a white handkerchief out of his suit jacket and wiped his forehead. Mark 7:20-23 states, "What comes out of a person is what defiles him. For from within, out of the heart of man, come evil thoughts, sexual immorality, theft, murder, adultery, coveting, wickedness, deceit, sensuality, envy, slander, pride, foolishness. All these evil things come from within, and they defile a person."

When he finished reading the scripture, church members yelled their approval. "Amen!" "Hallelujah!" "You better preach, pastor!"

Jeffrey looked out at the congregation and we locked eyes. He was many of those things the scripture was referring to. Somehow, he knew it and didn't care, because he smirked at me and tapped the top of his watch. The audacity of him. I quickly looked away. This time, my eyes fell upon my husband. I became uncomfortable as a twinge of guilt crept up inside me as I thought about how I deceived Brian. Knowing what I was doing, there were dire consequences to pay. Someone was bound to get hurt. In this instance, it was going to be Brian. I couldn't let that happen. I had to protect him from the truth at all cost.

## The Piper Must Be Paid

I was walking through the parking lot of Wells Fargo Bank towards my car carrying a briefcase filled with $500,000. I was lucky Brian and I had separate bank accounts. If not, I don't know how I would have pulled this off. Thankfully, he couldn't ask me anything about the large amount of cash being withdrawn.

Relieved, I made it to my car without getting bashed over the head and robbed, I quickly hopped inside and locked the doors. I sat my purse and briefcase down in the passenger seat, closed my eyes and started to pray.

As I backed my black Mercedes out of the parking lot, my cell phone rang. Brian's name and number displayed across the dashboard of my car, and nervous tension crept up the back of my neck. I held on to the steering wheel tightly and swallowed hard as I contemplated on whether I should answer his call.

I gathered my composure and quickly hit the talk button.

"Hello?" I answered warmly. Trying to disguise the pain that was truly in my voice.

"Hello, dear, how's your afternoon going?" The sound of his voice broke my heart. He sounded so upbeat and in a good mood.

"Fine."

"I missed you this morning. You were sleeping so peacefully compared to the other night and I didn't want to wake you. Where are you? It sounds like you are in the car."

"I am. I'm just leaving a business meeting." I lied.

"Okay. I know the group home has been keeping you busy. Do you think you'll be home by 5:00 in time for dinner tonight?"

"Actually, I have a stop to make when I leave the group home and then I'll be home. Can we make it six?" I asked, stopping at a red light.

"That won't be a problem. I'm having chef prepare a special meal for us. Afterwards, I arranged for us to have massages and then we can catch up on all the lovemaking we've been missing lately."

The thought of me being with Jeffrey yesterday crossed my mind. I have been deliberately avoiding sleeping with husband because I was betraying him with his brother. I never felt guiltier in my life.

"Are you there, dear?"

"Yes...um, I'm sorry. I just thought about one of the teen girls that came into the group home today."

"Is everything okay?"

"Yes. Nothing to worry about. I'm looking forward to our romantic evening."

"I'm glad you are. Well, I'll let you go. Sounds like you have a lot on your plate. Besides, Mya is calling in on my other line. I love you."

"I love you too."

As the light turned green, I proceeded through the intersection and my eyes became flooded with tears that were uncontrollably rolling down my cheeks. I couldn't take back what I had done. One thing was for sure... I was never going to hurt Brian again.

***

As I rounded the windy road, rain drops started to fall. "I didn't know we were calling for rain." I mumbled. I turned on my windshield wipers. Twenty minutes later, I arrived at an address that Jeffrey sent by text message. I turned onto a gravel road leading to a white ranch house. I parked my Mercedes in the driveway and turned off the ignition. I grabbed the briefcase of money from the passenger seat and slowly climbed out of the car.

The sun had already set, and the downpour made it impossible for me to see anything. I kept looking behind me as I walked briskly towards the house and up the steps. I stood in front of the unkept brick rancher home. White paint on the door frame flaked like dead skin. Wire stuck out of a small hole where the doorbell used to be. The cracked planks I stood on threatened to give way and send me plummeting toward the gates of hell.

I noticed the door was ajar and I called out Jeffrey's name, but he didn't answer. My skin prickled with unease. I pushed the door open and walked inside. I saw a dim light shining from the back of the house. The stilly silence that greeted me was nerve-wrecking. The type of silence where you couldn't hear a rat piss on cotton. I felt like I was surrounded by old. Not meaning old paintings or fixtures, but I felt the presence of old lingering in the air---it was unsettling.

Ignoring my common sense, I moved from the foyer and into the living room. Nothing prepared me for the grueling imagine that would forever be etched in my brain. Jeffrey's body lying motionless on the floor, surrounded by a pool of blood. His beady, glassy eyes staring upward as if he was making peace with God.

My fight-or-flight instincts kicked in and I spun on my heels and lunged for the door.

"You take another step and I'll shoot."

I froze and slowly turned around. I gasped in shock and my eyes widened.

"Surprised, bitch," her lips curled into an evil grin, pointing a gun towards me.

"Wh-wh-what're you doing here?"

"You'll find out soon enough. Get your ass in here," she demanded waving the gun at me.

I slowly moved inside the room, trying to avoid the dead body sprawled out on the floor. The stench from Jeffrey's body almost made me gag.

"Bitch, don't act like you never seen a dead body before."

Mya looked deranged. Disheveled hair, smeared make up, torn clothes, indicated there was a brawl between them and it didn't take a rocket scientist to know who won the fight. Never in a million years had I thought I'd see her here. I was confused.

Nervously I asked, "What happened to Jeffrey? Did you shoot him?"

"Duh, don't ask a dumb ass question," she rolled her eyes upward.

"What does it look like? He didn't do this to himself. As a matter of fact, you killed him."

"Are you serious? I didn't do this. Why would I kill Jeffrey? Why would you kill him?"

She shook her head. "You don't listen very well. I said you killed him."

"I didn't do this."

"You did," she insisted that I killed Jeffrey. "You're the one with plenty of motive. Let me see," she struck a thoughtful pose. "He was blackmailing you for sex and money. Although I got the pleasure out of sending you the threatening notes." She smiled wickedly.

"Oh my God. You were behind the notes." I couldn't believe what I was hearing. "Why? What have I ever done to you?"

Mya sighed. "You ruined my life, bitch!" The venom in her voice caused fear to pulse thorough my veins.

I gasped. "How did I ruin your life? What are you talking about?"

She snarled contemptuously. "You remember Bridgette, don't you?"

I was speechless.

"Speak, bitch!" she yelled, the gun wavered slightly in her hands as she blinked back tears.

I watched her tensely. "I-I-I'm sorry." My arms pits started to sweat, and my silk blouse was sticking to my clammy, wet skin.

"Is that all? You killed my mother and that is all you have to say. Well, revenge is a dish best served cold because I'm going to kill you. You heartless, whore!"

I swallowed audibly, my hand gripped the handle of the briefcase so tight that my knuckles ached. "You would never get away with this."

"That's what you think. I already staged your demise to prove that you killed Jeffrey then turned the gun on yourself. The police will call this a murder/suicide. It's simple," Mya said casually, as if she rehearsed the story for the one hundredth time. "Jeffrey found out about your past life as a former call girl who owned an escort business and served seven years in prison for tax invasion and pimping. He hated his brother so much that he blackmailed you into having sex with him and paying him $500,000 in exchange for his silence. You gave into his blackmail. You came here to pay him his money and a heated argument ensued between you two and you shot and killed him. Devastated that you betrayed your husband, and not wanting to face the backlash and shame you would receive from the church, you turned the gun on yourself." She held up the gun that was wrapped in a white cloth she used to kill Jeffrey. She looked over at his body. "It's a shame he had to be a pawn in all of this. I really did like the poor, old guy. To corroborate the story, I did the honors of writing your suicide/confession note. By time the police get here, I will be long gone and five hundred thousand dollars richer. The same amount of money you killed my mother over."

My heart pounded with fear as she walked closer to me with the gun. I took a small step backwards. "You don't have to do this."

"I can and I will." Mya snorted harshly.

A loud thump hit against the window pane and Mya looked over her shoulder. Taking advantage of the momentary distraction, I swung the briefcase and knocked the gun out of her hand.

Her mouth flew open in shock as she watched the gun clatter across the floor. We both dove for it at the same time, landing next to Jeffrey's dead body. I didn't have time to react at the scary looking corpse in front of me. I had to get to the gun before Mya did.

We fought and clawed at each other like wild alley cats. Mya was smaller but she was strong. My life was on the line and that made me much stronger. I managed to wrestle my way on top of her, throwing punches to her face and body. She dug her long sharp nails deep into my face, and I could feel my skin being peeled from my flesh like a banana. I hollered in excruciating pain. She managed to shove me from her and we both fiercely crawled our way to the gun.

We were in a tight race and both so close to the shiny black gun, when the door burst open. Brian's voice rang out at the sound of the gun going off.

## *Epilogue*
### *Six months later...*

As I stood outside the balcony of my villa, in Paris admiring the picturesque view, I thought about how much my life had changed since that fatal night six months earlier.

I was on pins and needles as I rushed to an address believing my brother, Jeffrey was in danger or something was wrong with Maxine. His text message said he needed to talk to me about my wife. Perplexed, I immediately called him, but he didn't answer. After several attempts. I decided to call Maxine. When she didn't answer, an uneasy feeling came over me.

When I saw Maxine's and Jeffrey's cars parked in the driveway, the uneasiness hauntingly increased. A commotion inside the house quickened my steps and I burst through the door like a mad man. The sound of a gunshot pierced my eardrums. All I could think about was Maxine, frantically racing to her side.

What shocked me more was seeing Mya. Her midsection bathed in a crimson stain. I was confused because she'd called me earlier to inform me that she had to leave and go back home due to a family emergency. So why was she there?

I demanded answers. Wracked with the pain of guilt, Maxine broke down and confessed to everything. According to her, she wanted to tell me the truth, but just didn't know how. I found that hard to believe. When Jeffrey threatened to expose her past, she felt she had no other choice, but to give into his demands.

"I was afraid of what you would think of me if you found out about my past. I couldn't take a chance on losing you. I love you, Brian." Those were her pleading words to me.

She wanted me to understand. How could she expect me to understand her not telling me about her past? How could she believe sleeping with my brother was the right thing to do? If she truly loved me, our relationship wouldn't have started off as a lie. She would have told me who she really was. She would have trusted me enough to make my own decisions and not judge her. If she really did love me, she wouldn't have slept with my brother and would have come to me about his demands.

She wanted me to believe she had no other choice. I told her we all have choices. As far as I was concerned, she chose him over me every step of the way. We are exercising choices every day, every minute, and every second. While people may think that they have no choice - I beg to differ.

Sadly, I didn't know who my wife was. I thought I did, but I was wrong. She was a stranger sleeping in my bed. Not only did my brother die that day, but so did my sham of a marriage. I'll admit, I will always love my wife, but I don't know if her betrayal could ever be forgiven.

***

"You ready to go?"

"Yeah, let's go." As I climbed into my sister's car, I took one more look at the beautiful house I was leaving behind. It's been six months since I saw or talked to Brian. If I could do it all over again, I would have told him the truth. As the saying goes, "the truth shall set you free."

I know I'll be seeing Mya again. She went through great lengths to try and destroy me. Lucky for her, the bullet missed her major organs. She was sentenced to 25 years in prison. Although I wasn't the one who actually killed her mother, I was the procuring cause. Mya never ratting me out to the police, meant only one thing...she would be hell bent on getting revenge.

As far as Jeffrey's concerned, he got what he deserved. Too bad I wasn't the one who got to spit on his grave. I leaned my head back on the head rest and closed my eyes. I thought about Brian and how much I loved him and was going to miss him. I don't think I will ever give up on my marriage. Brian will always be my husband. Nothing or no one will ever come between us again. I vow to make sure of that. After all, no matter what we've gone through, he's mine, until I kill him. The vows say, "to death do us part." Then he belongs to Jesus!

# PEARLS AND SHADOWS

## TONI SEATON

Kayla leaned in to the mirror and checked for stray hairs as she looked at herself one more time before walking downstairs. She was not one for that messy, bedhead tousled look. She was not on the beach. She was about her business today. Kayla stood up straight, took a step back and turned to her side to look in that full-length mirror at the end of the hall on the second floor of her and Pastor's home. The Waters home had not one, but three such mirrors. One in the master bedroom closet, one at the end of the hall just outside the bedroom and the last by the front door to the house.

This was a house that she and the Pastor made sure was as grand as it should be for an up and coming pastor and his first lady. As she tilted her head back, she looked at the crown molding that they had fought the builder over during the design process. A little smirk spread across her face as she admired her ensemble for the day and fiddled with her jewelry. Twisting her gold Bulgari bracelet and sighing heavily.

She pondered aloud, "the audacity of that man to actually think he could tell them what would be best considering their overall budget. He didn't know who he was dealing with let alone trying to match his working-class no taste with theirs. Maybe this bracelet is too much. Maybe I don't look humble enough. I have to look humble, but also show class and strength. I have got to get that busy body on my side."

No one, especially another church girl was going to ruin this for her. This is her time to shine. She had strived to be this person her whole life. In the Black community this position of power is reserved for very few, the pastor, the athlete, the entertainer; and their wives. She was determined not to be a powerless voice like her mother.

Her mother, Dayle Smith, was a hard-working single mother, a teacher who found solace in the church from a lonely life raising her daughter. After Kayla's father and mother divorced, she barely saw him. Her mother was not going to allow her daughter to have to deal with such a trifling man. She wanted her daughter to have a successful man of importance. Not a man that worked with his hands and was satisfied with that. Her mother would always say, "Dirty hands are for occasional yard work. Not every-day."

Dayle wanted her daughter to marry a man who would make her life easier. Put her on a pedestal and let her "work" from there managing others. She just didn't want her child to have to get up and work all the time worried about a paycheck. She wanted her child to matter, to be admired and respected, unlike herself.

"No one really admires teachers anymore. That's the polite lip service folk speak during the course of traditional conversation," her mother would say. "If they really meant it, they would be more involved with our schools."

She would often say these things to her daughter as she brushed her hair in the morning before school or church. Kayla learned early on that the people most admired by her mother were the church elite. Especially women with a husband - and power - who seemed to have the attention of everyone in the church. They were not unappreciated and forgotten, like she was. She taught her daughter to be like them, not her.

"Look how they dress, talk, walk. You have to carry yourself like a woman that has it all together and has made it to the top even before you get there. Get involved in those bake sales and volunteer some time," she would encourage, when Kayla became a teenager. "You gotta use what you got which is your skill at baking, talking and dressing. But of course, you got that from me!"

Kayla had to be the center of attention, at all costs. She had to stand out to gain her rightful position at the top. Her baking skills were good, but not outstanding. She could, however, carry on a conversation and manipulate her audience with the skill of a politician. But her true skill, revealed over time, was her ability to be the fashion trendsetter. She was complimented more on her clothes, accessories and how they were styled together no matter the occasion than anything else.

Kayla knew how to present herself to the world. Kayla Waters could grab the attention of any room. And once she got your attention, she would spin her words and turn you around to her way of thinking before you knew it. For Kayla presentation is and will always be everything. So, for this First Lady the cost of raiding the church accounts, especially the often ignored "Church Building Fund" to maintain her high fashion, a reflection of her position and importance was everything. The better you look, the more support your causes get. Becoming the Acting Treasurer for the church couldn't have come at a better time; even if it was borrowed time until the position was permanently filled.

She was finally making some inroads with the church elite around the state. She was being invited everywhere to everything. Her fashion sense was the talk of the state. The way she wore her hat, if she chose to wear one at all; along with the color of her dress or blouse and pants combination was on the tip of all the wagging tongues. She knew her designers and how to wear them. From her favorites - Dior and Bulgari - to the occasional Ralph Lauren, she was sure to have on at least one or two pieces of exquisite clothing or jewelry each and every day. And with each photo taken, came a new invite. A committee position, speaking engagement or party invite.

She was the new "it" woman in the Christian world and she was not about to relinquish that title. She was fulfilled in a way she had never been before. She was living up to her mother's expectations. It doesn't matter that sometimes she has no clue what to say or what the biblical stance was on some of the topics. As long as she presents herself right and tows the traditional viewpoint - right or wrong - she's right. And she and her husband reap the benefits. She was proud of her current status around the state and so was her husband. Afterall they were both living up to their ends of the bargain in their marriage.

Ten years ago, when Kayla met Andrew Waters, he had just received his master's degree from divinity school. He was home for a visit trying to figure out his next move. The word around church circles was that he was ready to find the right woman to marry and find a church to pastor. He would no longer be second in line and the woman he married had to be the right one. She had to look and act according to her position as well as bend to his will at all times. And that proved to be problematic for Andrew.

Most of the women he had been around were too independent and did not like to take direction from him. Or rather obey him, to hear Kayla tell it. Andrew learned quickly after coming home that he may not be able to find everything he wanted in one woman and he may have to be the one to compromise. The only woman who met most of his criteria was Kayla.

She always looked the part. It was only every now and then that she would not obey him and would go off the rails. At least that was done mostly at home where no one saw it and he was able to maintain his man-in-control public image. A man of class, education and power.

So, after dating for a while he and Kayla made an agreement. If they got married, she would always present herself as a woman of style, well spoken, and not embarrass him - no matter what - in public. If she did those things, he vowed to always make her happy with the material things she desired, and not to embarrass her with other women. And for Kayla that was pretty much what she wanted out of life and a marriage.

As Kayla walked down the staircase, she passed their wedding photo hung on the wall. "What a day!" she said and let out a huge sigh; as the realization of the importance of her big meeting today hit. "My lifestyle, my position, heck my dang marriage is on the line. This girl .... Ugggghhh!".

It's not that Kayla didn't know stealing money from the accounts was wrong, she just felt as long as the money was replaced it didn't count. She recalled a conversation she had with Maya an old friend from college shortly after she got married.

"Of course, I have read the Bible and I continue to on a regular basis. But I guess I just see things differently and can admit that I do. I kind of pick the verses to study and apply to my life. God, I feel is a personal god by virtue of Him knowing who we are; but He's hands off, not on. He's loving and forgiving, but man is not. Man, as far as I am concerned directs the here and now, day in day out of life. If you don't get to the top of the totem pole and do what's necessary to stay there; you won't last long. And to get to the top you have to look right even if you are not right. And the next person will come and take your spot that fulfills what the "people" want. And right now, I'm in the land of the living. I didn't get to the other side yet."

She explained herself even more when Maya began to push back on some of her ideas. "I do enough good on the committees I join to secure my spot in heaven. Or rather keep my spot. Afterall I'm not harming anyone. Girl listen, my redemption is sealed, and I don't think my behaviors are held against me. Borrowing money from church accounts and manipulating the staff and congregation from time to time really isn't harmful. I'm giving them what they want. A beautiful, stylish and successful First Couple beyond compare. We know what's best for them, Andrew and me; the longevity of the church. I'm exempt from prosecution!"

Although Kayla will not admit it, every now and then some of those long hours going to Bible studies or talks with one of the mothers of the church does give her pause. But it's never enough to actually cause a change of heart or action. Today may be different. Kayla grabbed her keys and "Louis V" off the foyer table, locked the front door to the house and started the twenty-minute drive to church.

Kayla turned the car radio off to be alone with her thoughts. No sooner than she had pushed the off button and looked up and into the rear-view mirror did she see her mother's image sitting in the back seat looking at her.

"Mama, I was waiting for you to show up. You always seem to show up when I'm stressed out don't you!

"I always told you I would be there when you needed me. Just because I died doesn't mean that changed." Dayle Smith said with a big grin on her face. Dayle reminded her daughter, "Kayla you remember when you met Andrew?"

"Of course, I do Mama. I had already graduated from college and was working for the accounting firm, I was semi-established. I just needed a great man like you taught me. I kind of hooked him fast. We met and married after only eight months of dating. I had and still have what most women want out of life."

"Yes," her mother said. "That's why I was of proud of you and made sure to tell you before I left. I didn't want you doing anything to mess up your life girl."

Kayla shook her head and looked back. Kayla said, "Dayle Smith, Lord knows you were hard to please then and still are now. Don't worry I got this under control. I will not lose. In fact, I remember everything you told me and taught me about what's important in this life."

"Oh really," quizzed Ms. Smith. "What else do you remember?"

Kayla looked up into the mirror and answered, "I remember you saying the other people in this world will fall in line if you tell them or show them what to believe. They don't want to think. Especially nowadays. Just look good and make whatever you have work for you Kayla. Child just do it. If you do it right, you won't have to go to TJ Maxx or Ross for your clothes. You'll be able to go directly to the designer's store. People will come to you and ask for your opinion on everything!" Kayla smiled, flipped her hair and said, "rings true Mama, everything you ever said."

People say what you look like doesn't matter. But where's the proof in that? How much money does the fashion industry make? Cosmetics and jewelry industries as well? Her appearance is paramount to her success. Whether it be a campaign she believes in for the moment or something her husband wants to get done in the community.

The first time she walked into the church with Andrew the all the ladies stared incredulously, but they were pleasant. Since most of their things were still in storage because the new house still had four days before it was ready; and she didn't have time to shop for a new suit, she had to wear what she had in the hotel room. She wore a simple navy-blue shirtdress with pearl earrings and flat ballerina shoes. It wasn't until she went to their second meeting with the church board that she wore her black pinstripe skirt suit with her high heels that she saw the sparkle in their eyes.

She just has to make sure she has Sister Brenda, the church bookkeeper, focused on the accomplishments they've had as the first couple since taking over the church two years ago. "I got to win her over and have her focus on something else besides the short fall in the account; and assure her that it's just an oversight on my part since planning for the busy holiday season." Kayla muttered.

Sister Brenda's good word went far within the church. Brenda grew up in this church and although she was rather mild mannered, she was one of those girls that everyone liked and trusted. Even in her dowdy clothes, as Kayla called them often, she had everyone's respect.

As Kayla pulled onto the church grounds and parked her car, she rehearsed what she might say. "Oh, Brenda, after all there are just like one or two misplaced deposit slips that will balance out the books. Give me just a little more time, I'll get those papers to you and all will be well."

Practicing the lines clearly upset Kayla, because the next statements revealed her displeasure. "I'll get receipts from somewhere even if I have to create them on the laptop myself. What's wrong with this girl anyway? It's only what like twenty or thirty thousand dollars missing? Please woman get a life. I just need to keep my husband from finding out."

Even though he's demanding and is strategic in all he does and the standards he keeps, Kayla also knows her husband is idealistic at times. He wants the church to be so perfect that he wouldn't understand that such a small amount really has no impact on what they do on a daily basis. Besides she thinks she will get the money back from the county bake sale and auction she's organizing. That usually brings in about four thousand dollars; a good start to fix the problem. And Kayla knows she's more than able to get at least three customized cakes from the leading bakeries in this part of the state. In fact, she plans to bring in more than that amount this year. There's also the women's conference which should easily clear around twenty-two to twenty-six thousand. "Oh, if Brenda would only mind her own business, I would have to be bothered with this foolishness."

Sister Brenda Fischer was too real and honest for her own good. Her nickname of "Real Ren" had been with her since a child. Although some would call her a tattle tale, she always believed in telling the truth, no matter how difficult it was. She learned from an early age to just be herself and those people that should be in her life will show up and compliment you. She couldn't stand liars and thieves. They were one in the same to her. She felt thieves were just people who lied about the things they didn't have. When the time was right (or convenient) they just took what they wanted from others. She felt the Bible laid out all the rules and they must be obeyed, period. She didn't understand grey areas or the people who lived there. She was loyal and loved her church family and would protect them at any cost. That was all she had.

Brenda would often say to others in conversation, "I believe the church is still the last and only authority on everything. If it doesn't come from the pulpit, it isn't relevant or true. And that's why I fight so hard to make sure the church runs smoothly. From the coffee pots in the kitchen to the lights in the vestibule, everything about the church must be impeccable, perfect. The church is the standard, the beacon of light in this dark world." First Baptist of Blue Heron has always been a stand out in the community, and Brenda's aim was to keep it that way.

This is one of the few churches that was able to stand the test of time and has managed, for the last one hundred and fifteen years, to bring together the most educated black minds in the state of Florida. A meeting place for conferences and campaigns, she sets the standards, for the black community. She basically tells them what to think and how to act. And Brenda and her extended family have been there from the beginning. Her family was one of the original founding families. Brenda and her cousin Malcolm, his wife and children are the last of the Fischers. So, for Brenda when she tells people the church is her family it is really true. When she's separated from them for long periods of time, she feels like a fish out of water.

She learned that long ago when she left the state for college. She only made it one semester in Tennessee at Fisk. She had to come back home and go to Bethune Cookman, that way she wouldn't be so far and could get home at least once or twice a semester for Sunday service in her home church. She truly doesn't always understand the outside world apart from First Baptist. The world scares her so much at times because she just can't relate to life without the influence of the church. That's why when she was asked to become the new permanent Treasurer by Pastor Waters she leaped at the chance. She knew there was no one else who could do the job like she could. Who cared as much about the bottom line as much as she did; with the exception apparently of the Pastor? Her certificates in QuickBooks and experience as an office manager the past four years at Don's Hardware, the largest chain in the southeastern United States after Loew's and Home Depot; set her up for this position.

This was her chance to show everyone she was the only choice to be the Treasurer at First Baptist. With First Baptist becoming the fastest growing mega-church in the state, this was her opportunity to shine. Brenda had to show off her best asset to the great "church-folk". They had to know her loyalty coupled with her math skills and accounting knowledge made her the perfect choice to assist in the church's overall growth. Growth not only in size but in influence.

Brenda was once overheard by Pastor Waters telling Malcolm, "how could anyone not know the importance of maintaining the church's influence in such a corrupt world? The church is the only thing left really that matters in this world that seems to have gone crazy overnight. At least that's what I think."

When scheduling today's meeting with First Lady Kayla, Brenda enthusiastically told her assistant Tasia, "We need to link up and straighten out the books to get ready for Thanksgiving, Christmas and the New Year. Replacing this missing money from the account will be one way I can contribute to the stability and continued growth of First Baptist. First Baptist has a legacy to create and a Creator to represent!"

So, that's why after a good two days of review Brenda had contacted the First Lady's office to let her know that irregularities were found, and she could not reconcile the account. Thirty thousand dollars may not seem like a lot of money to some, but it is something. It's part of the eighty thousand dollars needed to add on to the back-fellowship hall. That thirty thousand dollars could be used for the paint to change the trim on the church and place crown molding in the back hall. It is all Pastor had been talking about. So once Brenda got up the courage, she placed her call. She hoped Tasia didn't hear any nervousness in her voice as she agreed to the date the First Lady had free on her calendar.

She really didn't want anyone to know that not only was she intimidated by Lady Kayla, but they had never really spoken one on one before. The notes back and forth about the accounting and scheduling have been enough the last three weeks that she's been onboard. Lady Kayla had graciously said hello in passing, but they had never shared a real conversation.

Brenda has even told her cousin Malcolm, "It almost feels as if she's avoiding me on purpose. I mean like she just doesn't want to talk to me. But, I'm finally on her calendar and this is the perfect time to meet with First Lady Kayla and prove I'm the best one to be the Treasurer." She was almost giddy over this impending meeting.

Brenda knew if she made sure they were ready for their two biggest events, Thanksgiving Feed the Saints and the Christmas Gathering, she would be the talk of the church. Well - behind the First Lady - anyway. Not in a prideful way but in a helpful, Johnny on the spot type of way.

"I'm so excited to be around her finally Malcolm, "she said the night before meeting. "Like she seems to care so much about the women of the church especially the single ones that seem to be struggling; and she wants to be a part of this holiday season helping them to have the most memorable time ever. Shoot hopefully she might teach me some style tips, get me some attention and maybe a husband. I'm sure you would like me out of your hair a little bit."

Malcolm just rubbed the top of his bald head and said, "not so much. You're not annoying all the time." They both laughed. Malcolm went on, "you know Ren, you can't fully ignore the grumblings from some of the older saints in the church, that Lady Kayla, likes to spend too much money on the wrong things. Some people think she's over the top, just too much all the time. They actually say she looks down on them."

Brenda reluctantly responded, "yeah I've overheard some say she's fake. Putting on a show, but I know them shoes aren't fake. The ones she had on tonight at Bible study were well over three hundred! I know I checked them out before in the mall. But I do believe that overall most of the congregation is happy with her. Yes, maybe some of the out of town conferences are unnecessary, but Lady Kayla is okay, so far, I suppose."

Malcolm reiterated "Ren, just because she's a First Lady doesn't mean she's perfect or without flaws. I don't want to burst your bubble, remember for as much as Grandma loved the church, she would always say the biggest devils are in the church and most of the time show up wearing a fancy dress."

"You're right Malcolm. I just don't want to believe that the couple we chose to lead the church would bring scandal to it. But I do have just one concern about the Church Building Fund. That one dang account seems to be a short. But I'll remain hopeful that I and Lady Kayla can figure out where the mishap is and get the account all straightened out."

\*\*\*

Brenda stood at the end of the hall in the doorway of one of the conference rooms and saw First Lady Kayla as she entered the church. Brenda immediately began to ring her hands in anticipation. She smoothed out her favorite moss-green jacket with the gold buttons. As she waited to be acknowledged, under her breath she said, "I hope my outfit goes over well today. I know I look stylish today. My jacket over this white blouse and chocolate brown pants is classic. I may not be top notch, but I look like I know what I'm doing. I know for sure the First Lady will not only be pleased with my accounting skills but also my appearance."

But she quickly noticed that the First Lady didn't have that usual big bright smile she's so well known for as she walked in. It looked as if the First Lady just looked her up and down.

Brenda turned slightly away from the door frame, "So, wait a minute is she really sizing me up? No, she's just concerned that I've had to call her in and she's wondering what the real problem is. Right?"

Brenda repositioned herself and watched as Lady Kayla walked into the church greeting everyone, with one eye on her at the back. Truth be told if she was honest with herself and not trying to give the church lady the benefit of the doubt; the one eye was like a laser beam. She actually felt the hair on the back of her neck singe off. Lady Kayla glided in as if on ice. She walks like she's on ice even in heels.

"How does she walk in those things? And look what she has on today. A yellow, no that's not quite yellow. What is that? Gold or better yet a golden rod wrap dress over a rust colored tank and rust colored heels. Oh, and is that a Burberry wrap over her shoulder? Okay Brenda get it together, she is walking this way now? But why isn't she smiling? Oh, there it is!"

Lady Kayla extended her hand and although it looked like she was giving a big bright smile, she was actually gritting her teeth.

"Hello, Brenda, how are you?" she greeted her.

Brenda eagerly grabbed her hand with both of her hands and responded, "Hello First Lady how are you on this beautiful fall day?" Brenda quickly looked down and apologized, "I shouldn't have grabbed you that way. I am just eager to meet you for real and not just in passing. Please ... I really want this meeting to go well today. I mean this account needs to be reconciled, but I also want us to become close partners here in the church."

Brenda gave a sheepish smile and asked the First Lady if she was ready. Her faked smile lessened as she replied. "No, I need a few minutes. Let me check in with my assistant and I'll be right back."

She replied and dismissed her all in one swoop. She didn't even break her glide down the hall. She did however glance back at Brenda with a half-smile as she walked into her office where her assistant was sitting at a small desk across from hers.

"Oh, this may not be as hard as I thought," Kayla said aloud as she greeted Tasia and put her purse in her bottom desk draw. "That girl Brenda doesn't stand a chance against my charm." She motioned for Tasia to close the office door. Anastasia Brown was Kayla's "mini-me." Tasia got up and with a smile closed the office door.

She quickly spun around and asked, "What's wrong Lady Kayla? Is that dowdy Brenda getting on your nerves? I mean she's an alright girl but she ain't got no style and she seems to be a busy body with no life. If she's not at her job she's here. I almost think she works here and not at the hardware store anymore. I mean I think she wants to be here, and she is.... "

Lady Kayla held up her hand to get Tasia to stop. Once she starts it is hard to get a word in edge wise. "No, I just want her to wait a few minutes. Like ten to fifteen minutes. Let her wait on me awhile," said Lady Kayla. "I need to let her know she may have called this ridiculous meeting, but I'm in control. I will determine how this all turns out." Lady Kayla gave her desk one good solid pound just to punctuate her sentence.

"Understood" said Tasia.

"Nice outfit by the way. Who is that?"

"Well," said Tasia, "my skirt is nobody, the label was gone when I got it from the thrift shop. But my blouse is Nina Rinaldi. Do you like it?" Her voice went up a few octaves as she asked eagerly waiting on Lady Kayla's approval like a child waits on their mother. Lady Kayla just smiled and shook her head as she sat down and turned on her computer. Tasia was not her concern today. She decided to check a few emails before going across the hall to meet with Brenda.

Brenda stood in the doorway of the conference room, unsure about what just happened, but she simply offered and "okay" in the atmosphere and went back and sat down at the small table behind the big conference table. She shrugged her shoulders and decided to blow it off and chalk it up to the First Lady just needing to take care of some business.

Brenda continued to make excuses for Lady Kayla as she reviewed the matter at hand, "I can only imagine how much she must have to do in one day with the church growing so much in the last few months. I'll take this time and just take a few more minutes to review my notes and get ready. Afterall this is one of the most important meetings I'm going to possibly have for the rest of this year. This encounter could make or break me and possibly set me up for more responsibilities in the church."

Brenda sat down and read her notes. Then she looked up at the clock on the wall. A good ten minutes had passed, and Brenda was getting a little antsy. The meeting was only supposed to be about thirty minutes anyway because it was only one account with an issue; and she had only scheduled thirty minutes with Tasia. She nervously adjusted her pearls, stood up and began to pace.

She went over to the door and peered out across the hall. The First Lady's office door was still closed, which everyone knew meant she was busy. Her office door was always open reflecting the church's open-door policy for the saints. She went back to the desk and had to admit that now this was just a little rude, First Lady or not. But she would just wait and not ruffle any unnecessary feathers. Brenda started getting hot. A mad Brenda was not a good thing. She realized long ago that anytime her temperature began to rise it meant some type of confrontation was brewing. It was all she could do to remain calm and collected. She drank some cold water and tried to force herself to be positive.

Across the hall Lady Kayla was finished reading her emails. She didn't have too many today since she answered most of them yesterday before meeting the Choir Director for dinner to discuss the song choices for the Christmas Gathering. Lady Kayla however was actually finalizing how she would manage Brenda. She knew she sized her up well before going into her office. She could read people and that gift has served her well throughout her life.

She remembers her mother taught her from an early age that, "books aren't' the only things you need to read well. You need to read other people and their behavior well too Kayla. Especially other females."

Kayla had taken her mother's words to heart as she always did. Kayla even took classes in human behavior and social interactions in college to perfect this skill. She knew without a doubt that she intimidated Brenda with that sheepish grin she had on her face. She often did intimidate other women with her fashion sense and demeanor. Once again proving her right - appearance rules the day.

Brenda has no idea how finding that dent in the Church Building Fund affected Lady Kayla. It made her nervous. She had to maintain this façade of perfection she had created. Her position in the church and even her marriage depended on that. She just couldn't take the chance of losing, she would have nothing left. She decided Brenda had waited long enough and since fifteen minutes had passed, she only had to entertain her for another fifteen. Lady Kayla got up walked across the room and flung open her door while simultaneously calling Brenda's name.

"Brenda, Brenda are you there?" She crossed the hall and walked into the conference room. As she stepped in the room, she closed the door behind her. Brenda stood up and extended her hand again to Lady Kayla and thanked her for coming into the meeting.

Brenda with a shaky, but insistent voice said, "No, thank you for taking time out of your busy day. I'm sure Lady Kayla, that this is probably just a small oversight and a deposit was not documented."

Kayla sat down and with a snarky, condescending tone said, "I really don't make mistakes like that, but I'm not perfect and I'm sure with another set of eyes, especially my eyes on the accounts we'll figure it out."

Brenda agreed, and this time she sized up the First Lady and said, "You are so right; no one is perfect, just like the Good Book says." Brenda opened her notebook and pulled out the account balance she printed out last night in preparation for this meeting.

Lady Kayla shifted in her seat and commented, "Wow you are prepared, aren't you?"

Brenda, with a little more assurance in her voice, thanked her. "I'm always prepared when it comes to business. I know how important it is for the church to be on solid ground as we expand and become even more in the spotlight."

Lady Kayla shared, "I'm glad that you feel that way. I feel that way too. So, when my husband, Pastor, asked me to step in as acting treasurer I was glad to help out. I too want the church to be ready for anything that comes up in the community and I know how important it is to have the books in order. I'm sure it's just a deposit that may have been noted on the wrong day and not counted. Did you count it? I'm sure you counted it, that's what you do, right? Count?" Kayla gave a half smile and looked her up and down again.

Brenda quickly retorted, "I do more than count. In fact, I can tell you all that I do, if you'd like." Brenda was put off with Kayla's I'm better than you attitude. The First Lady's demeanor wasn't subtle at all. But Brenda still saw this as an opportunity to advocate for herself.

Before she could get started however, Lady Kayla held up her hand. She attempted to use this time and topic to control the conversation and avert Brenda's focus away from the missing money.

"You know I'm glad we're meeting today. This is really an opportunity for us to get to know one another and see if we could possibly work together. I mean even though this meeting is for something else there's no reason we can't use it for our benefit as well as the church's benefit." Lady Kayla said this as she reached for Brenda's notebook and acted as if she was reading it, waiting for Brenda's response with bated breath. She was becoming desperate to make this go her way. Brenda forgetting Kayla's bougie attitude ecstatically agreed with her and proceeded to basically give her entire resume and detail her desire to assist the church family in any way she could. Once she said that Lady Kayla knew how to play her.

Lady Kayla said, "you know what Brenda? I think I can trust you. You really seem to have the church's best interest at heart. I mean anyone who takes the time to review the accounts like you have and take such detailed notes is an asset to the church and should be used, I mean utilized as such. Have you ever thought of working for the church full-time? Or perhaps going into ministry? You seem to have not only a big heart but a calling for helping the church."

Brenda smiled and explained how much the success of the church means to her. She expressed to the First Lady, "the church is my family and my first priority."

Lady Kayla told her she could see that and just had to find a way to make this new position comfortable for her.

Kayla half-heartedly expressed to Brenda while leaning back in her chair "Especially since I'll still be overseeing everything with full access. You know at one point the board wanted to hire someone from the outside as the permanent treasurer, you know new blood, new eyes to take us into this new season of growth. But I assured them my husband's choice, someone with your keen eye, can be placed right here to keep watch over details. Or actually anywhere else in the church. Is there any other position you were interested in?"

Brenda thanked Lady Kayla but reminded her that most of her education and experience is in accounting.

Lady Kayla said, "that's unimportant. It's the skill and attention to detail that I'm talking about. That can be translated to many other areas. Don't you agree? I mean Brenda the church has many more needs and positions right now that we have to fill."

Brenda noticed the First Lady had actually closed the notebook. She also realized that they hadn't talked about the missing money at all.

Brenda interjected. "Yes, I agree with you and I think we can talk about that later, but I wanted to make sure today since we're short on time that we were on the right page about the missing thirty thousand dollars."

Lady Kayla shook her head, "Of course, of course. We are always on the same page. I think, and I don't like to admit this, that I forgot to write in a deposit from one of the offerings a couple of months ago. I think I have a deposit confirmation at home, and I'll bring it by and leave it for you one day next week so that when you come back the books will balance out. Would that be fine?"

Brenda asked with grave concern evident in her voice. "A couple of months ago? And you haven't brought it in yet? Why?" And although she hesitated, Brenda pressed on. "No. Next week will not work," she said. "I can wait an hour or two only. I have to close out this month's books today, and I can't have anything left outstanding; especially if it's from a couple of months ago. That's not acceptable. I'm sure you understand."

Kayla lost the smile on her face and said with as much lady-like force as she could without showing too much annoyance "Really? The accounts can usually go on for weeks despite the end of the month coming and going. I mean Brenda I'm only talking about until next week. Otherwise I would have to go all the way home and search for the deposit slip today?"

Brenda now annoyed responded, "Uh yes; maybe part of the problem is that everyone takes their time with doing things around here. We have to do better with being on time with these things because as we continue to grow it will become harder and harder to do this job. There will be too many items to reconcile."

"Brenda I'm telling you it will have to wait until next week. I've done that before and I'm going to do it now. I'm not about to run around like a chicken without a head just because you don't have any patience." Kayla stood up and hovered over Brenda defying her not to agree.

Although Brenda was surprised at this exchange, she was not about to be intimidated anymore by this woman and her posturing. Long ago Brenda learned that most of the time when people were bigging themselves up they were trying to hide something about their character.

A weakness if you will. Brenda stood up and realized for the first time that she was taller than Lady Kayla.

"Lady Kayla," she began. "I had no intention of this meeting becoming contentious. I truly just wanted to have a chance to interact with you on a one on one basis and rectify what I felt was a slight oversight in the accounting of the church building fund. Thirty thousand dollars is not accounted for and we need to find out where it is. Now I have no reason to believe what you say isn't true, but there's no reason this cannot be fixed today, period. I'm even willing to wait until 5:00 pm today since I'm not going to the bank until tomorrow to make a church deposit."

"You know Brenda although I think you are being a bit of a miser, I will comply with your request, this one time. This meeting has gone over by five minutes and my time is valuable. But let me remind you who I am and that you need to watch your tone. I'm sure you don't want to offend me and right now I feel a little attacked."

Brenda leaned back. "Attacked? All I did was ask you to bring in the deposit slip for the thirty thousand dollars. How is that attacking you? Either you have it, or you don't. You made the deposit, or you didn't. The money is in the bank, the church pocket or it isn't, or it is in your pocket or it isn't!" An awkward silence fell over the room. Brenda had just accused the First Lady of putting church money into her own pocket.

"Listen, Sister! I have never put anything in my pocket I did not earn from working hard. Which I do all the time. I will admit to delaying a deposit if I had to take care of something else first, but the deposit was always made."

Brenda threw down the pen she had in her hand and stepped back from the table. She took a breath and said, "You do realize that you just admitted to embezzling money from the church. You just said that you put money you earned in your pocket. Well it would explain how you afford some of the things I see you with. I do know how much the Pastor is paid for sheparding the church. I know how much that Burberry cape you wore today cost. Not that you would know, but Burberry is my favorite designer. I know for a fact that cape is at least fifteen hundred."

Lady Kayla flipped her hair, looked Brenda up and down again, "You are right. I didn't think you would know how much anything like my cape would cost. I don't see it, on you."

After a brief pause Brenda carefully worded her next statements. "Lady Kayla, it is not my intention to call anyone out to the church board. Especially someone who has done so much to help the church prosper and grow. However, an example can and will be made of anyone who steals from God, and that's what stealing from the church is. And I'm not about to play semantics with you. Put the money back and I'll let it be. But know I will be watching all accounts and all that have access to them. It's my duty as treasurer."

Lady Kayla stepped back a little more from the table. "Sister Brenda, maybe I came off defensive. I just have my way of doing things and don't liked to be challenged. No money has been stolen. It's just in the process of being placed in the right spot, accounts and there was a delay a few months back. I promise you that. Nevertheless, I will have Tasia get the information delivered to you by the end of the day as I have other things on the agenda."

Brenda quickly reacted to Lady Kayla's last statement, not wanting the meeting to end on a negative note. She leaned forward and almost apologetically began, "Lady Kayla I hope I didn't offend you or come off too pushy, but..."

Lady Kaya held up her hand and said, "this meeting is over. I have no more time for this today." At that she spun around and gave her back to Brenda.

Kayla quickly realized even though she was going to give Brenda what she wanted she couldn't let her think she won. If she did, she might continue taking a closer look at the books and realize there's actually more like forty thousand that's missing; going back to when she and Pastor took over the church. She was going to have to not only keep an eye on this girl, she was going to have to get her on her side and under her spell.

She turned back around and spoke softly. "Brenda, I know you're just fulfilling your responsibilities, I just wish it didn't take up so much time. I will get you that information." She gave a quick smile and gave Brenda a once over before saying as she backed way, "Oh, by the way, you actually look great today. Designer or not."

"Thank you. I suppose," said Brenda as she smoothed down her jacket and fixed her pearls again.

"I love pearls on a woman; don't you?" asked Lady Kayla. "Pearls are always the right thing to wear. The right accessory for a woman, especially church women such as ourselves. I love them in every color, but especially white like yours," she said as she caressed her own bare neck. "Pearls are effortlessly elegant and light up the face."

"I agree and the white ones represent purity," said Brenda as she looked at Lady Kayla's empty neck. With that, she walked Kayla to the door and opened it for her. "I'll be waiting and watching...for Tasia to give me the missing deposit slip or something so I can go to the bank tomorrow and finish reconciling the account."

As the door opened, she saw Pastor Waters across the hall talking to Tasia. He spun around and said, "hey there you are!" He stepped in to greet his wife as she stepped into the hall. He quickly stuck out his hand to shake Brenda's. Brenda greeted the Pastor as Lady Kayla leaned over to hug him. He asked what they were doing, and Brenda wasn't sure what to do. Lady Kayla did.

She waited a quick second to see what Brenda would do. When she hesitated Lady, Kayla stepped right up. "We were just finalizing the accounting that I've been helping with since I was acting treasurer. You remember Brenda does that kind of work and comes in to manage the accounts now once a week since taking over."

"Oh, right he said with a big smile on his face." All the while glaring at his wife. She was wearing her war paint today. That red lipstick always meant she was ready for war. He loved his wife, but she tended to hang out in the shadows a lot. She was always up to something and wouldn't cop to it until something shone a light on it. Now it wasn't always bad or negative, just secretive. Anyway, he was sure it would all be fine. It always was, at least so far.

Pastor Waters told Brenda it was good to see her, but he wanted to steal his wife for a few minutes. Brenda said, "sure Pastor we're done for now."

Lady Kayla, told Brenda she would get that confirmation for her by the end of the day. "No problem Lady Kayla I'll be here."

Lady Kayla smiled and as she said under breath to herself, "No, you nosey heifer I'm just going to keep you occupied and stroke that little ego a bit while doing so. All I need is an hour to get to the bank and put money in that account. I'll take it out of our household fund. Pastor won't notice. I'll tell him I put a down payment on the in-ground swimming pool we've been planning outside the game room off the patio."

Pastor had turned around to greet some of the congregation in the hall. Kayla sent a quick text message to Tasia telling her to type up a deposit slip for the amount of thirty thousand from two months ago and give it to Brenda. The text explained that they forgot to do it that week she was out sick.

Lady Kayla and Pastor Waters said good bye to Brenda walked down the hall toward his office. Brenda turned around and went back into the conference room to get her things. As she grabbed her purse and notebook, she looked up, exasperated.

"I can't believe what just happened here. I mean I did get tough, but she said she understood, and I feel we ended on a positive note, maybe. This is not what I wanted. But I will be respected and so will the church. But what really just happened here? I still can't believe she took that money and thought it was okay!" She laughed. "That devil was right up here in the church and had on a designer dress at that. But the truth always comes to the light from out of the shadows."

As she closed the doors to the room, she rubbed her hand over her pearls on the back of her neck and walked down the hall and finally out the front doors of the church.

Pastor Waters grabbed his wife by the elbow and directed her into his office, greeting church staff along the way. As soon as they entered the office, he closed the door and began to interrogate his wife. "Kay what's going on? I mean you got that war lip thing going on and you don't talk to girls like that Brenda on a regular, so what's up? I know you're not foolish enough to mess up this good thing we got going on? We are expanding and have growing influence in the town now, what's going on?"

Kayla started, "there's nothing going on I can't handle. Don't worry about it. I just had to get her clear on some things and fix some paperwork. It's fine Drew."

Now he knew something was wrong.

"Drew? You only call me Drew when you want something or you're hiding something. I don't know Kayla. I love you but not more than my church and the people I shepherd. I love you, but I will replace you. You are replaceable. I am not. I know I have my ways and standards, but I took a vow to look after this church. Don't mess this good thing up. You do remember your vows, I mean our vows to one another not to God?"

"Yes, I do," she responded sharply.

"Kayla, you have to keep it right and tight and dress it up pretty. We have places to go with this union."

"Drew I said I know, okay! It was a simple oversight that will be fixed. Brenda's just a busybody with no life. Yes, I got a little sloppy briefly with the deposits, but it's under control."

"Okay Kayla." He looked at her, then grimaced. "Where are your pearls? I think this is the first time on church property I've seen you without your pearls on. I mean you look nice and all, nice gold bracelet, but you're bare. Your neck is bare and exposed. Hmm. Seems like your slipping to me."

"No Drew I'm not. I just needed a little wake up call, a bit of a tune up that's all. Now can I go? I have to get Tasia to do something for me by the end of the day."

"Okay Kayla I'll let you go but don't forget what I said. There are others that can easily take your place. Quick. And I will oblige if you get too sloppy with your business. And that includes your appearance and your goings on."

Kayla jerked the door open and walked out.

Kayla went down to her office and caught Tasia before she left for lunch. She quickly explained to Tasia that she needed, giving more details from her text message. Two deposit slips typed up for thirty thousand dollars, split up almost evenly for one of the Sundays around two months ago. Kayla said "Now Tasia just do this for me okay. I just need to fix an error I made that Sister Brenda found. No problem."

Tasia said to Kayla's face, "okay I'll do it right after lunch." As Tasia turned around she smirked and said "You are slipping just enough for me to slide right into..."

"What'd you say? You talking to me Tasia?" Kayla said as she was walking out the door.

Tasia quickly yelled out to her, "No. I was just making a mental note of what I had to do. It's all good. I ain't crazy yet, just talking to myself. If I start answering, then we'll have a problem."

Kayla went to the bank and took twelve thousand out of their household fund and cashed out a personal IRA for the rest. She snapped as she folded into her luxury vehicle, "I hate having to use this money. There goes my trip to Dubai. That heifer is messing up my plans. But the money will be in the church bank account."

Kayla then made her next stop - the church's bank and deposited the full thirty thousand. On her last stop she went to the park for a semi-warm pretzel from the vendor that always sold near the water fountain.

She sat down at the table that she had dubbed her spot and flipped through the swimming pool brochure. She would have to choose the one she wanted to show the Pastor. When she looked up there was her mother's vision sitting across from her at the table.

"Kayla why are you stressing again? Twice in one day. I thought you had this under control."

"I do Mama. I do. All this was just unexpected. But it's fine now. I just had to think and come up with a new plan. See by the time I tell Andrew it's time to pay the builder to finish the pool I'll have the money from the women's conference. And that's all mine. I save money having it at the church and catered by the women's ministry. Besides we're serving breakfast which is cheaper than lunch or dinner." Kayla smiled as her other's image faded away.

As she got into her car, she grew giddy from a bright idea. "Maybe I can get that man to give me a bigger allowance for the household budget. Then I'll be able to spread around the money more for my personal shopping sprees and back off the church. At least for a while. Next year's church budget will have to include an overall clothing allowance for the both of us. We can handle it. With this year's church growth including the love offering and tithes, there's no way the board can turn the request down."

Pastor Waters went into the First Lady's office to see if she had left for lunch yet. But Kayla was gone. Tasia was about to leave for lunch herself. Pastor asked her what that meeting with Sister Brenda was about.

Tasia said, "Oh that was about some missing thirty thousand. But First Lady said it was a small oversight she had when I was out sick. No problem. I'm going to help fix it after lunch."

"Oh. Well alright then Tasia. 30 thousand dollars. Listen, if anything, else like that comes up let me know. That way I can help. Will you look out for your Pastor, like that?" Pastor Waters said with a smile as he held the door open for Tasia.

"I sure will," she said. I'll let you know everything." Tasia tilted her head to the side with a big grin as she passed by Pastor in the doorway.

"You look real nice today Tasia. Those pearls look good on you too. What are you having for lunch today?" He asked as he closed the door behind them.

# THIS IS NOT YOUR HOUSE

## E. CLAUDETTE FREEMAN

### COME SUNDAY

The First Sunday of August – an intruder disrupted the sanctuary of peace that was my life.

"Will there be one? Now is the acceptable time for salvation. I beseech you, do not let this opportunity slip through your hands. Will you accept Him as your Saviour today?" Pastor Luke Dickson's compassion was evident in his voice. His arms extended to welcome those wandering to the altar. The chandelier lights reflecting off his gold watch and cufflinks, added a theatrical effect. "The Father, the King of kings and Lord of lords is knocking at the door of your heart right now. Choose ye this day how you will answer." He unbuttoned the top clasp of his cassock. The black one with the purple sash that he reserved for first Sundays.

There was an increased regal atmosphere on these Sundays. The older mothers and the God's Essence Ministry assured it. Yet, there was no amount of preparation that could prepare the congregation for what God's knocking

on the door would reveal that day. "Perhaps you are here today, and you already know Christ as Saviour; but you have moved out of a place of fellowship. Our doors are open to you. We extend a family of believers who will help you live in the image of Christ and according to the statutes of Holy Writ. Will there be one?"

I have no idea how I had not seen her. From the alto section in the choir your eyes have full view of every seat – excluding the overflow – of Revealing Faith Church. She appeared from the door of the hallway that leads to the balcony. There is no way I did not see her before the fullness of her glory awakened that door frame. But there she was.

Being mindful of the movement of the choir and even more determined to show no concern of the moment, I slightly leaned over to Flo's ear. "Do you have something I can wipe my glasses off with? I'm seeing big red specks."

Flo's voice rose an octave, an off-key attempt to refrain from roaring in laughter I assumed. As the choir swayed to the right, she leaned into me, "There is no napkin, wipe or hem of a garment big enough to wipe what you see from your glasses."

Wearing a rich red, semi-fitted knit jacket dress. It seemed tailored to allow enough pleasurable view around her hips, while maintaining an air of modesty. The five-inch heels did not seem to slow her deliberate pageant stroll down the center aisle. An aisle she clearly chose to showcase her entry. I must admit I liked the hanging black feather earrings. Though I did question if they were overkill against the super wide red organza hat with ruffles and Black feathers clustered along the side.

I kept one eye on her and the other on Pas. Dickson. It was clear Flo was playing this tennis match with me. "You do know he is not going to look back here, right?"

And he did not look back. That was interesting and somewhat infuriating. There was never a time during the invitation to Christ that he did not look back at the choir and smile or give some signal of direction. But, scandalous Sheba in a red dress walks through the door and suddenly he behaves outside of the norm.

"Excuse me, Flo. I think I need to stand and receive the people with my husband this morning." I eased past her, as well as Enid. By the time, I hit the last step heading out of the choir stand, I had taken off the robe and was smoothing my dress down. Charlotte took the robe from my arm, pressed a handkerchief in my hand and offered some encouragement, "Let her know first lady, that there are rules to this thing." I smiled, pulling her into an embrace.

I hugged and shook hands with several of those who were either joining the church or accepting Christ. As my arms unfolded from around a young girl with black and purple box braids, I saw her extending her hand, and to me it seemed too much of her healthy bosom, towards the pastor as she strode past the second row of seats. Intent on signaling my presence, I placed my body against his, and without losing my stride or smile, planted my hand in hers. My shake was firm, and I planted my other hand atop our clasped ones and welcomed her. With me in charge of her, pastor moved on to the next person.

"Welcome. Thank you so much for coming forth today." I found her beige eyes to be cold and a bit disturbing. I was on assignment at the moment, however, and decided that no one in the 1500 blue padded seats that were placed about the sanctuary should sense my discomfort. "It's been quite some time since we've seen you. Is there something we can stand in agreement with or intercede for on your behalf?"

Before she could answer, Mother Ware hugged her about the waist and ushered her off with others who had come to the altar. Mother Ware taking charge of her concerned me. She loved the pastor and followed him to Revealing. Yet, she was consistent in voicing her displeasure with a pastor with big ideas trying to do things his way and not in line with tradition. She was even more vociferous about "that wife of his." She was always clear on one thing; I was not the type of first lady they were used to.

The type they were used to was once married to my husband, Luke. Though they were only married short of three years, she had come from the womb a first lady. I imagine she walked around as a toddler with a tambourine, wearing gloves and with matching Saint John suits and big hats. Mothers in the church loved her type because she is a little Xeroxed version of them. Dressed holy and sanctified. Wearing control with their pantyhose. Doling out hallelujah off-kilter wisdom with bottom of the purse peppermints.

And now, she had sashayed like a bride commanding the attention of wedding guests, down the aisle and joined the church we founded three years ago. The last time we saw her – well I saw her – because now I was wondering if perhaps, he had encountered her more recently. But the last time was in a hospital room. We prayed for her as she was preparing for surgery. Luke felt it was the least he could do. I did not see the need for it; but I rarely question his need to minister. The strange thing about that visit was the reaction of the nurses to our being there. I didn't get the impression that whatever the procedure was – and I don't believe we ever knew – was that big of a deal. Barbara Dickson convinced Luke that it was life or death and thus compelled him to come lay hands on her. The nurses were also concerned about how the pastor showed up with a wife. It seems, we learned later, that she had made it very clear that she was the present and active First Lady Dickson. I had a string of curse words eloquently perched on my lips. Yet, I held them and repented anyhow.

Watching her move through that side door almost compelled me to do the same and revisit speaking that string of words. Finally, Luke looked at me; his engaging smile softening the moment. His hand extended towards me to lead me back into the pulpit to join him for the closing prayer. His arms wrapped me tightly after he said amen.

"Can we hold this conversation for home? Because I do know we are going to have one." He smiled and stretched his eyes.

"Oh, sweetie, I have a feeling - that – is going to create several conversations." I softly kissed him, then wiped the luminous lilac lipstick from those thick lips that could still make me melt.

I spent another half hour greeting members, loving on the deaconesses, appreciating the choir and thanking the ushers for all the hard work they do. I made a point to thank as many volunteers as I could each and every service. Luke slipped away to his office as he often did, before he entertained quick meetings with various leaders and others. I strolled into his office, my hands lightly clasped in front of me. I stood just inside the door taking in the spiritually empowering artwork that he loved so much.

"Her joining the church does not have to be a major thing – if we don't allow it be." When he pulled me atop his lap, I couldn't help but wonder if I was about to be seduced for reassurance or to squash a heated discussion before it began.

"I really do not want any problems with the former first lady; but you have to admit when you make a theatrical, runway glide down the middle of the daggone church – you had reason to make an entrance. Question is, what is the reason." I leaned my head against the soft black leather headrest of his chair. I wished he would change this chair already. He swears it holds some kind of spiritual power. He says some of his most profound thinking is done in that chair. He leaves the house sometimes in the middle of the night to sit in this chair and ponder whatever has grabbed hold of his brain.

"I have a quick meeting with some of the deacons, and then I'll be home. You wanna eat out today?"

"No, I cooked after you left this morning. I'll grab Kezia from the kids' ministry and meet you at home."

"Vicki. I don't want this to stress you out. I'll talk to her. I promise you."

I rose from his embrace and his lap to head out the door. Retrieving my favorite Coach purse from the coat rack, a moment of oh-hell washed over me. I slowed my pace, then turned to see if I could find any idea of what was going through his head in his face. But he was tired. His head was buried in his hands as he massaged his temples. I walked back to his desk, lifted his head and kissed him again.

"You, I trust. Her, never and a day. We will talk to her. Together. Promise me."

He said nothing.

"Promise me."

"I promise you, sweetness. I promise you."

"Good. I'll have everything in place to help you destress when you get home. Don't get long-winded in your meeting. And whatever you do, don't let Deacon Allen pray. Y'all will be here until next Sunday."

"You wrong for that. I mean you right about it. But you so wrong for saying it."

Coach bag in hand, I headed for the east side of the church. I loved the kids' side of the church. They had a little garden, two or three play sets and jungle gyms, and today the workout bus was on site. The little people would go through the bus time and time again doing customized exercises and weight lifting. I always got a kick out of the way all of those little sticky hands, and glue and glitter-covered fingers always had to touch you somewhere before they hugged you. I think the touch is their way of asking permission.

I was returning one bear hug when I looked up and saw the devil in the red dress touching my child. I kissed Robert Willie's chubby beige cheeks and nearly sprinted to the doorway where Kezia, her teacher Rhonda, and Barbara Dickson were standing. She was holding my child's hand. The closer I got, the tighter my fists clenched.

"Mommy, mommy. I made a tree with leaves today. Fruit of the Spirit tree!" Kezia's high-pitched squeals broke my anger somewhat.

As she jumped into my arms, I found myself checking her, smelling her, looking for cuts or - scrapes. For one quick second, I even thought perhaps I should check for a tracking device.

"Well, go get that tree so I can see it. I bet your daddy is going to go crazy when he sees it. Get all your stuff too, we're heading home."

Rhonda smiled, "I think I should tell you, like I was just telling her aunt – they have a little can with seeds that they planted today. It's out back. We'll come back around as quickly as possible."

With that she took Kezia's hand and walked off. Barbara stood there like she needed to. She just stood there like she deserved to see what my child had created. This over-dressed serpent wanted me to beat her ass.

"Listen, Ms. Greene."

"It's still – Dickson. Dickson!"

"Listen, Ms. Greene. I have no idea why you are here. I have no idea why you would join a church that your ex-husband is pastoring knowing that he is remarried and knowing that your marriage ended on very questionable terms. What I do know is this – whatever game you are lining up to play – you will leave my daughter out of it."

"Don't you talk to me that way! If it weren't for you..."

"No, no, no – let's stay in the real world. You are about to drift off again. I had nothing to do with your marriage ending. And even if I did – I stress again – that you will stay away from my child. If you choose not to abide by that, understand there is nothing that will stop me from ..."

"I got my tree, mommy." Kezia waved it like a proud flag before me.

Barbara stormed off, one of her feather earrings falling to the ground. Deacon Small retrieved it as he approached and was taken aback when she snatched it from his hand and sucked her teeth. He looked at Rhonda and I, shook his head and stepped inside the class to get his son.

Rhonda was confused. "Is something wrong with your aunt?"

I smiled, then twisted my face hoping to squeeze out a tactful way to explain things. "Ms. Dickson is not a family member. She is pastor's former wife."

Rhonda twisted her neck in disbelief. "Oh, so she's a creative storyteller?"

"Yes. I like the way you put that. I'll talk to Pastor about what happened, but please let the others know that she is not Kezia's aunt. And, she is not to interact with her or ever take her off this property or away from this room."

"Absolutely!" Rhonda crossed her arms. "I think you should know, she did say Pastor told her to come take Kezia for ice cream. That's why I seemed confused when I saw you walk up."

"Glad I came back here when I did. You know what, watch her for a few more moments for me. Maybe I should go have a chat with him now."

I headed back to the administrative wing to the building, cutting through the parking lot so that I could give Mike Pritt, the head of the parking ministry, the gift card in my purse. That proved to be a bad decision. Twelve feet from Mike, I heard a motor rev up, heard someone yell slow down and move. Next thing I know, I feel a thump against me, and I was on the ground. Mike was at my side in seconds.

"You good? You good?" Mike was frantic, but careful not to touch me without my permission.

"I'm good. I don't think I was hit directly. I don't feel like anything is hurt or twisted. Help me up."

Mike lifted me and helped me find my purse, which seemed to take most of the impact. It had landed between some cars a row from where I was knocked down. He opened the bed of his truck and I sat there regaining my composure. Rhonda brought over a cup of water and wet wipes, so that we could assure there was no blood or bad cuts.

Attending to me seemed to become a major production. So much so that I didn't see Luke approach.

"What happened?" He was nervous, pacing and throwing the question all over the place. "WHAT HAPPENED?"

"Someone sped off like they were crazy. Looked like they opened their door to close it or something. Next thing you know first lady was on the ground." Mike's explanation answered some things for me as well.

Deacon Small added further details to the mystery. "It was the woman who dropped her earring over there."

Rhonda and I looked at each other. I averted my eyes away from Luke and reached for my purse from Mike. Rising from the truck, I assured everyone that I was okay and asked if anyone else was hit. Luke instructed Mike to file an incident and police report, although no one caught the tag number.

Luke's arm around my waist as he walked me to the car eased my trembling. "Sit here, I'll get Kezia. And I'll drive you home. I'll get one of the guys to bring my car."

"Luke, I'm okay. I can drive home."

"I think you heard me the first time, right?"

I knew there was no need to answer and no need to argue. Besides, I was scared. Within one hour of joining the church, Barbara had tried to assert her position as STILL DICKSON; tried to kidnap or perhaps just spend unapproved time with my child; and tried to run me over in the parking lot. I leaned back against the headrest.

"Well, Lord. The enemy may come in like a flood, but she will flee. I trust You for that. But, just to make sure her stupidity doesn't get special, I'll be pulling out that little 9MM beauty in the closet to keep me company for a while."

Kezia talked about her Fruit of the Spirit Tree until she fell asleep midsentence. I pulled her African princess blanket up to her waist where she liked it. Emotions from everywhere welled up in me. What would I have done if Barbara had taken her? What in God's name was she really planning to do? Why is she back?

Barbara's antics are not new to us. When we first got married, wherever Luke was preaching – there she was. And not just present. Present in full traditional old-world church first lady regalia. Present in the front row or one of the first three rows – depending on which one presented the best view of her. Luke put an end to it – for a moment - when we attended a convocation in Memphis, and she greeted him at the airport with a bottle of champagne and a hotel room key. The look of utter horror and disdain when she saw me come out of the bathroom and meet him at baggage claim where she and her five-inch stilettos stood. It was one of the few times through her shenanigans in that season that Luke not only got a tad indignant but a bit raw as well.

He took the bottle of champagne, but not the key, stood inches from her and declared, "It does a man good to know that a woman will travel all the way to Memphis to swing from his pole. But, Ms. B, every night of this convocation and every night until forever ends, this caramel queen will be the only thing riding dirty. But thank you for the bottle. Like Martin used to tell Gina – we can do some things with that."

That time, I almost felt bad for her.

When we moved into our first place, I thought she was doing something generous; turns out it was something from her mental disconnect. I heard a beeping sound just outside of the garage side door. When I stepped outside after seeing a truck backed in the yard from the kitchen window, there was this huge tan-colored dude – as big as a grizzly bear – unloading boxes. He said Mrs. Dickson told him to drop them off to her house. I assured him I did not. He blew me off and he was out of there.

I looked at the boxes in shock. Finally, I grabbed a knife from the kitchen and sliced open the biggest one and pulled a packing sheet from it. Four boxes of Le Creuset Cookware. I was impressed! Until … I'm dragging the second box in the house when a car pulls up and it's Barbara.

She rose from the car with polished intent, her designer bag in hand. I guess she assumed her fine gift would warrant an invite to Luke's castle. "A man like Luke deserves a meal prepared – not cooked and not thrown together – in the finest cookware. Le Creuset is historically fine cookware." She happened to glance down and noticed the knife on the ground. So, wisely, she folded her ultra-creased black pant suit back into the car. "Unfortunately, he won't know how well this cookware performs until I have the opportunity to show him."

The word in my head was not a nice one. I vowed never to call a woman that name because it is not one I want hurled at me. Instead I invited her to dinner that night so I could show her I could do the historically fine cookware justice. When she arrived at eight; we had eaten. I volunteered to take the trash out when I saw the lights of her car from the kitchen window.

As she stepped from the car, I was juggling two pieces of the cookware in the my arms. She looked at me like I was the lunatic, in the moment. I apologized and explained that Luke and I had eaten a little earlier. Then I threw the soup pot in the trash can. The sauce pan was meant to go in the trash as well, somehow it landed against the front driver's side of the car.

I was insulted that time. This time she has gotten my attention on a whole different level.

Luke stood on the patio smoking his La Clarita, from the line of Tres Lindas Cubanas Cigars. The Afro-Cuban sisters who own the line gave him a box as a gift, and it had become one of his favorites. I snuggled up behind him, leaning into his spine. He pulled me to his front side, pulling me into him.

"How are you feeling?" His warm lips brushed the side of my neck.

"I. Am. Fine." I paused, considering my next words. "The woman Deacon Small was talking about is Barbara."

His breathing grew deep. "I gathered that by how he described her when I went to get Kezia. He said she seemed unusually upset about dropping an earring."

I pulled away from him and sat in the padded patio chair. The coolness of it awakened the nerves in my thighs. It was a beautiful night and I considered whether or not I wanted Barbara to continue to infringe on our day.

"Did something happen?" He leaned against the pillar, his eyes watching me. Luke has this way of commanding a moment with his quiet. Looking at him with the cigar in his hand, and his bare chest shining lightly from remnants of cocoa butter were reason enough for me to let it go – at least for a couple of hours. "We can still do what you're thinking, but I'd like to know what happened."

I roared. Regaining my composure, I recounted what happened with Kezia. The look on his face, the tightness in his body worried me. It also made me feel good. I pressed on with the question I wanted answered when he didn't look back at the choir earlier.

"Did you know she was coming?"

He hesitated. I got mad.

"I knew that she was back. She left messages for me. She sent a couple of emails. I didn't respond to anything. I never thought she would show up and join the church."

"What are we going to do?"

He sat in the chair beside me, resting the cigar in its smoldering tray. "I've been thinking about that the past few minutes. I'm really in a get-it-over-here or get-it-over-there kinda situation."

"So – yeah – don't like that choice of words. You care to...."

"The woman joined the church. Above the history and personal possibilities, I have been positioned in her life to be her pastor. I now have soul responsibility. I cannot negate that."

"I do understand that. But weigh the seriousness of the personal possibilities Luke. It's not like this woman's behavior towards us has not been violent and imbalanced before. And it seems to me that she clearly laid out her plan today. She is still crazy. She is still not in her full right mind. She still wants to be first lady. She still thinks I'm the reason she's not!"

"What are you talking about? We didn't know each other when that marriage ended."

"I know that, and you know that. She doesn't care to know that. Me and you, together, interrupted her get-back-in plan."

I nearly knocked the smoldering cigar out of the tray when I huffed off. Luke caught up with me in the kitchen. I poured a glass of orange juice purposely not facing him. I was mad. And for some reason I was scared. I didn't want to come off like a jealous woman. Luke lifted his body onto the prep counter. He was quiet. I was quiet.

"Know, sweetness, that I have no desire for Barbara. I know who my wife is. I know – this time – that I am with the one God ordained for me. I do not think you and I should be involved with counseling her. I will not allow her to serve in any capacity where she has direct access to the kids. But I still have to handle this like a pastor. And, you still have to handle this like my support. Can we agree to that?"

I rinsed the empty juice glass and turned it upside down in the sink. Walking past him I knew he was right, and I didn't like that. I didn't like his spiritual logic. I didn't like that woman. And I didn't like her in that particular house of the Lord. I did like the feel of Luke's hands stopping me from storming off, removing my shirt and the feel of his body pressing me against the refrigerator.

## TROUBLE DON'T LAST ALWAYS

It was beginning to feel like I was stuck in a Lifetime TV movie. Barbara was a demonic interruption if I had ever experienced one. Despite warnings from Luke and other church leaders, she tried on three other occasions to get hold of Kezia. So disruptive was her behavior that when my baby saw her anywhere near, she would cower and cry. Two things that are out of character for an effervescent, perpetually chatty four-year-old.

Every week Barbara put out a new welcome mat to let me know she wanted her house back. Or, wanted my house. We, Luke and I, had been able to do things as a couple personally and in ministry that she never had the opportunity to do. Twice in their short marriage, Luke and her family had her committed. Finally, he ended the marriage when she broke into the home of their former church secretary. The woman touched Luke's arm one day while talking to him and that was a trigger for Barbara. From what I was told; she ignored the raging alarm system instead taking her time turning over furniture, pulling dishes out of cabinets and creating havoc upon havoc. When the police arrived, she insisted that her husband was hiding in the house. They arrested her. I think it hurt Luke. He is a gentle spirit and wise to a fault. Part of me thinks the way he is handling her now is out of a place of guilt. He has never admitted to anything with the other woman; and I don't believe he had an affair with her. Still, I think he feels bad that he wasn't able to help Barbara more effectively manage her lunacy.

My body was exhausted. I started running again to deal with this enormous stress factor that was now part of our routine. I hated it with every fiber in my being. I found myself thinking about taking Kezia and visiting my parents in Georgia for a while, just to breathe. Flo and Mother Bolt discouraged that. They were right. If I left, Barbara would literally move into my home and Luke would lose his mind and his ministry trying to manage her antics.

I now had a team of Barbara wranglers. Mike, Rhonda, Flo, Mother Bolt, Deacon Small and Deacon Rob were my team. Whatever they could cut off they did. Success wasn't always the order of the day, however. She would follow me. I would leave home in the morning and within 10 minutes, her blue Chrysler 300 would pull up behind me. I warned the staff at Kezia's school about her. Luke spoke to her. She showed up at the hair salon one day, looking like she hadn't slept in days, and demanded to know what I was doing with her husband. She threw bottles of shampoo, conditioners and brushes – whatever at me and whomever would try to stop her. Luke called her family to ask if she had gone off of her meds.

During an evening testimony and prayer service, she requested prayer for me. She asked that the intercessors pray that I release the witchcraft hold I have on her husband. She offered a generous financial gift in return for their favor towards her. When Evangelist Harris started warring and calling stuff out, she sweated profusely and seemed to be playing the dozens in prayer. She had gone up against the wrong one though. She ran out of the church throwing her shoes at Sister Harris. Luke asked that they continue to pray for her. He warned her family that he would call the police.

Things were tense between Luke and me. He keeps telling me to look at the whole matter from a calling perspective. There is nothing, in my mind, spiritual about Barbara's mission. In fact, it is very clear and direct. She intends to regain her position as Mrs. Barbara Dickson, wife of Luke, First Lady of Revealing, and head damn peanut in the cuckoo bin. The enemy is very crafty. While she wasn't winning the game, she was actually playing; she was gaining ground by default. Here is what I mean. Luke, in struggling to walk in his pastor's calling, was interestingly becoming a man managing two women – two Mrs. Dicksons.

Clearing my mind, I allowed Kezia to turn on her Disney show tunes in the living room so I could watch her dance as I cooked. She knew every word to every song and sang them loudly. But baby girl was happy and that made me happy. When Luke came in, she and I were munching on carrots and twirling to "It's A Small World". He lowered the music, and as I twirled to face him, I knew there was a problem. Barbara episode 256. Kezia flew into her daddy's arms, and he loved on her long enough to convince her to head up to her room for a few minutes. He promised he'd read her a story before dinner.

His steps were heavy as he followed me into the kitchen. I could feel his heat on the back of my neck.

"Are you just going to be a fire-breathing dragon or you going to tell me what's going on?"

His posture – straight spine, arms folded across his chest – pissed me off. He didn't even take that posture when he scolded our daughter.

"Explain to me why you did it?"

"If I know what it was – perhaps I could explain it. But since I don't ... perhaps you should be the one doing the explaining."

"I'm sitting in a meeting. The mayor in front of me. Commissioners and department heads all around me. I'm pushing an agenda item and my phone is going crazy." He looked at me as though I should have some degree of empathy. "I finally excuse myself. It's the church. Raul is there painting when a truck pulls up and proceeds to take furniture out of my office. While he's about ready to go ballistic on them, another truck pulls up delivering new furniture. They tell him a V. Dickson ordered everything."

"I did no such thing!" I slammed the knife down on the counter and approached him. "Why in the hell, preacher, would I do something like that? I have full run of this house and I have never changed a piece of furniture – one damn piece of furniture – without talking to you. Think man! You might be arguing with the wrong wife."

"Here we go with that again." His flailing arms was the wrong move.

"With that again? Did you look at the paperwork?"

Nothing.

"Did you look at the paperwork? Is it possible the man said B. Dickson? This is Raul we're talking about. You still don't know when the man is saying geesh or cheese."

His posture shifted drastically.

"Oh, now you're thinking perhaps coming in on attack mode was not a good idea? What the hell, man! Why would I do that Luke? Did you look at the furniture? Does it look like something I would buy?"

He distracted himself by rummaging through the refrigerator. "No, I didn't see any paperwork or any furniture. I came straight here. I thought you were pissed off about ..."

"I, in case you haven't noticed, I have been beyond pissed off for weeks now. About Barbara. About you serving as Barbara's pastor. About Barbara disrupting my day any freaking time she wants to. About Barbara stalking me. About Barbara stalking me while I'm with YOUR daughter."

I opened and slammed five of the kitchen cabinets as though I was creating a musical score. Everything in me poured out into one big yell. When I felt Luke move towards me, I held out my hand stopping him. Something in me shifted. This argument wasn't about furniture, or what Barbara did yesterday or last week or last month.

"Luke, sweetheart. You thought I was pissed off about what? What? This is something new?"

He slowly turned and moved into the living room, changing the Disney tunes to jazz. He raised the volume slightly.

"You didn't go to the ordination nomination meeting?" He plopped into the smoke gray side chair realizing one battle was about to escalate into something else.

"I did not go the meeting today. I picked up Kezia early and we had a girls' afternoon. This time we did so without intrusion from our obsessive shadow. Tell me ..."

"Sweetness ...."

"Yeah, she's not here right now. Tell me."

"Barbara has the three nominations needed to be considered for ordination. I have to give her ..."

"Okay, partner. Let me stop you right there. We have sung that tune so many times these last few months, that I am sick of it! Sick sick sick sick of it. Come on Luke! This is too much, man! Too much."

"Vik – I know the pressure has been a bit much. But ...."

"I have no more buts left Luke. I don't. I'm not pissed anymore. I'm not even scared anymore. I don't know that I have a word to tell you what I am."

He rose from the chair and again came toward me. I backed away, nearly falling across the arm of the couch. The room felt like an inferno suddenly and I wanted to run. He dug his hands in his pockets and rested his body in a sitting position on the back of that same couch. The one we picked out together and now he wants to be mad because he thinks I changed his precious damn furniture without asking.

Before I could speak, his phone rang. He pulled it from his pocket, glanced at it and hit the red key. It rang again.

"Answer it. On speaker."

Luke is not one for messiness. How he didn't see that his pattern of dealing with Barbara by not dealing with Barbara is messy escapes me.

"Hey, it's Barbara." She sounded like a giddy woman enjoying the touch of her own body. I placed my fingers across his lips. She continued. "I just wanted you to know I am excited about being considered for ordination. It's been a dream of mine since we were married. It has always been my plan – you and I being the ultimate power preaching couple."

I looked in his eyes and realized he really did not fully grasp her lack of what is real and what isn't. I pressed my fingers against his lips again urging him to listen; but most importantly – not to speak.

"I hope you like the furniture I sent to the office. I just really think our office needs a more corporate and polished look."

"Bar...." I cupped his mouth with my hand and pressed.

"Hello Barbara. This is Vicki. Luke mentioned the furniture to me. He hates it. He really hates that you got rid of his chair. Listen, I'm going to do you and he a favor. I'll have Raul hire someone to haul it out into the woods TONIGHT and burn it up. Now, listen Barbara, about the ordination thing --- well --- I think you know. I really have to run now. I need to calm my man down."

I snatched the phone from his hand and threw it into the bookcase. The ampersand bookend hit the ground. Luke didn't move. He was right. Whether he got hell from me or hell from her, he was going to get it.

"Is there any way we can put all of the emotions aside and talk for a while? Really talk. I didn't realize..."

"What didn't you realize Luke? That Barbara has cleverly found a way to get her husband back. You have a wonderful sense of duty and responsibility to her and for her. You call it being a pastor. She calls it being with her husband."

"Vi..."

"No, man. I AM YOUR WIFE! Your posture in this whole matter has given church leadership the approval to give her some kind of special treatment; so much so that she could garner three nominations to become a minister. And you want to tell me you have to consider it. I have to understand it. You have to understand that at some point the pastor needs to bring order to this damn confusion. What is it about her with you?"

"There is nothing." He walked back to the kitchen. Whatever he was feeling rose as tension in his hand and that tension forced the top off of the water bottle before he unscrewed it. "I guess I'm really just trying hard not to make it seem like I am denying her anything because we had a failed marriage."

I walked past him and turned the stove and the oven off. The smell of the overcooked roasted sweet potatoes and carrots reminded me that I was cooking. Burnt or not, dinner was done and over. Luke pulled my arm and held it around his waist.

"I really am not trying to hurt you. I ..."

I kissed his lips, his neck, his chest. "You have allowed your first wife to return to her position. She's on the front row. She still wears your name even though you guys don't share a child and you have a new wife. I knew I was the second Mrs. Dickson, but I refuse to be second to the first Mrs. Dickson. Baby, what you need to decide is which wife you plan to honor."

I yanked my arm away, stormed out of the kitchen and went upstairs to pack my bags. I told Luke I needed a few days to feel life in all of me again. Barbara had taken too much of it.


## STEAL AWAY


Kezia was excited about going to Georgia. She has only been a handful of times, but she loves my mother's house. It has so many rooms and when you're four, you can literally walk under part of the house. She liked it because everyone took the time to talk to her; and baby girl can hold her own. As normal, whenever we drive anywhere at night, she was asleep within five blocks of home.

I decided to stop by the church and drop off the fabric for the dancers' costumes. I told Flo to meet me there so that I could go over a couple of things with her as well. The parking lot was empty. I expected as much. I parked right outside of the entrance to Luke's office where it was well lit. Since Kezia was asleep, I decided to take the bundles of fabric out of the trunk first and then come back for her.

I turned the key in the lock and prepared to quickly punch in the alarm code. It beeped two times, instead of three – but I really didn't pay it a lot of attention. I was focused on the fabric, getting back out to get Kezia and running through all of my rebuttals for every argument Flo would certainly raise. I heard the door click behind me. A thud hit the side of my face knocking me to the ground, the spilling fabric bundles absorbing some of the impact. Barbara stood over me wearing one of Luke's spare dress shirts – assumedly from his office - preparing to hit me again with some kind of bag. My foot landed against her knee. The shirt opened more to reveal her red lace corset.

"You are getting on my nerves, Vicki! Why don't you just die?! You. Make. Me. Sick!"

She swung with every word it seemed. I kept kicking until I could pull myself up. When she swung again, I grabbed whatever was in her hand and swung her against the wall. She shook it off.

"This is what I mean. You are pissing me off little girl. Sit your ass down somewhere." She led with her left hand, and I ducked but she still managed to knock me back with her right hand.

My mind was reeling. Kezia is in the car. My gun was in the car. If this woman knocked me out or killed me, she was going to take my baby. I rose up to my hands and knees. She was looking for something. I crawled up behind her and bit into her leg, catching her off guard.

When she bent forward, I pushed myself up using her back, and kicked her between her breast. I turned to run, but inches from the door whatever she had been looking for landed against the back of my head. I felt darkness coming and I all I could see was my sweet baby girl asleep in her car seat.

## WHEN YOU'VE DONE ALL YOU CAN

For hours she tortured me. I just wanted to know where my baby was. I didn't see her. I didn't hear her. She had tied me to the chair she bought as part of Luke's new office furniture. Furniture covered in rose petals. She would ramble on and on as she fiddled with candles and drank wine.

"You know I figured you two made love in this office. On that desk. On that couch. I couldn't have that. Your little body scent all up in my space." She spat. "You. I hope you washed your filthy hands before you touched him." She pushed my head. "Look at you. You don't have so much mouth now, do you? Hell, naw. That fat lip shut you right up." She kicked my legs. "Don't worry though. I'm going to handle Luke like he hasn't been handled since – well – me." She held my breasts in her hand. "Do you like it when he does that? He is a breast man."

Rotating red lights shined through every window of the office. Probing white lights moving closer were seen through the curtains covering the window that opened to the other offices and conference rooms.

"Okay, fun's over. I'm going to untie you now and take that fabric out of your mouth. Here's the thing though. You still lose." She quickly cut the ropes loose and yanked the fabric from my mouth. I got up from the chair as quickly as I could, stumbling to get my balance. Suddenly, she screamed.

"Stop, please stop!" Like a scene from a movie she ran head first into a wall. Bloodied she fell. I stumbled on something, scurrying to get to the door. "Somebody, PLEASE. LUKE!  Pastor – please – help me! OH MY GOD!" She slashed herself across the arm, and then across the thigh. "VICKI PLEASE NO! NO!" She moved the knife diagonally across her throat and hit the floor.

The officers rushed in, weapons drawn. Luke was stopped at the door by one of them.

Through labored breaths she persisted, "Not let him come to me."

The officer moved him back down the hall. I watched the officer one place his hand against her neck wound. A female officer pulled me from the room. Flo, Luke and Kezia seemed like ghosts through my swollen eyes. I saw Flo move quickly with Kezia away from the office. I wanted to sleep, just close my eyes. I felt Luke's arms pull me in. His lips resting against my face.

***

Barbara didn't know Kezia was in the car.  When Flo got there and found her asleep in her seat, my trunk open and my purse on the front seat, she knew something was wrong. Barbara believed that if Luke thought I had assaulted her, he would be so repulsed by my behavior that he would run back into her arms. Crazy. Even crazier were the things they found in the office which she had decorated for a romantic evening, hoping Luke would come by.  Plane tickets to Greece. A pregnancy test. A note to me that she'd begun but never finished.

"Dear Little Girl.  You have intruded long enough. It is time for you to go bye-bye now. I must admit, you have had a good run. But I am home now. The Grand and Mighty Fine First Lady is home, and this is NOT your house. Now, go the hell on. Oh, and ..."

www.ingramcontent.com/pod-product-compliance
Lightning Source LLC
Chambersburg PA
CBHW071835020726
47502CB00004B/1361